When we arrived at the Chapman property, an ambulance, three fire trucks, and several police vehicles were parked off to the side of the house. Paramedics and firefighters huddled together, studying the beeyard out in the back field. Both the Waukesha Sheriff's Department and the Moraine Police Department were represented. I saw Johnny Jay, the Moraine police chief, off by himself, talking on his phone.

I'd never seen a dead person outside of a coffin, and seeing Manny lying there almost brought me to my knees. If I'd still had a champagne buzz after riding over in Hunter Wallace's truck, I instantly sobered up when I walked into the apiary and saw Manny Chapman's body.

I wanted to be alone someplace, crying my eyes out. I couldn't stop thinking that if I had been here, none of this would have happened. Logically, however, I knew that I couldn't fall apart. I was the only living and breathing person available at the moment who knew anything about bees. I had to help.

Buzz Off

Hannah Reed

BERKLEY PRIME CRIME, NEW YORK

THE BERKLEY PUBLISHING GROUP
Published by the Penguin Group
Penguin Group (USA) Inc.
375 Hudson Street, New York, New York 10014, USA
Penguin Group (Canada), 90 Eglinton Avenue East, Suite 700, Toronto, Ontario M4P 2Y3, Canada
(a division of Pearson Penguin Canada Inc.)
Penguin Books Ltd., 80 Strand, London WC2R 0RL, England
Penguin Group Ireland, 25 St. Stephen's Green, Dublin 2, Ireland (a division of Penguin Books Ltd.)
Penguin Group (Australia), 250 Camberwell Road, Camberwell, Victoria 3124, Australia
(a division of Pearson Australia Group Pty. Ltd.)
Penguin Books India Pvt. Ltd., 11 Community Centre, Panchsheel Park, New Delhi—110 017, India
Penguin Group (NZ), 67 Apollo Drive, Rosedale, North Shore 0632, New Zealand
(a division of Pearson New Zealand Ltd.)
Penguin Books (South Africa) (Pty.) Ltd., 24 Sturdee Avenue, Rosebank, Johannesburg 2196,
South Africa

Penguin Books Ltd., Registered Offices: 80 Strand, London WC2R 0RL, England

This is a work of fiction. Names, characters, places, and incidents either are the product of the author's
imagination or are used fictitiously, and any resemblance to actual persons, living or dead, business
establishments, events, or locales is entirely coincidental. The publisher does not have any control
over and does not assume any responsibility for author or third-party websites or their content.

PUBLISHER'S NOTE: The recipes contained in this book are to be followed exactly as written. The
publisher is not responsible for your specific health or allergy needs that may require medical supervision.
The publisher is not responsible for any adverse reactions to the recipes contained in this book.

BUZZ OFF

A Berkley Prime Crime Book / published by arrangement with the author

PRINTING HISTORY
Berkley Prime Crime mass-market edition / September 2010

Copyright © 2010 by Deb Baker.
Cover illustration by Trish Cramblet.
Cover design by Judith Lagerman.
Interior text design by Kristin del Rosario.

ISBN: 978-0-425-23642-0

BERKLEY® PRIME CRIME
Berkley Prime Crime Books are published by The Berkley Publishing Group,
a division of Penguin Group (USA) Inc.,
375 Hudson Street, New York, New York 10014.
BERKLEY® PRIME CRIME and the PRIME CRIME logo are trademarks of Penguin Group
(USA) Inc.

PRINTED IN THE UNITED STATES OF AMERICA

10 9 8 7 6 5 4 3 2 1

Acknowledgments

My deepest gratitude to:

- Jacky Sach, who got me this wonderful gig

- Andy Hemken, beekeeper extraordinaire (note—any mistakes are my own)

- Adam Baker, for his awesomely vivid map of the town of Moraine

- Doug Kennedy, K-9 police dog trainer, who shared canine stories and training methods

- Lisa Lickel, my first reader

- Heidi Cox, Mary Goll, and Jessica Stapp, who won places in the newsletter for their delicious recipes

- Shannon Jamieson Vazquez, for taking a rough sketch and bringing it to life

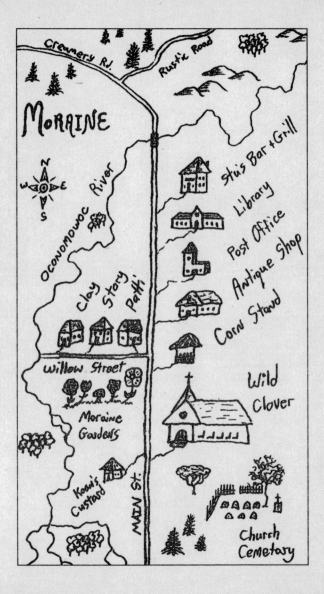

Buzz Off

One

If I hadn't been drinking champagne at noon on Friday, I would have been over at the honey house with Manny Chapman, my beekeeping mentor and owner of Queen Bee Honey, and possibly, just possibly, I might have saved him from what must have been a very painful death. Instead, oblivious to his pending demise and feeling slightly tipsy, I popped open bottle number three and filled more flutes.

I'm the only grocer in the unincorporated town of Moraine, Wisconsin, which has a population base climbing steadily toward eight hundred residents. I work hard to fill the needs of the community. Today, business was brisker than usual at my shop, The Wild Clover, mainly because of the free champagne and the one-day sale on everything in the store, including special bullet items such as:

- Wisconsin prize-winning cheeses
- Cranberries from the northern part of the state, dried and fresh
- Whole grains, including Wisconsin wild rice, which is really aquatic grass seeds
- Wines from Door County wineries
- Thirty-five varieties of organic vegetables
- Apples from the Country Delight Farm just up the road
- And of course honey products: comb honey, bottled honey, bulk honey, honey candy, beeswax, and bee pollen

There's nothing like the lure of freebies and discounts to bring out the best in people. Everyone in my little hometown made a point of stopping by my store to tip a glass and wish me well, whether they meant it or not.

Well, maybe not *everyone* stopped by. My ex-husband, Clay Lane, didn't show up, even though he lived only two blocks away and must have seen the banner tacked to the awning, announcing my freedom party.

"You should call him up, Story," Carrie Ann Retzlaff, my cousin and very part-time employee, said in her husky chain-smoker's voice. My cousin had close-cropped yellow-as-straw hair and a toothpick-thin body, since she ingested more nicotine and alcohol than nutrients. "Invite the ex to join us," she suggested.

I scowled playfully to let her know that was a bad idea. Celebrating a divorce is a lot like celebrating a successful heart transplant. They both hurt like hell, and your quality of life would be much better if the issues leading up to the situation had never happened in the first place. But at least I can say I'm still in the game, still alive and kicking. It's all about attitude.

"Cheers to all of you from me, Story *Fischer,*" I called out, placing special emphasis on my last name and noting by the clock above the register that I'd been a free woman for almost twenty-four breezy, wind-at-my-back hours. Fischer. My maiden name. The one I'd reclaimed yesterday afternoon. It sounded so right! Why had I ever given it up?

Story was my nickname, bestowed by childhood friends because I used to be quite the storyteller—in a friendly, silly sort of way, of course. I liked Story much better than my given name, Melissa, which my family shortened to Missy before I could even lift my bald baby head. As I grew up, Missy didn't exactly shout out strength and intelligence. Besides, the other kids came up with a bunch of variations for Missy that were truly mean and hurtful. Plus, Story has a bit of intrigue to it.

Story Fischer, that's me.

At the moment, I really missed my most loyal part-timers, twins Brent and Trent Craig, local college students in their sophomore years, working reduced hours at the store around gaps in their class schedules. That left me pretty much alone most days until they eventually reappeared like glorious gifts from heaven.

For this special event, I'd been forced to ask Carrie Ann, smoke-scented perfume and all, to work for me while I hosted the party. "Don't think anything of it," she said when I thanked her for the third time. She reached under the counter, then tipped back and drained an entire flute of champagne with one chug. "This is like hanging at Stu's Bar and Grill, only better because I get paid."

I plucked the empty glass out of her hand, ignored her startled expression, and said, "No drinking on the job, please."

"Why not? You're drinking," she pointed out.

"Yes, but that's why I asked *you* to handle the cash register."

"Crapola." My cousin shook her head at the injustice of it all.

I had a hunch that if I didn't watch the till, Carrie Ann would be giving away the store. How many glasses of champagne had she already had?

The Wild Clover was crammed from aisle to aisle as far as my quickly glazing-over eyes could see. The store's special sales and free-flowing champagne weren't just about my divorce. September was National Honey Month and this was our kick-off event. I lifted my head high and gazed at one of the stained-glass windows above me. The panes twinkled with sunlight, beaming rainbow-colored rays that gave the interior a certain magical light.

Two years ago, in more promising times, Clay and I had bought the Lutheran church for a song when the congregation outgrew the building and put it up for sale. The opportunity came about a year after we'd gotten married. What better way to begin our new lives together than to leave the city life in Milwaukee, move to my hometown of Moraine, buy the house I grew up in from my mother, and convert an early-twentieth-century church into a grocery store?

Our marriage had been doomed from the very beginning, but The Wild Clover was a success. Once we owned the building, I had removed the pews and the raised altar and converted the space into shelves, coolers, and freezers, but leaving all those fabulous stained-glass windows, three on each side, two in the back, and one above the massive double doors in front. From that beginning the store was born.

In addition to our house, we'd also purchased the house next door, which Clay had turned into a custom jewelry shop. Wire jewelry to be specific. Handcrafted, unique pieces guaranteed to attract a flock of females. The Wild Clover had been a beginning. The jewelry shop was the end.

I came back to the present and had to blink several

times before the store came back into focus, with all its artfully displayed produce and products and its fresh smells. A group of kids were crowded into the corner, picking out saltwater taffy and other treats from old-fashioned barrels. Several customers were planted right next to the champagne table and looked as if they were there for the duration of the party, or at least until the champagne ran out.

"I need a bagger," Carrie Ann called to me, and I quickly stepped over to help.

"Try the honey candy," I pointed out to those in line, indicating a honey jar filled with hard candy. "They have soft centers. Try one. They're free."

Honey! Sweet nectar from heaven. Most people don't know that honey comes in different flavors, depending on the bees' plant sources. Most honey is a blend, but if honeybees have an opportunity to forage in fields with only one type of available nectar, their honey reflects that.

In Wisconsin we have (listed from lightest to darkest):

- Alfalfa
- Clover
- Sunflower
- Cranberry Blossom
- Wildflower
- Buckwheat
- Blueberry Blossom

"Help yourselves," I encouraged my customers again, taking a piece of honey candy myself, unwrapping it, and popping it in my mouth.

I saw Manny Chapman's wife, Grace, walk in the front door, which reminded me that I'd promised to help Manny clean up his equipment later today, now that honey-harvesting and -processing season was over.

I'd been intrigued by honeybees as long as I could remember, so last spring when Manny Chapman taught a beginning course in beekeeping, I'd signed right up. Before long, my fascination had become a passion. When the class ended, I hung around to keep absorbing knowledge.

All of last year I helped Manny in his beeyard, extracting and bottling honey, learning every single thing I could from him about beekeeping. This spring, Manny gave me two strong hives of my own as payment for helping him out.

In fact, we worked so well as a team, he'd started talking about a partnership down the line, expanding the honey business with more aggressive marketing and higher honey yields. At last count, Manny had eighty-one hives, each one producing approximately one hundred and fifty pounds of honey, depending on the year. If he wanted to expand his business, he needed help. And I was right there, ready to go.

On a regular Friday afternoon, before the twins went back to college, I used to spend several hours in Manny's honey house, that sweet-smelling, homey building behind his home where he taught me how to extract wildflower honey and bottle it for sale.

Today wasn't a regular Friday, though.

"No, thank you," Grace said with a righteous air when I offered her a flute of bubbly. Grace Chapman was two years older than me, making her thirty-six. She was as plain as a donut without glaze. Her marriage to Manny eight years earlier had been the culmination of a May/September romance. He had at least twenty years on her, but you'd never know it. Manny had a love of nature and a joy for living, while Grace seemed to view life as a chore. "I don't drink," she said, glancing at her wristwatch in disapproval. "Especially during the workday."

I placed the filled flute on the table with one eye on Carrie Ann, who had edged closer. "When you get home," I said to Grace, "tell Manny I'm still coming out later."

Grace humphed and went down aisle two toward the cheese case.

"Isn't Manny coming to our party?" Carrie Ann asked, when I turned back to offer a flute to the next customer.

"You know Manny," I answered. "When it comes to his bees, he's obsessive. Although, he *did* say he'd stop by earlier if he could. Guess he got caught up in whatever bee project he's working on today."

Just then, Emily Nolan came in, carrying posters.

Emily, the library director, was Moraine's second-generation information specialist, meaning her mother had been the director of our library until her retirement. Then Emily, having prepared for this important career move her entire life, took over the position, and slid her own daughter into the wings to wait her turn. Our small library was stuffed with books from floor to ceiling, and although we, the residents, found it cozy and comfortable, the plain truth was that the town's needs were outgrowing the existing building. Something would have to be done soon.

In my humble opinion, libraries, once considered dusty dinosaurs destined for extinction, were reinventing themselves and emerging as important community centers like they were when I was a kid. I was pro-library all the way.

"Don't forget about the library event tomorrow afternoon," Emily reminded me. "A bluegrass band jam in the back. We've set up extra picnic tables."

"How could anybody forget?" I said. "We have posters plastered everywhere."

Carrie Ann snickered before she repeated, "Plastered," under her breath with a glance my way.

I was only getting started on the champagne, but that

one word spoken the way she said it reminded me to slow
down. I didn't refill my empty flute.

"I'll find a spot for at least one more poster," Emily
said.

As soon as the library director wandered off, my sister
made an entrance.

What can I say about my sister Holly? For starters,
she's beautiful. Add to that, filthy rich at thirty-one after
marrying a trust-fund baby the same month she graduated
from college, which had been the whole point of higher
education, according to her. She'd gone in for a good old-
fashioned M.R.S. degree. Max "The Money Machine"
Paine had come along her junior year, and it was love at
first sight. They now own a Milwaukee condo, a Naples
winter home, and a mansion on Pine Lake. They decided
not to have children, which means they can keep accumu-
lating as much stuff as they want.

Which is not to say that my sister doesn't have a generous side—Holly also loaned me enough cash to save the
store from certain death during the property split between
Clay and me.

Three years separated the two of us, which seemed huge
when we were growing up, but the gap was closing as time
went by. I liked her in spite of the fact that she was Mom's
favorite and spoiled rotten.

And I couldn't help comparing us. Here's me—sort of
pretty when I work at it, getting by with a lot of hard labor,
divorced, the oldest of two girls, Mom's problem child. But
who's keeping score?

My sister has so much time on her hands, she'd mem-
orized all one-thousand-plus text messaging acronyms
known to humankind. I've noticed lately, the abbreviations
are creeping into her spoken conversations. That's what
comes with too much money and too much spare time: use-
less habits. In Holly's case, she has a text-speak habit.

I try to keep up.

"HT (translation for those more normal: *hi there*)," she said, making her way over to me and picking up a filled flute. "Cool. A party. HUD (*how you doing*)?"

"Great. Free. Mellow. Did I mention free?"

"GR2BR (*good riddance to bad rubbish*)."

"Isn't that the truth!"

Holly had been in divorce court with me, along with Mom and Grams, so she knew Clay had been rotten to the core right until the bitter end.

"Who brings a new girlfriend to their divorce hearing?" I said.

"What an a-hole."

"See, you *can* speak proper English."

Holly laughed and took a sip of champagne.

We both glanced over at Carrie Ann when she gave a little shout of surprise before saying, "Look out the window. Isn't that Clay?"

Unfortunately, she said it much louder than necessary. Customers crowded around the front window to see what was happening outside. I saw my ex-husband standing right in front of the store.

He wasn't alone.

"Faye Tilley," someone said, recognizing the woman with him, the same one who had been in the courtroom the day before.

I couldn't help noticing Faye Tilley was younger, taller, and prettier than me.

"How old do you think she is?" a customer asked.

"Mid-twenties," someone else guessed.

I really hoped Clay and his girlfriend weren't going to come into the store.

"She's your spitting image, Story," someone else said.

That got them started.

"No way, Story's so much cuter."

"Look at the resemblance. He's trying to replace Story with someone exactly like her."

"You're right," someone behind me agreed. "They've got the exact same color hair."

Our hair *was* sort of similar. The color of fall wheat, I liked to think about mine. But hers was wild and untamed in a way mine never would be. Shorter and wavier. Not straight as a walking stick like mine.

Next to me, Emily Nolan said, "She's your doppelgänger, Story."

"Oh, no! Don't look at her!" Carrie Ann said to me. "You can't see your own doppelgänger."

"Why not?" my sister, Holly, said.

"It's bad luck, really bad luck." Carrie Ann tried to shield my eyes.

"That's ridiculous," I said, pushing her hands away.

Right then, Clay's new girlfriend spotted us at the window. Her eyes scanned, finding me before I could duck or fade into the background. She smiled coyly before turning to give Clay an openmouthed kiss.

I went back for more champagne.

Two

My hometown of Moraine is in southeastern Wisconsin, tucked between two ridges that were formed during the Ice Age when two enormous glaciers collided. Visitors to this part of Wisconsin are always surprised to find hills and valleys instead of flat cow country. Like most small towns, Moraine's enterprising founders planned the community along a highway to take advantage of travelers passing through. Since those times, however, faster, more efficient roads have been built that pass by us instead of through.

Besides The Wild Clover, which is the only grocery story within ten miles, we have:

- Koon's Custard Shop: frozen custard is a Wisconsin favorite, much like soft-serve ice cream only softer and richer

- A popular antique store with the less-than-original name of The Antique Shop

- Stu's Bar and Grill for beer, pizza, and other bar food, mostly breaded and fried

- Moraine Library, with its herb garden outside and extensive collection of local history inside

- A postage-stamp-sized post office

- Moraine Gardens, across the street from my house, specializing in native plants

- A seasonal roasted-corn-on-the-cob stand with all the trimmings that opens for several months in late summer and fall—like now

- And Clay's jewelry business—although I prefer to pretend that doesn't exist

I stepped out onto The Wild Clover's front lawn into the sunny September afternoon and plunked myself down in one of the brightly colored Adirondack chairs I'd painted.

The church that housed my store had been constructed with Cream City brick, which was made from a special clay found only along the banks of the western shore of Lake Michigan, mostly in the Milwaukee area. When it was fired, the clay turned a creamy light yellow color. The church's steeple and bell tower were whitewashed and wood-framed, and the church bells were still intact.

Milwaukee was forty minutes away, close enough to Moraine to visit whenever we needed culture and fine dining. I'd spent enough years living in the city to appreciate what it had to offer. All the same, when I first left home to move to Milwaukee, I couldn't wait to get away; but by the time we decided to relocate, I couldn't wait to come back. It's weird how your priorities change over time.

While I sat admiring my store, Holly came out, waved good-bye, and roared away in her Jag. A few minutes later my grandmother's Cadillac Fleetwood pulled over, its tires kissing the curb. Mom was on the passenger's side as usual, since Grams, at eighty years old, refused to give up the driver's seat.

The Caddy's window slid down, and Mom poked her head out.

"What's going on inside the store?" Mom asked, even though she knew perfectly well.

"September is National Honey Month," I said. "The store is celebrating."

"Looks to me like you've been drinking."

Now how could she tell from where she was? Then I noticed that I had an empty flute in my hand. "Only a little," I said, walking over to the car.

My mother had done me a huge favor when Clay and I decided to move to Moraine, by selling us the family home for a very low price—making it affordable enough for us to also buy the house next door as well as the market. My dad had died several years ago, dropping at the age of fifty-nine from a massive heart attack, and Mom never got used to living alone. After the house closing, Mom moved in with her mother, my sweet-apple-pie Grams, who was presently looking happy and pretty with a daisy from her garden tucked into her little gray bun.

Unfortunately, all my mother's genes came from my ornery grandfather's side, not from my grandmother's. Mom had a negative outlook on life. Worse, since the house sale, she thought she owned me.

"Are you coming in?" I asked, noticing that they weren't getting out of the car.

Grams leaned over Mom to join the conversation. "We're going to the beauty shop over in Stone Bank," she said. "We only stopped because we saw you outside and wanted to say hi."

"You shouldn't be drinking on the job," Mom said, puckering her lips in disapproval. "You aren't serving alcohol inside the store, are you?"

"When's your appointment?" I said to Grams, who caught my hint.

"We have to go, Helen," she said to my mom. "Or we'll be late."

My mother hated being late for anything. "Fine," Mom said.

Grams pulled out at a snail's pace and disappeared from sight.

I stood on the curb, considering the virtues of a hot cup of coffee.

While I went over my limited beverage options—coffee from Koon's Custard Shop or more champagne, which would have been the absolute wrong decision—Hunter Wallace, my first high school flame, pulled up at the curb in a Waukesha sheriff's SUV and decided for me.

I'd get neither.

As Hunter rounded the SUV, his body language screamed official business. He's a member of the Critical Incident Team, aka C.I.T., which comprises law enforcement officials from the surrounding towns and villages. They respond to anything considered high risk. The C.I.T. would swing into action, for example, if we had a hostage situation or a gunman entrenched on a rooftop. Not that we get much of that kind of crime. C.I.T. also handles potentially risky situations like search warrants and arrests, but again, not much of that action around here.

Although last year, when Stanley Peck had summer workers staying at his farmhouse, C.I.T. had to break up a drunken shooting incident that left poor Stanley with a hole in his foot.

Stanley, all sixty-plus years of him, still owned one of Wisconsin's disappearing farms, although he leased out most of his acreage to other farmers. His wife, Carol, had died that year. I thought about how lonely he must've been without her, and how that emptiness might have been the reason he invited temporary summer workers to stay with him in the first place. Rumor has it Stanley did the shooting himself and blamed it on his houseguests, but since he has deep-rooted family ties and is as local as you can get, the town sided with him and sent the so-called rabble-rousers packing.

Stanley still had a slight limp.

Because Hunter looked so businesslike, my eyes swept up to The Wild Clover's bell tower. I didn't see any gunmen up there. Stanley Peck was inside the store, but last I looked, he hadn't been toting any dangerous weapons—visible ones, at least.

"Hey, Hunter," I greeted him, taking in his tight jeans and untucked, button-down blue shirt with rolled sleeves. The shirt matched the blue of his eyes.

Hunter lived about ten miles north of Moraine and worked in the City of Waukesha, which was twenty-five miles southeast of my town. Our paths hadn't crossed on a daily or even weekly basis in the two years I'd been back in Moraine. We didn't see much of each other in the fourteen years that I had lived in Milwaukee, either (between the time I went to college there and when I came back, with a lot of baggage in the form of Clay Lane). Still, Hunter was usually happy to see me when we came face-to-face here and there. But today he wasn't in a joking, flirtatious mood.

"Story, I need your help," he said. "Right now."

"Sure."

"I see Grace Chapman's car. Is she inside?" He motioned to the market.

I nodded, sensing this wasn't the best time to invite him in to toast my newly single status. "What's up?"

"I have bad news. Stay put. I'll be right back."

With that he yanked open the door and disappeared inside.

What could Hunter possibly need me for? What bad news was he about to deliver? Was it bad news for me? Or for Grace?

Before I could ponder the cryptic message further, Hunter came out, leading Grace by her elbow and carrying a small bag of groceries tucked under his arm.

"What's going on?" Grace asked him.

"Just get in, please." He held open the front passenger's side door. "You, too, Story. Please. Hurry. I'll tell you on the way." Grace slipped in first, and I got into the backseat. Hunter handed me Grace's bag of groceries, slammed the door, and trotted around to the driver's side.

I heard heavy breathing behind me, glanced back, and saw a crate in the cargo area. Dark canine eyes peered back at me. Large or small, dogs get the hairs on my arms standing at rigid attention. The big ones have big teeth and most of them think they are the leaders of the pack, which includes any humans around. The little ones are even worse, all hyper and ready to latch on to sensitive body parts.

Getting bitten by a dog as a kid has made me leery of all canines.

This one was big. I scooted closer to the door.

As we pulled out to make the short run to the north side of town where Manny and Grace lived, Hunter was more serious than I'd ever seen him. "Have you been home in the last few hours?" he asked Grace.

"Not since earlier this morning. I've been visiting my

brother and sister-in-law. Why? Did something happen to Manny? Is my husband okay?"

"I'm sorry to have to tell you this, Grace," Hunter said. "But Manny's unconscious out by the beehives, and it doesn't look good."

"Oh, no!" Grace said.

"Who called you?" I asked.

"Ray Goodwin stopped by to pick up a honey delivery and found him."

Hunter glanced back at me. Grace looked over at him, and I could see the shock on her face and how pale she was, before I met Hunter's blue eyes. The message they conveyed wasn't good. He was preparing her for even worse news.

"Hunter, you have to be wrong!" I said, a little too quickly, a little too loudly in such a confined space, but I'd been caught off guard. "Manny was perfectly fine yesterday morning when I saw him."

"I came from their place just now," he said, looking at me in the rearview mirror, "and saw it with my own eyes. That's why I need your help, Story. Manny's covered with bees and we can't get near him." Then to Grace, "I can't tell you how bad I feel. You'd better brace yourself for the worst possible case."

Three

When we arrived at the Chapman property, an ambulance, three fire trucks, and several police vehicles were parked off to the side of the house. Paramedics and firefighters huddled together, studying the beeyard out in the back field. Both the Waukesha Sheriff's Department and the Moraine Police Department were there. I saw Johnny Jay, the Moraine police chief, off by himself, talking on his phone.

I'd never seen a dead person outside of a coffin, and seeing Manny lying there almost brought me to my knees. If I'd still had a champagne buzz after riding over in Hunter Wallace's SUV, I instantly sobered up when I walked into the aviary and saw Manny Chapman's body.

Emotionally, I wanted to be alone someplace, crying my eyes out. I couldn't stop thinking that if I had been here, none of this would have happened. Logically, however, I knew that I couldn't fall apart. I was the only living and breathing person available at the moment who knew anything about bees. I had to help.

Manny was lying in the center of the beeyard, sprawled squarely between the hive boxes. He was dressed in a loose long-sleeved shirt rumpled up around his armpits, and sweat pants tucked into a pair of high boots, the same kind I wore to keep bees from crawling inside my clothes.

And, as Hunter had said, Manny was covered with honeybees.

When Manny fell, he must have overturned a plastic five-gallon bucket filled with honey. Some of it had landed on his body, and bees were crawling around, feasting on the thick sweet line that had run out onto his chest from the bucket. My beekeeping friend's staring eyes were all the indication I needed that he was gone.

This was September. Bees were starting to get extra hungry. Their pollen sources were drying up, and they were busy trying to store enough food for the winter. Contrary to what some people believe, bees don't hibernate. They tough it out the best they can by huddling together inside their dark homes, protecting their queen from the cold while surviving on honey reserves.

"I've always hated those bees," Grace sobbed, from a distance. She had a knot on her forehead that had swelled like a bag of Jiffy Pop popcorn. When we'd arrived, she'd climbed out of the SUV and had taken one look at her husband's body lying in the beeyard, then pitched forward in a faint. I'd tried to catch her, but she had forty pounds on me, and we'd both gone down. I'd been lucky, I'd only scraped my right elbow and banged my knee. Even though I'd cushioned her fall, Grace had bounced backward and clunked her head on the side of the SUV.

Grace had never liked Manny's bees, but whether it was the bees themselves or her husband's obsession with them,

I wasn't sure. Either way, she refused to have anything to do with them.

"He's dead," she said. "I can tell. And the damn bees did it."

"You're not really blaming his bees?" I said, astonished that anyone—least of all Grace, who lived among them—would think that honeybees were dangerous, let alone deadly.

"Well, it sure looks like they killed him," one of the officers said from behind me. "Was he allergic?"

"No," Grace said.

"Absolutely not," I agreed. Some beekeepers would start out without problems, but then developed allergic reactions to stings over time. Manny wasn't one of them.

Police Chief Johnny Jay stood by himself, still talking on his cell phone, but he had one eye on me and it was clear he didn't like what he saw.

Johnny Jay didn't fit any of the physical or mental stereotypes associated with small-town cops. He wasn't overweight and didn't eat donuts. He didn't wear mirrored sunglasses or talk around a toothpick. Johnny looked like a choirboy or a boy scout—clean-cut, good teeth, and even though he was approaching thirty-four, he looked much younger. He was smart, calculating, and serious about his position. This wasn't your typical Mayberry cop.

But Johnny had enough buffed-up muscle to let you know that he had a major vain streak, and when he opened his mouth and you heard the garbage come out, you knew something was seriously wrong with the boy. That is, if you were listening hard.

Way back when, if I had known that the biggest bully in school would grow up to be the chief lawman in the same town I lived in, I wouldn't have gone up against him so many times. Okay, maybe that's not true. I would have anyway. Johnny Jay didn't fool me then, and he didn't fool me now. He was still a bully, but he'd become sneakier at it.

"A man can only stand so many stings before the venom will poison him to death," one of the uniformed county sheriff deputies said.

Which was true. Even someone like Manny, who wasn't allergic, would die from too much toxin.

Hunter put a hand on my shoulder and gave me a nod of encouragement.

I felt isolated from my own species as I forced myself closer to Manny's body, ending with my feet grounded not a foot away from him. I'm not afraid of honeybees, having spent all of this year and last discovering how gentle and industrious they are. Everyone else was a good distance behind me, ready to turn and run at the slightest sign of trouble from the bees.

"Let's go put some ice on that bump, Mrs. Chapman," a paramedic said to Grace, leading her toward the house. "You don't need to watch this."

I'd been trying to avoid looking at Manny's exposed head and stomach, concentrating instead on the bees by the bucket. Now I forced a peek. His face was red and his lips were swollen. So was the lower, bare area around his stomach. That was almost more than I could stand. Nightmares were sure to haunt me that night and for a lot of nights afterward. I stayed focused on his chest area and the immediate problem of removing the bees.

A few yellow jackets had joined the foray, which was common. None of them attacked Manny or me. They just wanted the honey, like the others did.

"Are they eating him?" another of our fine law enforcement officials asked.

"Honey bees are herbivores," I said. "They only eat plant products."

I didn't think it was necessary to inform them that yellow jackets were the ones that were carnivores. They would eat dead, decaying carrion just like a vulture would.

I shut my eyes, but the image of my fallen friend remained vivid. I snapped them back open and looked away.

A police dog leashed to a fire truck bumper studied the situation as gravely as the humans, outwardly calm but alert. Hunter's dog. The one that had locked eyes with me in the SUV.

Hunter and several other C.I.T.s I recognized from the neighboring communities also studied the situation. To them, this must be worse than a barricaded gunman—much worse. They could negotiate a hostage situation or bring in a sharpshooter to pick off a gunman, but they didn't have a clue how to handle hundreds of bees.

I squatted next to the beekeeper's body. If I didn't have a rudimentary knowledge of bees and their nature, I would have suspected the same thing that the others did—that Manny's honeybees had killed him. He certainly looked like he'd been stung one too many times. However, these weren't honeybee stings.

I put a shaky hand out, steadied it the best I could, and poked a finger into the gathered bees as they lapped up honey. They didn't react to my intrusion, which was exactly how nonaggressive bees would behave.

"Are they still stinging him?" I heard behind me.

"They aren't stinging him at all," I said. "They're eating the honey. If you'd come closer than ten yards you'd be able to see for yourself. Come on over here, but move slowly. You don't want to scare them."

Hunter was the only one willing to take me up on my offer. I checked out his attire, especially the button-down shirt he wore.

"Bees are curious," I said to him. "They'll crawl in

through your shirt collar or up your pant legs. I'd suggest you button up around your neck."

Hunter adjusted his clothing, then squatted down next to me while bees buzzed overhead, checking us out and planning their landings onto Manny. Not a single one of them tried to sting us. Once Hunter acclimated himself to the unfamiliar environment and discovered that he wasn't a bull's-eye on a bee's target, he leaned over Manny and looked more closely. "There are welts all over his exposed skin."

I'd been afraid he'd notice that. "Let me get the bees off him," I said, standing up, grateful that I had been born with a strong stomach.

But I had a dilemma. I had no idea what to do next.

"What can I do to help?" Hunter asked.

"I'm not sure. Stand back while I get rid of the bucket."

I slowly moved the bucket away from Manny's body, careful not to put my fingers down on top of any bees. Then I pondered my next move. Some of the honeybees had followed the pail, but a significant number of them remained with the honey on Manny's chest.

What to do? I glanced at the honey house.

Manny's honey house was the size of a two-car garage and the shape of a very large garden shed, with windowless double doors. It contained all the standard beekeeper's equipment and gear and was set up to harvest, process, and store wildflower honey. Since Manny had been working around the beeyard, the honey house wasn't padlocked. A good thing, since I didn't have my key with me.

But I didn't want to use a bee suit and smoker with Hunter and his group looking on. Encasing myself in armor and toting a weapon would only cement their belief that honeybees were dangerous, and that in turn would feed the rumor mill. In a small town like Moraine, the panic button is always within easy reach.

Instead, I set my sights on the bee blower. Bees don't mind a strong wind. To them, it's part of nature and they don't consider it an aggressive act from an enemy. So when Manny and I wanted to get honeycombs from the hives without a bunch of bees tagging along, we blew them away with the bee blower.

Only I couldn't find it. In the end, I sent one of the officers into the Chapmans' home. He came out with an extension cord and a large fan.

Jackson Davis, the county medical examiner, had been hiding inside a circle of firefighters, probably wishing he'd chosen a different career. "I'm not going in there," he said, indicating the flying insects. "I'd have to be nuts."

"You're the M.E. for Christ's sake," Police Chief Johnny Jay said. "Get your butt in there. Or do you need a shove?"

"We'll put you in a bee suit," I said, changing my mind about the armor idea, since it would be the M.E. going in. If one single honeybee stung him, I'd hear about it for the rest of my life. "You'll be perfectly fine. Most of them will fly away when the fan starts up."

I directed a silent plea to the remaining bees, hoping my message of peaceful interaction resonated through the universe and came to rest where it should. One could always hope.

With more coaxing and reassurances, Jackson let me help him into Manny's bee suit. I adjusted the veil for him. Hunter blew the fan at high speed and we watched most of the bees blow away, which gave the M.E. renewed confidence. He went in and went to work. Not long afterward, he gave us a thumbs-down.

The official verdict, the one we'd all known was coming: Manny was dead.

I went into the house and cried with Grace. Up until now we hadn't been more than polite acquaintances in spite of all the hours I'd spent at her house learning beekeeping from Manny. I'd never been comfortable around her, sensing that she was an insecure woman who resented the interest in bees I shared with her husband. But for now, we put our unspoken differences aside.

After the cop cars and fire trucks pulled away and Grace headed to her bedroom to rest, I went outside on the porch. Hunter was still studying the apiary. The dog I'd seen earlier was on a short leash at his side. Manny's death hadn't slowed the bee activity. Honeybees poured in and out of the hives.

Hunter walked over with the dog to join me. I took a few steps back, keeping some distance between us. He didn't seem to notice that his dog was way too close.

My nose was running, I had a wad of tissues clutched in my hands, and my eyes felt almost swollen shut. "I didn't know you had a dog," I said.

"He's one of our police dogs."

"What happened after I went in the house with Grace?"

"I seem to be the one delivering all the bad news today," Hunter said. "Johnny Jay wants to destroy the beehives. He's right, you know."

No! Not the bees! I thought, temporarily forgetting the dog. "Nobody knows yet what killed Manny. Isn't his decision a little premature, not to mention drastic?" I'd square off against the police chief and every cop in the county to protect those honeybees.

"Anyone could see that Manny had been stung all over his body," Hunter said. "The bees have to go."

"Please don't let Johnny Jay kill them! I can prove they weren't responsible."

"You'll have to make it good, if I'm going to have a case. It's never easy convincing Johnny Jay of anything."

"Manny's bees aren't Africanized, if that's the worry." Africanized honeybees, also known as killer bees, had escaped from a breeding program in the tropics and began to crossbreed with European bees, their gentler cousins. Africanized honeybees were extremely defensive—they had a larger number of guard bees, protected a larger zone around their hives, and would chase for longer distances. "Killer bees can't survive our cold winters." Which was true. Wisconsin didn't have killer bees.

Hunter sighed. "That's it?" he said. "That's your whole argument? They aren't killer bees? Of course you want to protect them, but you have to face facts."

I leaned against the porch rail. "Listen up," I said. "Bullet point number one."

Hunter smiled at that. Bullet points had always been my favorite way of listing pertinent facts and he knew it.

"Bullet point number one," I said again, "honeybees have barbed stingers. That means that when they attack they leave their stingers behind, imbedded in flesh. Did you see any stingers in Manny?"

"No, but you have my attention." He could tell that I was just warming up. "Are you sure about the barbed stingers?"

"Of course," I said like a confident pro rather than the rookie that I really was. "Bullet point number two: These bees knew Manny wasn't a threat. He worked with them every day. The only time he was ever stung was if he accidently put his hand down on one. Number three, honeybees die after stinging. Did you see piles of dead bees around Manny?"

"I didn't notice, but I'll take another look." Hunter's eyes crinkled when he smiled. He still had those laughing eyes I'd fallen so hard for in high school. He'd also had great feet; I have a secret thing about beautiful male feet. A fetish, I suppose you'd call it. Like some women admire butts or chests or pecs. Me? I'm a foot woman. I glanced down to check out Hunter's feet, but they were encased in his Harley Davidson boots.

"I can tell you have another bullet point ready to go," Hunter said.

I'd lost focus when my thoughts went south. How could I be thinking of feet at a time like this? "Where was I?"

"Number four."

"Right. Bullet point number four," I said, back on track. "The only reason honeybees would attack is if they thought their hive and queen were in danger. But Manny's bees weren't agitated like they would've been if they'd had to defend their colonies. They weren't upset at all. There's no denying he'd been stung all over, but the real culprit had to have been yellow jackets. They don't lose their stingers, so they can sting over and over."

"Okay. Okay." He raised his free hand in mock surrender while the dog watched me carefully. "You should have been an investigator. You missed your calling. Nice observations, especially considering the circumstances. I'll suggest we wait until we hear back from the M.E. before carrying out any apiary death sentences. I'll convince the others, including Johnny Jay."

Yes! A short reprieve.

I was so excited, I wanted to hug him, but the dog stood between us.

"What is it? A German shepherd?" I asked, pointing to the dog. Not that I knew anything about dog breeds—as far as I'm concerned, they just come in big or small versions.

"Ben is not an *it*. He's a Belgian Malinois." The dog looked up at Hunter when he heard his name. "His markings are similar to a German shepherd's, but Ben would be offended by the comparison. He's faster, more driven to please. Ben has tackled shooters on command. Once he pulled an armed robber right out of a vehicle window to prevent him from escaping. Ben's a very bad good guy."

The dog *looked* bad. Despite his reserved calm, I sensed

he was alert to the possibility of danger and looking forward to the opportunity to wield steel-jawed force.

"If I hug you, will he attack me?"

"You want to hug me?"

"Not if Ben's going to attack."

"Of course, he won't. Ben, stay." Hunter walked forward. Ben didn't move a muscle, but I had a feeling he'd be a flash of lightning if Hunter gave him the proper command. With a cautious eye on the dog, I hugged Hunter. "Thanks for offering to help save the bees. That means a lot to me."

"I heard about your divorce," he said, softening his voice and leaning against the rail right next to me, so our arms touched. "Should I congratulate you or express my condolences?"

"I'm relieved it's over. We were only married three years, but it seemed like a very long time."

"I hear he's living next door to you," Hunter said.

"I can't get rid of him."

"That must be awkward."

"Yup."

"How's your mother?"

"Same as always. Disapproving and loud about it."

His dog watched me every second like he was just waiting for me to make the wrong move. It was kind of creepy.

Hunter and I shared a few minutes of thoughtful silence. I'd always liked that about Hunter. He didn't feel a need to fill every quiet moment. The sound of a car turning into the driveway finally distracted us.

I recognized Grace's brother, Carl, and his wife, Betty, from several times when they'd been visiting while I'd been working in Manny's beeyard. They leaped out of a Ford Bronco and hurried toward us. Grace's sister-in-law was expecting her first baby and looked about three months overdue.

"Where is she?" Carl asked.

"Lying down," I answered, getting what I thought was a cold glare from Betty. Or maybe that's how she came across when she was shocked by tragedy.

We all handle bad news differently.

Four

"How many times are you going to arrange that same shelf?" Stanley Peck asked. I'd been rearranging a honey display back at The Wild Clover while trying to clear the image of my dead mentor from my head. The day was like a bad dream, only I wasn't going to wake up from this one.

My loyal part-time employees, the twins Trent and Brent Craig, had arrived at the market ahead of me. They were working the counter, checking out customers and bagging.

"Carrie Ann got wasted and went home as soon as we got here," Trent had said when Hunter dropped me off.

Just great. I'd have to deal with her at some point.

Word spreads fast in a small town, and Moraine is no exception. Customers flowed through the door of the store, hanging around to get more details and to commiserate.

"Manny started me out with my first queen bee," I said to nearby customers. "When I wanted to have hives in my backyard, he gave me thousands of worker bees. And when he realized I was serious about beekeeping, he included me in his business, teaching me what he knew and giving me a cut on any sales I made."

I wasn't telling anybody anything they didn't already know. Everybody knew how Manny had taken me under his wing, but we were all reminiscing and sharing stories. I wiped away a renegade tear and continued, "Other beekeepers have lots of problems with diseases and mites. Not Manny. He was the best beekeeper and he left some big shoes to fill." Which was true. Bee management came with all kinds of problems—parasites, pests like ants and mice getting into the hives, predators, and diseases, both old and new. Manny was always on the cutting edge of new technology and preventive care.

"We target practiced together," Stanley said. "Right out in his backyard with Grace and Carol egging us on and critiquing every shot."

"Manny was one of a kind," Milly Hopticourt added. Milly was a seventyish retired schoolteacher built like Julia Child and, like the famous chef, she loved to cook so much that I'd made her the official tester for all of the recipes that appeared in The Wild Clover newsletters.

"He'll be missed plenty," other folks agreed.

That was an understatement from my point of view, and not only from a personal perspective. The future of his honey business was in serious jeopardy with his death. I'd secretly counted on a full partnership at some point in the near future, and with him gone, that dream was totally shattered.

Manny, or rather Grace now, owned the honey house, the land, the equipment, and most of the bees. All the bees, actually, except for the two hives in my backyard I kept to pollinate the neighborhood gardens and to provide me with a little honey for my own personal use. Could I carry on without him, keep Queen Bee Honey going? Would Grace even agree to sell the business to me?

Not to mention another pressing business-related problem—my total lack of expertise at managing bees. I'd been in training for a year and a half, but it was only this spring that I started with my own hives. Could I manage eighty hives alone? If Grace would give me the opportunity, I'd make it work. Manny had known what he was talking about when he said that bees would get into my blood. They had.

I gave up on reshuffling the honey products, since it wasn't helping numb the pain I felt, and went outside where people were loitering in front of the store. The crowd not only filled the assortment of Adirondack chairs lined up on the grass, it spilled out onto the sidewalk. "I heard the sirens early on," Emily Nolan, the librarian, said. Her presence made me realize how the day had flown. If Emily was here, the library must be closed, meaning that it had to be after five. "Didn't all of you hear the sirens?" she asked.

I hadn't, but then I'd been focused on myself, living inside my own head, laughing and celebrating, boozing it up while Manny's life oozed away.

I must be a slow learner because it took a while after I went back into the shop for the reality of the situation to sink in. I suddenly realized I had bigger worries than an employee drinking on the job and an ex-husband living next door to me. It didn't take long for the news of Manny's death to spread, for people to find out that I'd been at the scene and saw some of what happened. My presence in his beeyard and the manner and place where Manny died didn't help matters one bit.

It only took one excited town gossip named P. P. Patti Dwyre to put what I feared the most into words. P. P. Patti, short for Pity-Party Patti, lived next door to me (on the opposite side of Clay) and spent most of her time trying to convince people to feel sorry for her, making sure everyone knew just how crappy her life was. Her life wasn't one bit worse than anyone else's. She just complained more.

"Raccoons got into my attic," P. P. Patti whined to me, handing over a cloth grocery bag. I rang up her items and began placing them in the bag. "It's probably going to cost a gazillion dollars to repair the damage, and I just don't know where the money will come from or where to find anyone to help with the handy work."

"Put a notice on the board." I waved to the bulletin board next to the entryway where customers sold their litters of puppies and kittens, or looked for work, or offered to deliver topsoil and mulch in the summer months or plow snow in the winter.

Patti's head swung in the general direction, but I could tell she had other things on her mind.

"I heard," she said in front of everyone inside the store, "that Manny was murdered by killer bees."

That's all it took.

"Was Manny really stung to death by bees?" Stanley asked the group in general.

"We won't know anything for sure until the medical examiner finishes up," I said.

I counted on a favorable verdict, so I kept quiet, mainly because it was easiest. But looking back, I should have made it clear that there was no way honeybees could've been involved in Manny's death. Yellow jackets were the most likely culprits, having the ability to sting multiple times. Yellow jackets were loners, not traveling as a group, but if one got angry and stung, it released a chemical that alerted other yellow jackets. Then they would arrive on the scene and join in the attack.

Whether venom killed Manny or something else caused his death, only Jackson would be able to say conclusively after performing his medical examiner's miracles.

I felt so bad for Grace that my heart ached.

I heard a truck's backup alarm and spotted Ray Goodwin's delivery truck sliding in to park in the back of the store. Trent came out to unload produce. He carried in boxes filled with vegetables while Ray ticked things off on a supply sheet. I joined him.

"I need a signature," Ray said, handing me the clipboard. "Awful about Manny and those bees."

"His bees didn't kill him." I signed off on the order, thinking I'd be saying that a lot in the upcoming days.

"Sure looked like they did," he said. "I'm the one who found him right after I stopped at Kenny's Bees."

I glanced up from the clipboard. Hunter had already told me that Ray found Manny, but that wasn't what caught my attention. "Kenny Langley's?"

Although I knew of the Langley family through my grandmother, I'd officially met Kenny just once, in the spring, when he and Manny sat down to negotiate sales territories. I didn't like him from the start, because he'd treated me with an exaggerated indifference. Plus, he'd called me "the girl."

I'd been working in the honey house right next to where he and Manny had had their little chat. So I knew what the old-fashioned handshake entailed. Manny would take Waukesha County, Kenny would stay in Washington County—a logical solution, since they each lived and worked in his own territory. It was a truce that seemed to satisfy both of them. As the two fastest-growing producers in both counties, they didn't seem at all concerned about the little guys who operated hobby honey farms and dabbled in a sale here and there. Manny had introduced me to Kenny when they first sat down, Kenny more or less ignored me, then before the meeting broke up, Manny asked me to be the official contact person if there were any issues.

That had been a pleasant surprise, in spite of my not liking

Kenny. Anything to be involved. Manny wasn't interested in the sales and negotiation end of his business, which led me to hope that I would be able to take that burden off his shoulders completely in the future. Marketing was second nature to me after owning a small business like The Wild Clover. In any case, there hadn't been any problems that caused me and Kenny to meet again, which suited me just fine.

"What were you doing at Kenny Langley's?" I asked.

"Oops." Ray looked uncomfortable. His eyes flitted away and his coloring deepened like he'd been caught with his hand in the cash register.

"You're distributing honey from Kenny's?" I said with narrowing eyes. Kenny's Bees should definitely have been off-limits to Ray. Every since he took over deliveries two years ago, Manny and Ray had had an exclusive agreement regarding honey. Ray helped Manny get his honey onto other grocers' shelves, and Ray received a deeper discount. Since I had a small piece of the action based on my own sales' efforts, Ray's actions cut into my profits, too. I shoved the clipboard back at him. "You have an agreement with Queen Bee Honey, and you know it. How long has this been going on with Kenny's Bees?"

"Only once," Ray said, which is exactly what my ex, Clay, had said the first time I caught *him*. "And I feel real bad about it."

"I bet you do, and you're going to feel worse when I take a percentage off this invoice you just handed me to compensate for you reneging on an agreement, which, by the way, is now null and void."

"Come on, Story. It won't happen again."

"Manny's not even in his grave," I said, laying on the guilt with a spatula. "Or he'd be turning in it."

"I promise. I really do. What if I take a few more cases than usual and find new buyers? My route's expanding. I can sell more."

"We'll talk about it later." I gave him a hard look, but my voice changed to small and pained. "Now tell me about finding Manny."

"Not much to tell." Ray tipped his ball cap back and scratched his head. "I was supposed to pick up cases of honey between nine and ten this morning. I got there a little before ten and found him covered in bees. I called nine-one-one."

"Was he dead?"

"I don't know—he wasn't moving, and I wasn't about to check his vital signs with bees flying everywhere."

"I didn't see you there this afternoon."

"I freaked out after I called for help. That never happened to me before, a crisis like that with me the only one around. I've never been too good in emergencies. I should have stayed, I know. The sheriff let me have it good for leaving."

When he drove off, I went inside through the back door thinking about Ray Goodwin. When our long-time deliveryman retired, Ray managed to land the job. But he'd always been a loser with a capital *L*, moving from one job after another, most of them finishing fast with his termination. I made a mental note to keep a better eye on him in the future.

The store buzzed with activity, giving me another brief moment of guilty pain; I felt bad that my store was benefiting from Manny's death, but it clearly was—I had the evidence of that right before my eyes. A line at the register kept Brent busy ringing up orders. I took over behind the counter so he could help his brother unpack cases of fresh produce from Ray's truck—apples, corn on the cob, cabbage, beets, and a variety of late potatoes, including my favorite, fingerlings. Today's delivery was only a small sampling of the abundant produce Wisconsin had to offer at this time of year.

For the rest of the evening, while the twins and I worked,

through the pizza we shared from Stu's Bar and Grill, until eight o'clock when we closed up, I could hear the growing concern in customers' voices.

I walked the two short blocks home, knowing it was only a matter of time before the residents of the town would come hunting for killers in my own backyard. I had to think of something to prove that Manny's bees were innocent.

Lights were off in my ex-husband's jewelry shop next door, but they were on in Clay's small living area behind the shop, meaning he was entertaining. Why else would he be home on a Friday night? I wondered if he was still with Faye, or if he'd already moved on to someone new.

Faye Tilley, as the entire town knew thanks to their performance outside my store, was only Clay's latest in a long line of females extending way back into our history as a couple. While I expected my ex to have the unmitigated gall and extreme bad taste to bring her to the divorce proceeding, I blamed Faye just as much for going along with something like that. To top it off, she'd come wearing dragonfly earrings and a wire butterfly barrette in her hair, original pieces I recognized as Clay's handmade jewelry.

For some twisted reason, it was comforting to know there were other women in the world with judgment as awful as mine. I felt slightly guilty for being happy that it wasn't me lying in his bed, but it didn't last more than a second or two. Let someone else think they could change him. The man was like a shell—beautiful on the outside, hollow on the inside.

I turned away from Clay's house and considered taking my kayak out. It was a routine of mine almost every night. Late in the evening, right before bed, was the best time to be on the Oconomowoc River. I'd added reflective tape to the sides of my kayak and a few strips of it on my life jacket and, on nights when the moon wasn't shining to light my way, I wore a waterproof headlamp.

But tonight the river didn't beckon me. I would probably see death in every shadow. Besides, I was drop-dead tired from the day's stress.

Those nightmares I'd been worrying about after seeing Manny's dead body caught up with me. I woke up in the middle of the night, startled, thinking I had heard loud voices followed by a scream. I flipped on the outside lights, but didn't see anything unusual in the backyard. My bees had bunked down at the first fading light. Nothing moved.

I went back to bed and waited for morning, convinced that the scream had come out of my own unconscious mind.

Five

Clouds rolled in overnight. The early-morning air smelled of gathering rain when I sat down at my backyard patio table with a hot cup of coffee—and fresh pain over Manny.

I'd been too tired and distraught last night to gloat over how the old family house was finally totally mine. Of course, I'd lived in it most of my life, first as a child, then with Clay, but the deed had never been in only my name.

Now it was mine.

My house.

It belonged to me. I loved the sound of that.

The lot was narrow, but what it didn't have in width, it made up for in depth, going all the way back to the Oconomowoc River. I'd repainted the house from faded gray to sunshine yellow, given the wraparound front porch a splash of the same color, and added bright white trim. I added three colorful Adirondacks to the porch, the same kind as at the store. The beehives were in the backyard, closer to the river than to the house, placed strategically in a protected spot near my vegetable garden.

On the other side of my garden, an old coop still stood where we had raised chickens when I was growing up. I'd been seriously considering getting back into raising a few chickens of my own for the benefit of fresh, organic eggs.

The weeping willows, which hung over the riverbed, had inspired the town founders to name the short street in front of my home Willow Street. Nature enthusiasts could turn off Main Street, drive past my house and Clay's, and launch their canoes and kayaks from the end of the street.

Besides my ex to the west, cedars flanked the east side of my property, giving me some relief from Pity-Party Patti's gossip antennas, although her two-story home rose above my privacy hedge, and if she really wanted to spy, she could. Not that there was anything worth watching at my house.

Being sandwiched between my ex-husband and the town gossip wasn't the best of situations, but I wouldn't give up my place for anything in the world because in spite of my undesirable neighbors, I owned a tiny slice of paradise.

The river formed the northern boundary, and a hedge of viburnum along the front walkway gave the front porch a little privacy. I'd planted flowers and herbs everywhere. All the bee's favorites, especially:

- Purple coneflowers—these lavender beauties are a member of the sunflower family, which bees love

- Phlox—the tall garden variety, mine are white and pink

- Yarrow—its leaves can be eaten like spinach, although I haven't tried it

- Butterfly weed—an orange species of milkweed, which all nectar-loving creatures are attracted to

- Lavender—for potpourris and dried bouquets

- Coreopsis—a cheerful yellow flower that blooms all summer, which is what I like about it

When my busy worker bees weren't helping themselves to my varieties, they were across the street, gathering pollen to mix with mine from Moraine Gardens, a perennial nursery that specialized in native Wisconsin plants.

I decided to take my kayak out on the river, since it was Saturday and the twins didn't expect me in at the store until sometime in the afternoon. Kayaking was like meditation to me. The river and nature, the sounds and smells, calmed me like nothing else could. And after what had happened to Manny, I needed peace and quiet.

Except my kayak wasn't on the grassy spot beside the river where I always kept it. This wasn't the first time someone had "borrowed" it.

Clay answered his door after I banged on it several times. His physical presence in the doorway provided his alibi, proving him innocent of this particular watercraft theft. Damn. I'd really hoped the thieves weren't those kids again.

Clay wore silk pajamas and had bed creases in his face. A diamond stud glistened from his left ear, something new since the divorce hearing two days ago. His dishwater blond hair had sleep spikes in it.

"Have you seen my kayak?" I said, refusing to lower my gaze to his bare feet, which beckoned from my peripheral view. His gorgeous feet had caused me to overlook his fatal flaws in the past. "It's missing again."

"Too bad, but I haven't seen it. You can search my body

if you want, honey." He opened the door wider, spread his arms, and grinned wolfishly.

"Don't call me honey," I said. "And where's Faye? Did she take it?" I didn't bother masking the disgust in my voice.

"She isn't . . . uh . . . available," Clay said. "And she didn't take your kayak. Faye, uh . . . is . . ." His eyes shifted toward the bedroom. "Uh . . . indisposed."

"Never mind," I said, turning and stalking away back toward my house.

I showered, dressed in shorts and a halter top, slipped on purple flip-flops from my vast flip-flop collection, breakfasted on toast spread with peanut butter and honey, and drove out to Grace's in my pickup truck. I had purchased the used truck right after Clay and I moved into town. It was over a decade old, a rusty blue with a few dings and more than one hundred thousand miles. But she never let me down.

Grace's sister-in-law, Betty, answered the door, talking to me through the screen. I noticed again how enormous she looked and wondered if she was having twins.

"Grace is at the funeral home with her brother," she said, without a trace of friendliness. "Making arrangements. She won't be back until later."

"When's the funeral?" I asked, unintentionally matching her tone.

"Tuesday," Betty said.

"What about the autopsy?"

"There isn't going to be one."

"What?" I couldn't believe my ears. I was counting on an autopsy to clear the bees' good name. "How is that possible? Doesn't Grace want to know why Manny died?"

"She already knows. The bees killed him. Cut and dry." Over her enormous stomach, Betty chopped one hand into the other for effect. "Besides, the medical examiner didn't order one, and Grace didn't want it. She just wants a traditional burial without a lot of fuss. The M.E. said it wasn't a suspicious death, so he approved her request."

"I think it's pretty suspicious." That comment came right out of my big mouth without any thought at all. What I meant to say was that I thought yellow jackets were the bad guys, but apparently Betty took my comment the wrong way.

"Don't go stirring up things," she said. "This family doesn't need any more trouble from the likes of you."

"There's no need to get nasty." Jeez, Betty was a mean mom-to-be!

Betty clamped her lips into a thin line. We glared at each other through the screen door.

I gave in first, since I was dealing with a grieving family member. "I guess it's Grace's call. If you don't mind, I'll check on the bees and get a few cases of honey from the honey house."

Betty didn't look pleased. She sighed a big sigh, whether from frustration or her enormous pregnant body, I wasn't sure. "Help yourself to the honey, but say good-bye to the bees. Somebody from the bee association is coming tonight to get them."

"What?" I said, stunned by this news. "Why wouldn't Grace have talked to me first? Who's taking them?"

Betty shrugged. "Darn if I know. But good riddance."

"Listen, when is Grace coming back? Precisely." I tried to hide my outrage, but it was dripping from my mouth like rabies foam. First, no autopsy; now the bees were being taken away? This was too much to bear. It would mean the end of Queen Bee Honey.

"I said she will be back later. You'll have to be satisfied with that." Betty's eyes narrowed. If I was getting mad, so was she.

I faked a smile. "Sorry, everybody's on edge after what happened."

"Not me," Betty said.

She watched from the doorway while I went into the beeyard. Honeybees flew in and out of the hive openings like aircrafts arriving and departing from a finely tuned airport. Guard bees made sure the incoming flights belonged there, ready to turn away any intruders if they smelled different from the hive's members. Beehives might all look the same to us, but the bees knew the difference.

Honeybees circled my head, curious and harmless.

I closed my eyes and pretended that everything was as it had been before Manny died. I listened to the buzzing, smelling the freshness of the day and its accompanying promise of rain. When I opened my eyes, my loss felt even more pronounced.

Knowing this could be my last time ever in Manny's beeyard hit me like a ton of bricks. After dark, when the bees were all inside their hives for the night, someone was going to take them away. Manny wouldn't have wanted just anybody to take the bees. He would have wanted *me* to have them.

He'd rarely attended bee association meetings because the meetings were mostly social gatherings, beekeepers talking shop, and that wasn't Manny's way. Although he knew most of the members, he wasn't overly friendly with any of them, though if they needed advice, he was right there for them.

I had to talk to Grace before it was too late. What was she thinking to let an outsider have Manny's bees? Would she even give me a chance to buy some of the equipment, or was that going, too? I felt so helpless.

I approached the honey house. The weathered, graying wood gave it a rustic look, but if it had been mine, I'd have painted it bright yellow with white trim. Yellow was absolutely my favorite color. I slipped a key into the padlock, letting myself in. The smell of honey was strong.

I looked around the room at the extracting equipment, then at a stack of frames in the corner. I saw familiar rows of empty honey jars and lids on a tabletop and cases of filled jars everywhere.

Manny and I had packaged some of the honey right from the hives to sell as comb honey, delicious when spread on bread. The rest went into a special machine that spun around and extracted the honey from the combs for bottling. In bee lingo the process is called spinning honey.

After loading two cases of bottled honey into my truck, I selected several honeybee reference books to take with me, ones that I'd purchased myself. Then I decided at the last minute to also take our bee journal.

Well, okay, it wasn't exactly "our" journal. It had really belonged to Manny, but some of the entries were mine, so I felt a certain ownership. Manny had kept detailed information on his progress against mites and diseases that might come in handy with my two remaining hives. He had also been a great experimenter, testing ways to increase production of different components like royal jelly and propolis.

Honey production wasn't the only source of income for a beekeeper. Royal jelly was the stuff nurse bees fed to larvae to produce queens. Besides its anti-aging benefits, which made it a favorite ingredient in skin creams, royal jelly had anti-cancer properties, a hot commodity, health-wise. Then there was the propolis, a special glue bees made from trees to seal their homes from extreme temperatures. Scientists, including backyard scientists like Manny, were finding out that it had powerful antibiotic components, and serious beekeepers were keeping track of their results, studying the market.

And he was scientific about his research into colony collapse disorder, something that was threatening honeybees all across the country. Whatever he had been doing seemed to be working, because he had strong hives. Some

beekeepers were reporting unexplained hive losses, entire
hives dying at the same time. Not Manny.

I planned to read through the journal, make copies of
some of the pages, then return it to Grace, if she cared
enough to want it back.

Except the journal wasn't on the table or in the drawer
where Manny usually kept it. And it didn't show up in my
search.

Giving up, I locked the honey house, took one last long
look at it and at the activity in the beeyard, and drove away.
As I left, my thoughts turned criminal. What if I came back
after dark but before the association folks came, and loaded
as many hives into my truck as possible? Then Grace would
think the association had taken them, right? By the time she
found out, I'd have them safely hidden away. Besides, what
would she care? They would be gone and, as Betty said,
good riddance. Right? After that, I'd buy the entire honey
house from her, equipment and all, and have the house
moved as one big piece on a gigantic truck, the kind you
see with the "Wide Load" flags on the side.

There was room for a honey house in my large backyard, I thought. I'd just have to do some measuring.

Me and my pipe dreams.

But it's all about having a positive attitude.

Six

Clouds overhead were darkening, but still no rain. Since I couldn't paddle down the river because my kayak was missing and my effort to see Grace had been a complete bust, I decided that healthy physical labor might improve my day. The Wild Clover was next on my to-do list.

"Business has been steady all morning," Brent said, nodding his carrot head. The twins both had red hair and a healthy dose of freckles, but telling them apart wasn't hard, because they weren't identical. Trent's hair was browner, and he wore it longer. Plus I've known them their entire lives. "This is the first slow-down," he added.

Trent appeared from aisle four. "You're early."

"My morning isn't going so well. I thought I'd improve it by coming here."

"I hope you aren't sending us home yet," Brent said.

"We need the money for all those expensive textbooks we have to buy."

"You can stay all day," I promised. I could use the time to find my kayak and track down Grace. "Think you could bring in two cases of honey from the back of my truck?" Trent promptly took on the task.

Third-grade teacher Bruce Cook came in, greeted us, and wandered away with a shopping list in his hand. Then Police Chief Johnny Jay showed up.

"Well, if it isn't Missy Fischer," he said, still refusing to call me Story after all these years. "I've been looking for you."

"Don't act so surprised to find me," I said. "After all, this is my store. It shouldn't have been too hard, Johnny."

"It's Police Chief Jay to you."

"Whatever." I bent over to add more honey sticks to the almost-empty containers, careful not to mix the orange ones with the clover ones, trying to ignore him. Maybe he'd go away.

"Heard you were serving alcohol inside this establishment yesterday."

I glanced up and grinned. "Did I forget to invite you to the party? Shucks. Don't know how that slipped my mind."

"I'd like to see your permit."

"Brent," I said with a cattish grin, "show Johnny the temporary permit. It's under the five-dollar bills in the register."

Brent pulled the piece of paper out of the drawer with a sigh of relief that said he sure was glad I'd managed to stay ahead of Johnny one more time. Even Johnny looked surprised. It pays to be a smart business owner, especially when dealing with authority figures who don't like you.

Our police chief scanned the permit. I could sense the wheels turning in his overblown brain while he looked for a loophole to nail me. He practically threw the permit back at Brent.

More customers arrived, signaling the end of the lull. Either they had been on their way to the store anyway and it was pure chance that the police chief was inside, or they'd seen his SUV and didn't want to miss any late-breaking news. Glancing through the window, I noticed that none of my customers had parked near him, though. Johnny Jay had been known to deflate tires if a driver parked too close to his vehicle. And Johnny Jay made up his own rules about what was or wasn't too close.

He's a mean one. Yes, he is.

I straightened from my task. "I heard there isn't going to be an autopsy," I said. "Why not?"

Customers craned to hear. Johnny noticed and frowned.

"Normally I wouldn't dignify that kind of question with an answer but I want you to get the facts right—something you don't always do—so witnesses to my reply are more than welcome."

Well, *that* was nasty and totally uncalled for. When had I ever gotten facts wrong?

Customers edged closer, pretending to study the shelves, their ears practically quivering.

"Manny Chapman's death was not suspicious in any way," Johnny said. "His body isn't going to the crematory, which could have changed things. He's having a normal burial, and his death wasn't an accident involving other people. According to the medical examiner, Chapman died from toxic stings, in particular stings in his mouth, which caused his throat to swell and obstruct his airway. And that's that. Why on earth would you suggest an autopsy?"

"Honeybees didn't kill him," I said, remembering Manny's swollen lips. How awful! "Some kind of wasps killed him, and since we have tons of yellow jackets at this time of year, it's perfectly obvious they did it. I sort of hoped to have that reinforced, so the entire community wouldn't go into some kind of panic over *my* honeybees."

"You want us to prove exactly what kind of bee was responsible by slicing up the poor man? By sawing off his brain and making a mess of his innards? Grace didn't want an autopsy. Do you want to upset the poor woman more than she already is?"

I felt all eyes burning into me, waiting for my reply. The cash register was completely silent. "Of course not," I said, conceding a small win to Johnny Jay, who made disgustingly smug noises with his lips. "But why is everybody having such a hard time distinguishing between bees and wasps?"

No one replied, mainly because they couldn't tell the difference and they didn't care.

Just when I thought the day couldn't get any worse, Lori Spandle, our resident real estate agent, came in wearing a bee veil.

"Oh come on, Lori," I said. "What in the world are you doing?"

"Protecting myself while I organize a spray committee," she said. "We're going to eliminate this immediate threat to our lives before it's too late. This is a preemptive strike. Anybody here want to help save the town?"

I can read body language pretty well. My customers leaned toward Lori, giving me looks that said I would lose them to the other side if I didn't think of something quick.

"Bullet point number one, you'd be killing innocent bees," I told them, in case Lori was thinking of including my bees in her mad attack, which I was certain she was. "Think about what you're considering. Bullet point number two, some of you could lose your livelihoods with that kind of talk. We count on those bees to pollinate our crops. We'd be stabbing ourselves in the back. Bullet point number three, we now know for sure that Manny died from stings, thanks to the chief, but they could only have come from *wasps*, not bees."

"But one of us could be next," Lori said, ignoring all my bullet points.

The only bees Lori had ever had to worry about were the ones she'd disturbed when she snuck over to visit Clay while he was still my husband. She'd knocked around in the bees' territory and riled a few attentive scouts into giving her warning stings. I had watched from the window, knowing what she was up to. By then it was common knowledge that I'd filed for divorce, but Lori was married to Grant Spandle, our town chairman and local land developer, and he wouldn't have been too happy with his wife if he'd found out.

"We have to take action," Lori said, intent on rallying the masses.

"What you *aren't* going to do is recruit in my store." I glared at her round, cunning face camouflaged behind the netting.

Johnny Jay butted in. "Maybe you should stock some of those veils," he said during the pregnant pause while Lori and I squared off. "They'd go like hotcakes."

"Besides," I said, ignoring that last remark from the police chief, "I have news to share with you that'll end this foolishness right now. Grace's sister-in-law told me the beehives are being picked up tonight by someone from the bee association. They'll be gone. You won't have to worry anymore."

"What about your bees?" Lori said, confirming my suspicion that she was after me more than anything. "They might be killer bees, too."

"My bees? Killer bees?" I snorted in disgust. "Yeah, right." Then I addressed the others, "Any of you are welcome to come over and check out my hives."

Bruce Cook was hanging at the edge of the group, listening in. His third-grade class had toured my backyard beehives. "Bruce," I said. "Did any of your kids get stung?"

"You know they didn't," Bruce said. "It was a fun day."

"See," I pointed to Lori. "Come on over and see for yourself if you don't believe Bruce."

"No, thanks," Lori said. "I've already had first-hand experience with your aggressive bees."

"Should I explain to everyone why my bees went after you? And what you were doing at the time?"

"That won't be necessary," Lori said, taking a step back like I'd slapped her. I noticed her tone evened out instantly as she rethought her strategy. I'd never threatened to expose her before, but my back was up against the wall. I'd thrown away the rule book, especially the chapter on fair play. It had been surprisingly easy to stoop to her level.

No one else took me up on the offer to visit, either, but they did agree to rein in the mob for one more day when I promised to deliver positive proof that the bees were gone from Manny's.

"That won't help protect *my* residents from *your* bees," Johnny Jay said. "They should be destroyed, too, just to make absolutely certain no one gets hurt."

Murmurs of agreement.

Personally, I thought destroying the police chief would go furthest in protecting all of us. "I'm also going to prove that honeybees didn't kill Manny," I said, instead of voicing my murderous thoughts regarding Johnny Jay. I had no idea *how* to prove my claim, though. "But one thing at a time. Give me a chance."

The fight had temporarily gone out of Lori, and once the police chief got a call from dispatch, sending him on his way, the rest of the group disbanded.

Things settled down after that because of the event at the library. There had been talk of canceling the bluegrass band jam because of Manny's death, but everybody agreed that we needed each other at a time like this, so the jam was on. Free lemonade and the chance to listen to music were big bonuses on a cloudy Saturday afternoon. Emily had planned smart with a giant tent, just in case, so the event was on rain or shine.

I walked over to Stu's Bar and Grill, planning to borrow Stu's canoe to scout for my kayak, hoping to find it and get back and over to the library as soon as possible.

"Hey, Story," Stu called out from behind the bar. I waved. Stu Trembly had bedroom eyes, those smoldering kind that show a little white just under the irises. He was also engaged to Becky Hellman and had been for years. Most of the local women had given up on him long ago and moved on to more available men.

As unlikely as it was, I saw that my cousin Carrie Ann Retzlaff and Hunter Wallace were having lunch together. I sat down with them and swiped a French fry from what was left of Hunter's hamburger platter before calling out to Stu, "Do you still keep your canoe down by the river?"

"It's there. Why? Want to use it?"

"My kayak is missing again."

"Kids messing around like last time?" Carrie Ann suggested.

"Probably." Two weeks ago I'd discovered my kayak ditched about half a mile from my house after kids had filled it with water and sunk it. "I'll need a piece of rope to tie it to the canoe. That is, if I get lucky and find it."

"We're done with lunch. I'll help you look," Hunter offered. He reached in his back pocket, removed a wallet, and placed a few bills on the table. He wasn't working, judging by his attire. That meant well-worn jeans, a white T-shirt that set off his tan, and . . . were his bare toes exposed? I suppressed an urge to look down.

"You better get going before it starts raining," Stu said, coming around the bar with a piece of rope. "A storm is moving in."

"Want to come along, Carrie Ann?" I asked as we stood up. Hunter's feet were definitely bare except for a pair of sandals.

"No thanks," Carrie Ann said, running both hands through her short head of hair to refresh the spiky look she liked so much. "I have errands. I'll see you later, Hunter."

"I'll pick you up," he said to her.

"When will you need me again at The Wild Clover?" Carrie Ann asked me.

"I'll call you after I look at the twins' schedules." Never again, was my best guess, and I planned to deliver that exact message to her in private. Carrie Ann wasn't a stable employee—she's been late or even a no-show to work several times, took cigarette breaks every ten minutes, and had a perpetual hangover written across her face. It was too bad. She and I had been friends growing up and had shared a lot of good times together before she'd spiraled into a bottle of beer. The family had all been trying to tell her she had a drinking problem for years. Even after her husband left her five years ago and got custody of their two kids, she still hadn't been ready to face the truth.

Stu's piece of property ran along the Oconomowoc River just like mine did. The Winnebago Indians named the waterway, which is quite a mouthful for outsiders. *Oconomowoc* means "River of Lakes," which sounds confusing unless you know that this area is lake country and the Oconomowoc River intersects with many of our other lakes.

"Where's Ben?" I hadn't seen Hunter's dog.

"In my truck. He can wait there as long as we aren't gone too long."

"We'll do this quickly."

Hunter wrapped a windbreaker around his waist, and we

dragged Stu's canoe into the water, threw our shoes and the rope into the bottom of it, waded in a few feet, and hopped in at the same time, one of us on each side. Smooth as silk, right as rain.

The air smelled sweet and warm, but cloud formations swirled above us.

The wind began to blow as soon as we set off.

Seven

We headed upstream, Hunter in the stern for muscle power and steering, me up front in the bow, paddling and scouting for rocks and shallow spots. Once we left Moraine behind us, hardwoods flanked ridges following the banks of the river. Then the trees on the east side opened up and the slope tapered off into cattail marshes. Red-winged blackbirds perched on top of cattails and wetland grasses, calling to each other. When they flew off almost simultaneously, it should have been an indication of things to come. But we missed the warning.

Hunter and I hadn't said much until now, although I was bursting with curiosity. "What's new with Carrie Ann?" I finally asked. I couldn't help myself. Call me nosy, but I really wanted to know what they were doing together. Back when Carrie Ann and I hung out in high school, Hunter hadn't cared for her personality. Of course, times and people change. I still couldn't see the two of them being close, though.

Hunter laughed easy behind me. "Jealous?"

"That's the arrogant man I know so well," I teased. "Sorry to disappoint you, but I was just wondering." Which wasn't exactly true. Hunter and I had spent some time together recently and I liked what I saw.

He chuckled again, but didn't answer my question.

I pressed on. "I have to tell Carrie Ann she won't be working for me anymore." I kept a keen eye out for any sign of my kayak, first scanning the sides of the river in case the pint-sized troublemakers had pulled it ashore, then peering mid-stream in case they'd sunk it like last time. Those kids could have left it anywhere.

"I wouldn't fire her if I were you," Hunter said.

"I can't handle any more of her erratic behavior. She's an alcoholic."

"She needs a job, and she needs the stability you can provide her."

"Listen to you defending her." I switched my paddle to the other side, dipped the blade while I watched ripples of wind glide across the water. All bird life had vanished from sight because of the incoming storm.

"Would you reconsider your decision if I told you she's going to AA meetings?" Hunter said.

"Since when? She was drunk at the store yesterday."

"She just had her first one."

That surprised me. Carrie Ann had come a long way if she was ready to finally admit she had a drinking problem.

Now that Hunter mentioned her newfound sobriety, I couldn't remember seeing any beer bottles on their lunch table.

"She didn't say anything to me about AA," I said. "Carrie Ann didn't mention one word to me, and I'm family."

"Maybe she didn't tell you *because* you're family."

"I wouldn't have told anybody else. She could have trusted me."

"Give her another chance?"

"I don't know. I'll have to think about it." I stopped paddling and twisted around to look at Hunter. "Should we head back?" He looked up. So did I. The sky had darkened significantly since we'd set out.

"I don't hear thunder in the distance," he said. "I'm not afraid of a little water. Unless you want to turn around?"

I listened for rumbling. "I don't hear anything, either."

"Then onward, Pocahontas."

It figured that soon after, the sky let loose. I could hear rain slapping at the treetops, driving through to the next layer of canopy before pounding into the water around the canoe like buckshot. We guided the canoe under as much cover as we could find along the wooded side of the shoreline, then met in the middle of the canoe to huddle under the windbreaker Hunter had had the foresight to bring along.

In better weather, this was my favorite part of the Oconomowoc River, where it continued all the way to Loew Lake, which nestled in a valley within one of our state forests. I'd completed that scenic journey many times. From where we sat I could see the Ice Age Trail following the west side of the river.

Before long, rain was falling in sheets and the windbreaker broke down as a working tarp. Hunter held the canoe in place with a firm grip on a thick maple branch, otherwise we would be spinning out of control in what I feared might develop into funnel weather.

If the firehouse tornado siren went off, it meant we were in big trouble.

I remembered fantasizing about an adventure similar to this when I watched Michael Douglas and Kathleen Turner fight their way through a Colombian rain forest in *Romancing the Stone*. And again when I saw *Six Days,*

Seven Nights, where Harrison Ford and Anne Heche crash-land on a deserted island. How she couldn't adore him from the very beginning was beyond my comprehension.

Recklessness and romance. That's what I craved.

Hunter had that same starlike male sexiness that Ford and Douglas had. But I didn't look half as good as Kathleen or Anne did with mud all over and their hair plastered to their faces. Not to mention the cold. Suddenly, I was freezing to death in wet clothes that clamped onto my body like cling wrap. It didn't feel good at all, and totally not sexy.

"How are you doing?" Hunter asked, with water streaming down his face.

"I need a hot shower." I tried to keep the whimper out of my voice. My kayak could go fly a kite for all I cared.

"You'll have to settle for hot conversation instead," Hunter said, still holding us in place with one hand clutching the branch. The other arm squeezed me closer to his body, where I got a really good view of his feet.

They were tanned and toned and shiny wet from the rain, with wisps of man hair on each toe.

I needed to redirect my thoughts before he tuned into them, an ability I've discovered that most men possess as long as it involved sexual context. "I wanted to thank you for trying to get Grace to agree to an autopsy," I said, wiping mascara from my face. Movie stars never lost their makeup, even after a night between the sheets. So much for this particular fantasy.

"Grace is a stubborn woman when she makes up her mind," Hunter said.

"Her sister-in-law said someone from the beekeepers association was picking up the honeybees tonight."

"Don't you want them?"

"Of course I do, but apparently Grace didn't think I was the best choice. And the bees aren't really mine, at least not legally. Manny owned them. Grace can do what she wants."

"Maybe she felt that if you had them, the bees would be too close to home for her. They'd be a constant reminder of the day she lost her husband."

I shivered as the wind gusted again, driving rain into my skin like pinpricks. "Let's get out of here."

"We'll have the wind at our back. We can give it a try." He pulled me closer, if that was even possible. "First, promise to give Carrie Ann another chance."

"What's it to you?" I blurted out, pulling away enough to meet his eyes. "Why all the sudden concern?"

"Because she came to me for help."

"Why would she do that?"

He shrugged. "What do you say?" he pressed. "Give her another chance?"

I couldn't refuse those deep blue eyes. I sighed. "As long as she stays sober, comes in on time, and does her job. Yes, I'll give her another chance. But you owe me."

"Thanks. Come on. Let's go. The storm is passing."

Which was true. As quickly as the rain had started, it was ending. The clouds didn't exactly part and the sun didn't shine, but the end was in sight. If only the wind would die down. When Hunter pulled away from me, I tried to wring some of the water out of my halter top.

The adventurous romantic fantasy I had envisioned was completely ruined.

"Is that your kayak?" Hunter called out. I followed his gaze.

"That's it!"

My kayak must have been lodged between clumps of cattails in the marsh, and the wind and torrential downpour had set it free. Designed for speed, it came at us fast with the wind gusting at its stern and vegetation streaming behind it like it had risen from a watery grave. We paddled like mad to intercept it before it crashed into the rocky bank on our side of the river or had a chance to change course and take off downstream ahead of us.

We came within reaching distance. I dropped the paddle into the bow of the canoe and stretched out both hands to get a firm grip on the kayak.

What I saw made me sit back down hard. I couldn't form words. My mind couldn't get past the image of the body sprawled faceup inside the kayak, hair knotted and plastered to her face, her red top drenched and splattered to her body like thick paint.

"Dammit!" I heard behind me.

Eight

Hunter scrambled toward the front of the canoe, almost tipping us out into the river. I clutched both sides, lifting up and shifting my weight in the direction I thought would steady us, but my brain wasn't working like it should.

"Sit down," Hunter shouted.

Too late. The canoe flipped faster than my numb mind could register the action. Splashes and sputters later, we came up clinging to the canoe's underside.

Hunter had a few choice words for the situation, which I won't bother repeating. Nor did I acknowledge the glare he shot my way before we managed to right the canoe and get back inside.

By then the kayak had banged up alongside the river-bank, and we had to paddle over.

"Who is it?" he asked, jumping out of the canoe and

grabbing the kayak before it could move away. "Do you know?"

I nodded, not that he was looking my way. "Her name is Faye Tilley."

I'd seen the dead woman on my ex-husband's arm at our divorce trial, and most recently, making a spectacle in front of The Wild Clover. Faye was wearing the same jewelry she'd worn at the hearing—a butterfly barrette in her hair, and one of the dragonfly earrings was dangling from her right ear. The left one was missing.

I stumbled out of the canoe onto solid ground and considered passing out. But that wouldn't accomplish anything productive. Instead I sat down hard and watched Hunter spring into action. I made a mental bullet-point list of what happened next:

- Hunter secured both the canoe and kayak, then used his cell phone, which had been inside his waterproof jacket, to call for assistance.

- It took a lifetime for backup to arrive, some on land, some by water. The approximate location where we'd first seen the kayak was marked with a buoy.

- The far shore area was marked in grids, and the search began for evidence.

- Divers went down, hunting for weapons or other clues.

- Jackson Davis, the M.E., and Johnny Jay, the police chief, both arrived. Hunter and I gave our statements, and Johnny Jay was too busy to torture me with verbal abuse, which was a huge relief.

- Afterward, we couldn't just leave Stu's canoe in the middle of nowhere, so despite being soaking wet, we declined an offer of a ride back to town and went back in the canoe.

The music from the library's bluegrass band event wasn't playing when we paddled into Moraine near Stu's. A few bar patrons standing along the river watched us come in. Hunter jumped out of the canoe and ran for his truck and took off back to join the other professionals in their search for answers. My thoughts were a jumble. I couldn't get poor Faye's face out of my head.

And Clay. He would have to be told. Did I have to be the one to tell him the horrible news?

After securing the canoe, I stood on the shore—barefoot, wet, and wind-whipped. Where had my flip-flops gone? Oh, yes, I remembered—into the river when the canoe tipped.

More people were beginning to gather at the river's edge. Word was spreading. I had to get out of here before they heard that Clay's ex-wife had found his girlfriend's dead body in her kayak.

It was true that I'd wished Clay Lane dead a bunch of times, sometimes even verbally in front of witnesses, but I'd never extended that sentiment to any of his conquests. I figured they would be punished enough when they figured out that Clay wasn't what he seemed.

A terrible idea flittered across my mind. What if Clay had killed her? Impossible. The man wasn't capable of that kind of extreme emotion. Through our entire relationship, he'd never displayed passion for anything other than his own creature comforts. Good food and sex without borders, those were his most important needs.

Someone wrapped a towel around my shoulders. My mom and grandmother appeared out of nowhere and rescued me from the crowd of spectators, guiding me to Grams's Cadillac Fleetwood, refusing to let anyone interfere with our progress.

I heard the band tuning back up.

* * *

After I took a hot shower at home, Mom handed me a cup of steaming tea, settled me in a kitchen chair, put on her everyday scowl, and went to work on my confidence. "What were you thinking to get involved in something like this?"

My defensive hackles went up. I forced them down.

Being the oldest sucks. Personally, I've always suspected our mother/daughter conflict has everything to do with me being the firstborn female. I had a theory about relationships between mothers and oldest daughters. They couldn't get along no matter how hard they tried. I'd seen it time and time again by observing other families. While Mom had a hot, poisonous tongue and spoke out before thinking about how harsh her comments were, most mother/daughter relationships were cooler and crisper. Sometimes I wished for a cold, restrained version of Mom.

Since most of my immediate family lives within a ten-mile radius of each other, I really try to get along with them the best I can. But I seem to be the only one who has unresolved issues with Mom.

Grams squeezed my arm to show support. She had her gray hair pulled up in her standard cute little bun with a new, fresh daisy tucked into it. Grams, at eighty, was an avid flower gardener, card player, and amateur photographer.

"You didn't kill that girl, did you?" Mom asked. "Please tell me you didn't."

"Of course not. I just found her. That's all there is to it."

"What must people think?" That's my mom, she really focused on the important things in life.

"Now, Helen," Grams scolded my mother. "It's your daughter we should be most concerned about, not the neighbors."

With a little coaxing from Grams, I told them what I knew, which was next to nothing other than that my kayak had gone missing and Clay had given me the impression this morning that Faye was with him, when all along she must've been lying dead in my kayak.

"You're still shaking," Grams said when I tried to take a sip of my tea and my trembling hand gave me away. "I'll get you a sweater."

"I'm fine," I said.

Grams didn't believe me about being fine. She went into my bedroom to find a cover-up. Her departure gave Mom another opportunity.

"When are you going to stop causing problems for us?" she complained. "This is killing your grandmother. First, you marry the wrong man . . ."

True. I had liked Clay more than I should have simply because my mother hadn't.

"Your personal life is spread over the entire town like a B movie . . ."

Not my fault that Clay tried to sleep with every woman in town.

"And poor Manny Chapman is killed by the same kind of bees you have, and I can look right out this window and see them all over the place. What do you have, a death wish?"

Heavy sigh.

"Now you're linked to what might turn out to be murder, through some kind of sex triangle!"

"Okay, that's going too far," I said. "I have a few bullet points for you. One, I have no control over Clay's actions. Two, Manny's death has hit me hard enough without you going through this big lecture, okay? Three, he was killed by wasps, not honeybees. Four, I'm not involved in any triangle. And five, I refuse to take responsibility for Clay's bad behavior ever again."

"Not taking responsibility has been your problem all along." Mom made a sour expression. Worry lines were permanently etched in her forehead. I knew that if I pointed them out to her, she'd blame those on me, too.

Grams came out of my bedroom carrying a cardigan.

"Mom's ready to leave," I said to her, taking the sweater and putting it on. But my goose bumps and shivers weren't from coldness. Extra layers wouldn't help bring back Manny or Faye. "Thanks for rescuing me at the river."

Grams beamed. "You're welcome, sweetie. Take care of yourself. If you don't want to be alone, you can come stay with us for a while."

"I'll remember that." *No, thanks!* Eating poisonous mushrooms would be less painful than staying with my mother.

"I'll drive," Mom said to Grams at the door, picking up an ongoing conversation that they carried from one scene to another. You'd think she'd have given up by now.

"I'm perfectly capable, Helen." Grams refused to give up the driver's seat, which annoyed my mom no end. The Cadillac Fleetwood was Grams's pride and joy. It had been the height of luxury in the mid-nineties, she took great care with it, and she never, ever allowed anyone else to drive it.

Mom gave me an eye-roll and grimace that implied we were on the same side. It said, *Look what I have to put up with*.

Grams is third-generation Morainian, Mom is fourth, making me fifth, and our family one of the oldest in town. The old cemetery, next to The Wild Clover, is filled with names from both sides, since my father came from this area, too. If you've been in Moraine as long as we have and you're from Grams's generation, you get automatic acceptance in the old guard's eyes. They watch out for each other and know more of the goings-on than they'd ever admit.

My cousin Carrie Ann came up the sidewalk as Grams and Mom were leaving.

"How are you doing, Carrie Ann?" Mom said, rather stiffly. Carrie Ann was my dad's sister Marla's daughter. Mom had never gotten along with Aunt Marla and she didn't have any use for my cousin or her hard ways, but she was bound by her manners.

"Pretty good," Carrie Ann said. "Thanks for asking."

We watched them drive away at a max of ten miles per hour with a jerky stop at the Main Street crossing.

"I'm ready to chew off my left arm," Carrie Ann said. I noticed she had a hunk of gum in her mouth. She was a visual gum chewer, rolling it around while she talked. I couldn't help staring at it. "I quit smoking this morning and it's killing me. This nicotine gum is the only thing saving my sanity." She pulled a piece out of her pocket, peeled off the foil and popped it in her mouth right along with the old one.

It was beyond me how my cousin could pull off quitting two addictions at once. But it was her business, not mine. Hunter had refused to date smokers in high school and probably still avoided it. Was she quitting for him? I wanted to ask her about AA but I didn't know if I'd blow a confidence if I did. I was sure she wouldn't have wanted Hunter telling me.

"You smell nice, instead of like smoke," I said, trying to give her encouragement. I knew she expected to be invited in, but I just couldn't entertain at the moment. "Like lilacs."

"Hey, thanks."

"I heard hypnotism helps if your willpower starts breaking down."

"Ha. I'll keep it in mind. Right now I'd like to beat my head against a wall. Anything to numb my brain. And my hands. I don't know what to do with them." She gave me a studied look. "I heard about what happened. Are you okay?"

"I'm fine. "

"You're awfully pale."

"I'm fine. Really."

"Okay, if you insist." Then Carrie Ann got to the point of her visit. "Did you figure out when I work again? I know this isn't the best time to talk about it with a dead person in your kayak and all, but I need to pay my rent and I'm a little strapped right now."

I took a moment to realize how lucky I was that The Wild Clover market was doing well enough that I could hire extra help. Times were tough. The twins needed to pay for college; Carrie Ann had rent due. Financially, I wasn't in bad shape. Although, if things had gone like Manny and I had planned and we had expanded Queen Bee Honey, my future finances would have been even more secure.

"Come by the store tomorrow afternoon," I told her. "We'll talk about it and work up a plan."

With that, Carrie Ann took her leave and went off down the street. I wondered where she was heading—home or to the bar. I hoped it was the former.

I went back inside and lay low, watching the world through the cracks in the blinds. Cop cars came down Willow Street and parked behind each other. Law officials began canvassing the neighborhood. A team swarmed into my backyard, staying wide of the beehives. They began searching along the waterline. I saw a deputy go into Moraine Gardens across the street. Clay's car was next door, so he was home. The police chief's SUV pulled up to the curb. Johnny Jay rang my bell. I had been surprised when none of the others had bothered to check to see if I was home, but now I knew—they must have been ordered to stay clear. It seemed that the police chief wanted first crack at me.

I decided to ignore him. I was all worn out emotionally and didn't have the strength to take on Johnny Jay in the manner in which I had become accustomed. When I didn't answer my door, he went over to Clay's house. My phone rang multiple times, but I didn't answer that, either, preferring to let the answering machine take over.

Nine

Not only are bullet points important in life, so are priority lists. My heart was heavy from the loss of Manny and the discovery of Faye's body. All I wanted to do was stuff myself in my bedroom closet for the rest of eternity. But I still had a bee mission to complete. I didn't want to lose them, too. Time was running out. Before long, someone was going to show up at Grace Chapman's and take the beehives.

So when the sun began its descent over the horizon and the cops had finished in my backyard, and when the squad cars disappeared from my street, I cleared my mind of all whiny, self-pitying thoughts and called Grace.

"Grace, it's Story Fischer."

"My sister-in-law had a few rather unpleasant things to say about you," she said, making this one of the poorest beginnings to a conversation in my history.

"I was upset," I said. "And rightly so, I might add. She was rather unpleasant herself. But please, tell me about the bees. Where are they going?"

"Someone called and offered to take them off my hands. What else was I going to do with them?"

"What about giving them to me?" Was Grace really this dense?

"I never thought you'd be interested."

Yeah, right!

"I love those bees. So did Manny. You can't give them to just anybody. I'll buy them from you."

"Story, they killed Manny. How could you get up every morning and look out on a bunch of killer bees after what they did? Besides, I'm already getting paid for them. I tried to explain the risk, but this beekeeper didn't seem worried."

"I know they didn't do anything to Manny. It had to have been—"

But Grace wasn't going to listen. "I won't discuss it with you anymore. I've made my decision and I'm sticking to it."

"What about the equipment and some of the other things? Can you give me first dibs on the honey extractor and Manny's journal?"

"I haven't thought that far ahead yet. And, trust me, I'm not doing an inventory any time soon. I never set foot in the honey house when Manny was alive and I'm not changing that now. I'll allow you to come out and get honey, though. To sell, I mean, and I'm counting on you to be honest with the proceeds."

"Of course." I was so relieved that I let the honesty shot fly by without comment. At least she would be open to working with me in some capacity. But she was one unbending woman.

"What's the name of the bee association member who's taking the bees?" I wanted to know.

"Gerald Smith," she said. "He's coming in an hour or so."

"I'm so sorry about Manny," I said, but Grace had already hung up.

I knew now what I had to do. My motive was crystal clear and there would be no turning back.

I was going to steal as many of Manny's beehives as I could.

Black is a cool color. For starters, it's slimming. You can wear it for any occasion—working out, sleeping, dressing up, and for blending in to the dark of night.

I pulled on black sweats and a black tee. Then added a black fleece after I opened the door and realized that the night air was a bit brisk. I had a black ball cap on my head with my hair tucked up inside.

I'd left my truck at The Wild Clover, which was standard operating procedure for me. Living two blocks away, I didn't see the need to drive it back and forth constantly, and I used it more for work than for personal errands anyway. Once I was sure that there were no more cops on the street, I headed out, careful to stay in the shadows.

I worked on a plan as I snuck over. Beehives aren't the lightest things to move, so I'd be physically handicapped working alone. And I couldn't transport all of them in the short time I had. But I could take a few, disappear into the night, then work later on getting the rest of them in a less-covert manner.

My brilliant plan blew apart when the police chief honed in on me the second I tried to pull my truck out from its parking space at The Wild Clover. Johnny Jay blocked me in, got out of his vehicle, hitched his pants, and approached my truck. I refused to roll down the windows or step out of the truck until he threatened to smash my windshield with the butt of his gun. Then I rolled down the window on the passenger's side, but only partway. He was standing on the driver's side, so he had to walk around to the other side.

"What?" I said, glaring over and acting annoyed, an offensive response I learned from the master of emotional manipulation—my mother.

"We need to talk," Johnny Jay said. "Right now."

"I'm a little busy." I glanced at my watch. If I didn't get moving, Gerald Smith would beat me to Manny's place and I'd lose my window of opportunity. "Move your SUV."

"This isn't an optional request. We can do it nice and easy or we can do it my favorite way." He dangled a pair of handcuffs.

"Where's Hunter?" I wanted to know. Johnny had local jurisdiction, but Hunter's Waukesha County credentials might trump Johnny Jay's. Or so I hoped.

"Hunter Wallace doesn't have anything to do with official business in this town," the police chief said, dashing my hopes. "Other than responding with C.I.T. when we have a situation."

He played with the cuffs.

"This might be one of those situations," I suggested.

"Besides, how do you think a dog trainer can help you? Don't you know he transferred from being a real cop to the K-9 unit to train mutts?" Johnny snickered, like the K-9 unit and dog training were the lowest of the low.

When Hunter had shown up with a dog in the back of his SUV, I never imagined police dogs were his full-time job. Since he and I usually stuck to flirting, and more recently to finding dead bodies, that wasn't a subject we'd covered yet.

Johnny Jay tried to open the truck door, but I'd locked it. He reached in the window, unlocked the door, opened it, and said, "Get out. Now!"

After that, I ended up "downtown" just like in the movies.

Only the station wasn't downtown because the new build-ing was way too enormous to fit inside the business section of town. Why is it that every small town thinks it needs its very own, state-of-the-art, big-tax-drain fire station? In Moraine's case, at least they combined fire with police in the multimillion-dollar taxpayer-funded monument. After 9/11, fire and police were high on everyone's referendum agenda, and that's how Johnny Jay got his special facility.

My interrogation was conducted in a sterile conference room that contained nothing more than an empty table, six chairs, and a picture of an eagle hanging on the wall. The police chief grilled me back and forth and sideways about Hunter and the kayak and the ill-fated canoe trip. My story stayed straight and simple, focusing mostly on Hunter as guide and decision maker. I already knew that Johnny Jay was not my friend.

And based on the intensity of his questioning, chances were good that Faye Tilley had been murdered. I'd been worried about that even though I hadn't spotted any blood in the kayak or any other signs of an attack. My first thought was, if she had to get herself killed, why did she have to do it in *my* kayak? Then I felt bad for having the thought.

But steel bars did *not* go with any of my outfits, includ-ing the black one I was wearing at the moment.

"I've told you what happened at least sixteen times," I said, exaggerating. "And Hunter told you, too. How much more information do you think you can squeeze out of me? That's it. The whole deal."

"You still haven't explained why the deceased was in your kayak."

Johnny Jay was flopped back in a swivel chair with his feet plopped up on the table, crossed at the ankles.

"How should I know why she was in my kayak? It was missing. I thought kids took it for a joy ride again. Hunter helped me look for it, we found it, she was in it."

"You have to do better than that."

I sighed as heavy and disgusted as possible.

Suddenly Johnny Jay's feet came up off the table so he could lean into my face. I wanted to smirk and tell him where he could go, but it might not be in my best interest to go with my first impulse. What he said next scared me almost to death. "Let's talk about the night before," he said. "And you can tell me what you were doing out on the bank of the river behind your house with Faye Tilley?"

I felt a chill. That question had come out of nowhere. "What?" I managed to croak out.

"Someone saw you two, said it sounded like you were arguing."

My gasp of shocked indignation sounded good even to my terrified ears. "Who would say such a horrible thing?" *Well, who would?* This was crazy.

I saw it in his eyes. Johnny Jay thought I had killed her.

"Are you trying to tell me it isn't true?" he demanded.

"Absolutely not. I mean, er, yes!"

"Which is it, yes or no?"

"I wasn't arguing with Faye. I didn't even see her. Someone's lying big-time."

"So is the answer yes or no?"

That's one of Johnny Jay's tricks to trip people up. He asks questions that will sink you no matter which response you give. Whether you say yes or no, he comes at you.

I went on. "Where did that lie come from?"

Johnny Jay had his head tilted back and he was watching me down his nose. "A tip."

"Well, I demand to know who this ridiculous tip came from."

"You don't get to make demands, not even for a lawyer. Unless I decide to arrest you."

"And are you arresting me?" I really expected him to say yes once I thought about it—a body in my kayak and not just any body, my ex-husband's girlfriend's body. And a tip. Big-time incrimination evidence. So I was surprised when he said, "Not yet. Too bad the tip was anonymous. Once we find the witness, I'll be paying you another visit."

"Then I'm out of here." I jumped up.

"Missy Fischer," he said, getting in the last word. "I'll be watching you. Closely. We aren't finished with this."

On the way out I stopped in dispatch. Sally Maylor, one of my steady customers and a good person, was working the airwaves.

"Hey, Sally," I said.

"He let you go," she said, smiling. "Good for you. I was worried."

"So was I. So Faye Tilley *was* murdered?"

"I can't say until the chief makes a public statement," Sally nodded, giving me the answer anyway.

"Why is he after me?" I asked. "Sure, it was my kayak, but that can't be enough."

"He sure doesn't cut you any slack, that's for sure. Maybe the police chief knows how to hold a grudge."

"About what?"

"Now, do you regret turning him down for prom?"

"That was more than fifteen years ago! You're kidding, right? Is that really why he gives me such a hard time?"

"That's the talk."

I shook my head in disbelief. "Somebody called in a tip," I said. "Saying they saw me with Faye."

"I heard about that."

"Who called?"

"We don't know."

"With all the technology around here"—I gestured at all the gadgets and blinking lights—"surely you can trace a phone call."

"It came from a computer—e-mail."

"Well, trace it!"

"We did. It came from one of the library's public computers, we know that, but the account used to send the e-mail was untraceable."

Damn. That meant it could be anyone.

Ten

I couldn't sleep that night, considering that my friend and mentor Manny Chapman was dead and gone, and my ex's latest girlfriend, Faye Tilley, had been found dead in my kayak. Not to mention the fact that someone was trying to frame me for Faye's murder and doing a bang-up job of it.

Worse yet, the most obvious suspect in Faye's death was the man I'd married and divorced: Clay Lane. He could have argued with Faye. I froze, suddenly recalling the loud voices I'd heard in the night. I remembered the scream that I'd chalked up to a bad dream. Only instead of a nightmare, it must've been Faye.

Could Clay have killed his girlfriend?

But even if the pieces fit together regarding means and opportunity, I couldn't come up with a motive strong enough. Why would Clay go to all the trouble? Sure, he messed around on me and on every other woman, too, but when his flings ended, he didn't really care. He was all passionate and lovey-dovey at the beginning, cold and impersonal at the end.

If anyone should be dead, it should be Clay. Some woman should have killed him by now.

Which led me to wonder at the possibility of one of his other women committing the crime. There are all kinds of nutcases in the world; maybe some crazy woman was picking off her competition? Even if, in my opinion, she'd have to be totally insane to go to those drastic measures for someone as superficial as Clay. But whether the killer was Clay or one of his women, based on what Johnny Jay told me about the tip he'd received, someone was trying to pin this on me!

By the time the sun rose, I was cranky from lack of sleep and ready for hand-to-hand combat with Clay.

But my number one priority every morning, the very first thing I did even before coffee, was go check on my bees. I did a quick buzz past my honeybees. They were happy and busy.

Then I banged on Clay's door until I noticed that his car was missing from the drive. I never was at my sharpest when operating on zero sleep. Clay wasn't exactly an early riser, so my guess was he had stayed someplace else last night. Was there another woman already? That would be rotten, even for that scum.

I was so crabby at the moment, I couldn't stand myself.

Annoyed that Clay wasn't home but knowing he never locked his door, I let myself in. I wasn't sure what I was looking for, but figured I'd know it when I saw it.

One thing I will say for the man, Clay kept his lair clean and tidy. Sexy feet and neatness were two attributes I had admired in him once upon a time. But now I'd take a sloppy, loyal man over one like my ex any day of the week.

Clay lived in several rooms in the back of his jewelry shop. The space wasn't large—small bedroom and living room, and a very tiny kitchen—so I was through it in less than a few minutes, ignoring the array of sex toys in the nightstand and girly magazines stacked in the closet and next to the toilet. The man needed therapy. Sex addiction is a major relationship buster, as he should have figured out by now.

His wire-making jewelry workshop would take longer to search. There were a zillion hiding places. His work-bench looked like a carpenter's table—pliers, file hammers, vises, torches, wire cutters—and the shelves above the bench were stacked with containers filled with supplies he needed to create his art: wires in copper, silver, yellow brass, gold, beads, gems. Half-finished projects took up another major section.

Then there was the showroom where he displayed his pieces, some of which, and I really hated to admit this, were fabulous.

I had hardly started rummaging through the workshop when I saw his car pull into the driveway. Clay got out and headed for the door. I didn't have the energy to panic or to hide. Instead, I met him in his living room.

"What are you doing here?" He said, surprised to find me on his sofa. Clay looked like he'd had a bad night, too. His eyes were puffy and red-rimmed. He moved past me like a sleepwalker and sank into the sofa next to me without waiting for a response. "This is hell," he said.

"At last we agree on something." I was on guard, ready for anything, convinced that I could take him, what with all that rage I'd worked up through the night. But seeing Clay like this, all messed up and miserable, reminded me of his nonviolent, albeit totally selfish, nature. He just wanted to be loved. And loved. And loved.

"Did you kill Faye?" I blurted.

Clay bent forward and buried his hands in his face, ignoring me. "I can't believe she's dead," he said, or at least I think that's what I heard. The sound was muffled.

"I'm sorry for her and for her family. And for you," I said. "But did you know the police chief pulled me in last night and all but accused me of killing her?"

Clay uncovered his face and focused on me for the first time. "I didn't see you down there. They kept me all night. Police Chief Jay thinks I killed her."

"I thought Johnny Jay had *me* in his scope."

"He does," Clay said. "He thinks we're in it together."

"That's ridiculous!" I said. "Everybody in town knows how I feel about you. I just threw a party celebrating our divorce! I'd never do anything with you. I wouldn't even share the same side of the street with you if I could help it, let alone murder your girlfriend with you."

"That's what I tried to tell him."

I had a few more accusations to throw his way before I went back home. "Why did you tell me Faye was in your bedroom when I came asking about my kayak?" I said. "She must've been already dead."

"We had a fight and she left. I never said she was here."

"I'm pretty sure you did." Or he'd implied it, at least, with his gestures and facial expressions. *Would that hold up in court?*

"We argued," he said.

"About what?"

Clay's eyes went to the ceiling, a sure indication that he was concocting a lie. "Um."

"Don't lie to me."

His eyes came back down. "I'm not talking about it."

"Okay, fine, you argued with her. Then what?"

"She stomped out. At first, I thought she was outside cooling off. When she didn't come back, I figured she'd walked down to Stu's and called for a ride home."

That seemed reasonable. I assumed she'd had friends who would have picked her up.

Clay tucked his feet in and rolled up in a ball.

"Clay, look at me," I said.

Clay glanced up.

"Meet my eyes." Toward the end of our rocky marriage, I'd perfected the ability to sense when he lied to me. His mouth told all sorts of stories, but his eyes didn't know how to play along. "Did you or did you not murder your girlfriend?"

His eyes never left mine. "I did *not* kill Faye. There, are you happy? Besides, I wouldn't have made love to her in your kayak if I planned to kill her in it. That would take a crazy man!"

"What? You had sex in *my* kayak?"

"In the afternoon. While you were having your divorce party at the store."

"You are so gross!"

I slammed out of his house, disgusted and thinking of a zillion names to call Clay. But I was 99 percent certain *killer* wasn't one of them, which meant I'd wasted a whole night's sleep for nothing. It also left the field wide open, if I was right. Did Faye have any enemies who hated her enough to kill her? Did I have any who hated me enough to frame me for it? I tended to blurt out things without thinking them through sometimes, but I'd never intentionally hurt anybody. Well, nobody other than Johnny Jay, but that was mutual.

I showered, made a pot of strong coffee, poured it into a carafe, and carried it down the street to open up The Wild Clover.

Milly Hopticourt, my recipe tester, arrived at the store at the same time I did, carrying a cardboard box filled with bouquets of flowers from her garden—cosmos, sunflowers, Russian sage, borage, Shasta daisies, globe thistles, baby's breath.

"Every last bunch I brought in yesterday sold," Milly said proudly.

"They are *so* beautiful. Come on in." I held the door open for her then set the carafe on a counter.

After turning on lights and flipping the open sign around, I helped Milly arrange the bouquets in a big bin. I added a few inches of water to them, wiped my wet hands on my jeans, and surveyed my dream come true.

Everything was bright and shiny and inviting. Buying the church and opening the store had been the right decision.

"What recipes should we put in the next newsletter?" Milly asked. "I should start testing soon."

"I found some wild grape vines next to the river bank, in my secret place. How about whipping up something with ripe grapes as the main ingredient? I'll pick them for you tomorrow."

"Perfect. I'll start with that."

"Tell me, Milly, were you at the library yesterday afternoon?" I poured a cup of coffee and handed it to her.

"Me and the rest of the town," she said, taking the cup.

"That many people came?"

Milly nodded. "Tons. It was so much fun even with the rain, because we were all dry there under the tent. But when the news came about Faye, the place cleared out like there'd been a bomb threat, with everybody running to the river by Stu's for news. You can imagine what we all thought when we heard you were out on the river with your ex-husband's dead girlfriend's body."

"Yes, well, that must have kept everybody busy." I'd gotten out of there just in time, thanks to Grams.

"You bet. And now we hear that she really was murdered."

"We did?"

"It's all over town that she drowned, and it wasn't an accident, either."

Secrets don't last long in a town this size. If Johnny Jay wanted to hold back information, he'd have his hands full. And I had to hope our conversation at the police station didn't leak out. That's all people needed to hear, rumors that I'd been overheard fighting with Faye before her death.

"Was Clay at the library, too, when you found out about Faye?" I reached for another cup to pour coffee for myself, waiting for her answer. The false tip had to have been made sometime on Saturday, after Faye was found but before the library closed for the day. If Clay hadn't been there, he couldn't have used the computer to send the e-mail and he was totally clear in my book.

Milly scrunched her forehead. "Um, I don't think so. But there were so many people in and out." She paused. "No, he definitely wasn't outside when Larry Koon came rushing over to tell us the awful news. Wouldn't that have been a terrible shock for him? Not that it wasn't bad enough for him later, I'm sure."

"I'm relieved I wasn't the one to have to tell him," I said.

"Now I remember," Milly said. "Emily told me later about how pleased she had been to see Clay because he'd never set foot in the library before. And I said to her, maybe he was turning over a new leaf, a book leaf, and how he would need some distractions to help him get over this and reading might help." She took a sip of coffee. "Emily said she went inside after the news came, but he was gone by then. What's wrong with you?"

The coffee I was pouring missed the cup and splattered across the top of the counter.

Eleven

I tried to stay calm after learning that my ex-husband had been at the library that afternoon and could have sent the incriminating e-mail. I reminded myself that almost the entire community had been there as well. Anybody could have done it. Anybody.

Thankfully, to keep my mind out of dark corners, Sundays are always busy days at the store. My honey sticks were the most popular item with the kids. That and all the penny candy in bins, though it cost a lot more than a penny these days. Locals came in to gossip and buy ingredients for Sunday family dinners. P. P. Patti bought a half dozen ears of corn and tried to twist as much information about Faye's death from my lips as possible.

"I can't talk about it," I improvised, refusing to add *gossiper* to my list of personal faults. "The police chief is investigating and he asked me to keep everything I know confidential for now."

"That means you know something important to the case," Patti pointed out. "I heard you were taken in for questioning."

"*Consulting*," I corrected her. My mother must be having a *bird*—her word for a fit—over what was going around.

Stanley Peck had his own angle. "Maybe something illegal was going on somewhere up the river," he said, filling his shopping basket with beer and pretzels. "Thieves with their loot or something worse. And Faye happened right into the middle of it. They couldn't let her go because she could identify them."

"You should tell the police chief about your theory," Patti said.

Stanley was on a roll. "I just might do that. You be careful down by that river, you hear? You, too, Story. At least until the police solve the case. We haven't had this much action since I shot my foot. I mean, since I got shot in the foot." He had the decency to blush at his slip of tongue. So the rumor was true. Stanley had shot his own foot.

Lori Spandle came in to remind me that I still had to prove the bees were gone to pacify the masses and time was running out, she said, as though I didn't know that. Lori still had on her bee veil. "You should be in marketing," I said just to bug her. "You really know how to brand your product."

"I *am* in marketing, in case you've forgotten," the real estate agent said. "As soon as Manny's funeral is over, I have to talk to Grace about selling out."

The woman was like a barracuda. And her husband, the land developer, wasn't any better. The Spandles made quite a team. She squeezed the landowner, so her husband could sweep in to develop the land.

"Manny would never approve of selling," I said.

"Manny's gone," Lori said. "It's Grace's decision now. Don't forget," she added again, "you have to prove that those bees are out of attack range."

"The ones at Manny's, yes," I said. "I'll go out and take pictures of the empty beeyard after I close at five. They're really gone. Grace told me." Thanks to the police chief and his interrogation drama last night that prevented me from saving some of the hives, they *were* all gone. My heart ached at the thought.

"Your bees, too," she said next. "They have to go."

I shook my head. "You stay away from my bees. They haven't done anything to anybody and I still will prove that honeybees didn't kill Manny Chapman."

"We'll see about that at the meeting tomorrow night." Lori wore prebattle triumph on her face.

"What meeting?"

"The regular monthly town meeting, except this time we have extremely pressing business to discuss and we're taking a vote. Your bees are going."

I groaned. Usually the monthly town meetings were b.o.r.i.n.g. But, by the gleam in Lori's eyes, I suspected major trouble at this one. Lori was obsessed with shutting down my bee operation by extending killer-bee fear to all corners of the county and she wasn't above using her husband's position as town chair to further her cause.

"I'm looking forward to it," I lied. "But doesn't the board have to give me some kind of notice?"

"Not if it's a threat to the community. Your say doesn't count."

"It sure does. I'll be there and my vote will count just as much as yours." Another thing about small community boards—they bend the rules to suit themselves.

Pity-Party Patti ate up our exchange like it was chocolate mousse at an all-you-can-eat dessert table. "I have to see a doctor," she said, launching into her current problem after Lori flounced out the door. "Look at my hand shaking." Her hand quivered in my face.

"Too much coffee?" I guessed.

"I gave up all caffeinated beverages. It might be Parkinson's," she said. "Then what would I do? I have nobody to take care of me or that big house and yard or all those raccoon attacks."

"You're stronger than you give yourself credit for."

"Being a single woman is hard in this world. That's why I'm glad at least one of us has found a man."

I looked at Patti. "You're in a relationship?" As long as I'd known Patti, I'd never heard of her even going out once with a man.

"Not me, Carrie Ann. I saw her making out with Hunter Wallace. Talk about hot!"

Gawd, I didn't want to hear what Patti just told me. So that was pretty much it. I had barely felt the rustling of interest in Hunter before it was snatched away. I might be a lot of things, but I'm no relationship buster. I'd been on the receiving end of that with Clay, and it wasn't a good place to be.

Thankfully, business picked up right then and I was able to make my escape from Patti.

Stu came in for a Sunday paper and confirmed that Carrie Ann hadn't been in the bar since I'd seen her there for lunch yesterday. Unless she was slinking into taverns outside of town or drinking at home, she had made it twenty-four hours.

Good for her. And good for Hunter for supporting her efforts, and whatever else he was supporting.

Every time business tapered off, I tried to imagine what had happened to Manny and what a person without bee experience might do if a swarm of stinging insects attacked him. He'd instinctively run, but an experienced beekeeper like Manny would also know to pull his shirt up to protect his head and eyes. That could explain why his stomach had been exposed. But here was the clincher: Why wouldn't he have kept running? He wasn't that far from his house. Even his car was within reachable distance. He could have saved himself by getting into his car. All he had to do was keep moving toward safety.

I supposed that most accidental deaths carry this kind of after-the-fact analysis and helpless sense of regret for those who feel they could have changed the outcome. If only things had been different. If only I'd been there when it happened. If only Grace had been home when the attack occurred. *If only.*

Although it would take only one sting in the wrong place (like inside his mouth as the medical examiner had told Johnny Jay) to finish him off. I wondered whether or not he'd realized he was going to die. How long had he suffered? Please, let it have been easier and faster for him than I imagined.

At two o'clock Carrie Ann came by the store. She didn't look good.

"I'm having a hell of a time," she said, gnawing on her fingernails. "But I haven't smoked, not a single drag." She still hadn't mentioned the whole not-drinking thing to me.

"Just keep busy and try to think of other things," I said, knowing how hard that was.

"Do I have some hours at the market?"

"Let's see," I said, studying the schedule, not at all positive Carrie Ann could make it without falling off the wagon. I'd promised Hunter, and I really could use the help.

Before we could get down to the details, I spotted my sister Holly's red Jaguar convertible through the front window, its glossy finish gleaming in the warm September sunlight. My blue truck looked like a bucket of rusty bolts next to it.

I could use her company and support to go take pictures of the missing hives over at Manny's. And I needed somebody to talk to about Faye.

"Want to work right now?" I asked Carrie Ann.

My cousin looked puzzled, as if she hadn't thought I'd agree to giving her hours at all. "I suppose."

"I have to go take some photographs. And tomorrow, can you work the morning for me?"

Carrie Ann smiled as I dashed for the door. "Sure. Cool."

"There you are." Holly stalked toward me, wearing the same kind of casual clothes I wore—jeans, V-necked cotton pullover, casual summer footwear. The only difference was everything she wore looked like it cost ten times more than mine. Which it had. "Mom sent me to spy on you," she said.

"I'm on my way out to Manny Chapman's. Want to come?"

"'K. I'll drive." Holly had a lot of Grams in her, except thankfully her driving was much better. "What's going on out there? I heard Manny Chapman died. I'm so sorry, I know he was a good friend of yours."

"Thanks." I started to well up but fought it back and focused on my mission. "I have to go take pictures of his apiary. I'll explain on the way. But you can't tell Mom anything about what I do or say. Okay? Say 'okay.'"

Holly gazed at me with the same hazel eyes I had. "'K."

I didn't tell her this was also a hastily hatched surveillance run, and that I planned to clear the honeybees' good name if it was the last thing I ever did.

Twelve

We pulled up in Grace's driveway in Holly's Jag about the time I finished telling her about the bee scare. After one quick glance told me the hives were gone, I couldn't bring myself to look that way again. "I can't do it," I said. "I just can't."

"SC (translation: *stay cool*). I'll take the pictures," Holly said. "You just want empty-space pictures, right? Where the hives used to be?"

I nodded. "With some of the house in the background, so everybody can see that the photos were taken right here in Manny's yard. Knowing Lori, she'll accuse me of manipulating the photos anyway." Holly headed over to the remains of the beeyard with her cell phone while I went to the house and knocked on the door. No one was home. Perfect. The honey house beckoned to me.

I used my key to unlock the padlock and drew in a sweet breath of the honey aroma. I flipped on all the lights and began a thorough search. Holly joined me a few minutes later.

"What are you doing?" she wanted to know.

"I'm not sure. Could you check around the outside of the honey house? Look for signs of yellow jackets."

"Ick," Holly said. "I'm staying right here with you."

My sister wasn't exactly Discovery Channel material.

I took my time, unlike during my last visit. Manny's missing journal didn't surface, which was starting to worry me, but I found two dead yellow jackets on the floor of the honey house. Not concrete evidence of anything, but I was in a suspicious frame of mind. "Yellow jackets," I announced.

Holly peered at the dead insects, keeping her distance. "How can you tell? They all look the same to me."

"These don't have hairy back legs to carry pollen like honeybees do. See." I picked one up and pointed to its smooth legs, which she couldn't see anyway since she was so far away. I placed it and the other one on a worktable in case they were important to my investigation, and we went outside.

"Now what are you doing?" Holly seemed slightly impatient. "I thought we were going to take a few pictures then leave."

"In a minute. Help me look for more signs of yellow jackets. But be careful."

"OMG (*Oh, My, Gawd*), no! I'm waiting in the car."

Holly headed for her Jag.

Yellow jackets sometimes make their homes in the ground rather than in more traditional nests, but I didn't see any buzzing activity at earth level. I had to take several deep breaths before walking in a wide circle around the perimeter of what used to be the apiary. Nothing. Yellow jackets also liked trees, sheds, eaves, even holes in walls, so I widened my search, without any luck.

If I could find an aggressive yellow jacket nest close to the empty apiary, I might be able to convince the bee-hungry jurists to reach a unanimous decision to acquit the honeybees. I had to do it, had to know for sure, and that meant facing my fear and going right into what was once a thriving apiary.

It was a beautiful fall day, as Wisconsin Septembers usually are, when I forced myself into the beeyard. I heard birds in the trees and flying insects *did* wander by, including an occasional yellow jacket, but as much as I wished for it, there wasn't enough activity to indicate a hive or nest close by. I instinctively strained to hear familiar sounds, but all I heard was emptiness.

After that, I rounded the honey house, looking up to search the eaves. I almost tripped over the bee blower, the same one I'd looked for without success when I'd needed to remove bees from Manny's body. What was it doing back here? Manny was fussy about his equipment, almost to the point of obsessive compulsiveness. He never would have left it outside in the elements.

Then I spotted an object so small I almost missed it. A tiny shred, but I knew exactly what it was. A piece of a paper nest, the kind made by yellow jackets when they chewed wood into pulp to make their homes.

I looked up, but nothing above my head indicated that a nest had been under the eave. Still . . .

Had Manny discovered the nest and tried to destroy it? Had the wasps attacked him? But he was a professional beekeeper—he was more than smart enough to know to wait until dark, and he would never have been foolish enough to try to take a nest down with live yellow jackets inside. He would have sprayed the nest with massive doses of poison first.

What had Manny been thinking?

I put the bee blower back inside the honey house. Then I wrapped up the two dead yellow jackets and the piece of nest in a tissue and put them all in a plastic bag.

"What's that?" Holly asked when I returned to the car.

"Nothing much."

"Fine, don't tell me."

So I did. About how the entire community was about to wage war on honeybees, which I'd explained some of on the way over. About how Grace wouldn't allow an autopsy that could have proved that wasps killed Manny, and about Grace giving away the bees that should have come to me. "I'm taking what I found to the police chief," I finished.

Holly laughed. "AYSOS?"

"What does that mean?"

"Are you stupid or something?"

"I resent that."

"I have to be there when you talk to the police chief. I can hear you now. 'Hey, Johnny Jay. Look, yellow jackets really did kill Manny, not bees. And my evidence is this dead yellow jacket I found in Manny's honey house and this little piece of nesting material.'"

It did sound lame. But Holly wasn't through mocking me. "'Now, Johnny Jay, I want you to go out there in the community and make an announcement and warn everybody that there will be legal consequences if they don't leave me alone.'"

I didn't know what to say because she was right.

"Story, maybe it's best to just let it go. I know you cared about Manny a lot, but he's gone. BON (*Believe it Or Not*)."

"I've got to find out exactly what happened."

"No, you don't. SS (*So Sorry*), but maybe Mom was right."

"What is that supposed to mean?"

"She thinks you're working too hard and getting nutty."

"Thanks for sharing."

We were still sitting in front of Manny's house. "I wonder where Manny's journal went," I said, talking to myself more than Holly. "It must be in the house. We better get out of here before Grace comes home and catches us."

Holly pulled out, heading for town, and that's when the subject of Faye Tilley and Clay came up for the first time. Holly must have sensed that I wasn't ready to talk about it earlier, because she waited for me to bring it up.

"Mom called and told me about it, but she didn't go into any details. It must have been awful," she said when I was done telling her about the events on the river—the storm, the cold and wind, and finding Faye's dead body in my kayak.

"It sure wasn't what I had expected to find," I said.

"Why would somebody want to kill her?"

"Who knows?" I remembered how Faye had flounced into the courtroom during the divorce hearing and how smug she'd looked later when she lip-locked with Clay for my benefit. "But she definitely wasn't a woman's woman."

"Absolutely, not." Holly knew exactly what I meant. Some women managed to be popular with both men and women, but Faye was too catty and competitive to fall into that category.

The only piece of information I kept from Holly was the damaging news about the e-mail tip. I wanted to save that until she wasn't behind the steering wheel. I don't have a death wish.

Back at The Wild Clover, we headed for my office, which amounted to a desk jammed at the back end of all the storage shelves. We downloaded two copies of the missing beehive pictures onto my work computer and printed them out.

"Stay right here," I said to Holly. "I have something important to tell you." I rushed out to tape one set of evidence to the front door. I left the other set with Carrie Ann.

"If anybody asks about the bees," I said to her, "point them to these photos."

"You got it."

Then I hurried back to the storage room and closed the door as quietly as I could. I didn't want anyone, especially Carrie Ann, to try to listen in. Nobody, but nobody else, could know my secret.

"Promise you won't scream when I tell you this," I began.

"OMG," Holly said. "You're pregnant."

"Shush. Keep your voice down."

How I wished that were the breaking news. How much simpler it would be to bring someone new into the world rather than get involved with one going out.

I shook my head. "You better sit down." Holly sat down in my office chair. "A tip relating to Faye's death was sent from a library computer to the police station."

"Okay."

"The tip wasn't true, but Johnny Jay believes it, and he's looking for the person who made the accusation." Holly started frowning like she wasn't following me. "So in my thinking," I continued, "the person who sent the tip has to be someone with a big grudge against me. Right?"

Holly looked totally confused. "What are you trying to say? What tip? What accusation?"

I crouched down and clutched her hands. "This person says they saw me arguing with Faye by the river the night before Hunter and I found her body in—"

"—your kayak," Holly finished for me, light bulbs going on inside her head.

I nodded.

"Oh, hell," Holly said, jumping up from the chair and knocking me over on my butt. "SNAFU! (*Situation normal: All F#@&%! Up*). What have you gotten yourself into?"

Thirteen

Early Monday morning before work, still stinging from Holly's barbs and the angry tirade I'd had to endure, I sat down at my patio table with a cup of red clover tea. My sister hadn't been exactly sympathetic, although eventually she'd settled down. We both were pretty sure the liar who claimed to have seen me would never come forward. But even without eyewitness evidence, Johnny Jay might think I had sufficient motive. Jealousy, he'd tell the jury, Story Fischer couldn't bear to see Clay Lane with another woman.

I wondered how the authorities knew for sure Faye had been murdered. For that matter, how were they so positive Manny's death was an accident?

How many death certificates are prepared every year where the cause of death is either accidental or natural?

Bunches, I bet. And how many of those innocent-seeming incidents could have been murder? Who knows?

Consider the elderly. When they die alone at home, none of the family members think an autopsy is important. Grandpa died of old age. Right? But what if Cousin Frankie had been adjusting Grandpa's medication? Or feeding him arsenic? Or helped him along with a pillow to the face? Who would be the wiser?

And those so-called accidental deaths? Say someone's husband falls off his roof still clutching his beer and lands right on his head? An accident, right? But what if he was pushed? Or what if the missus, sensing her lucky day, finished him off with an additional bang to the head?

I couldn't stop thinking bad thoughts and concocting gruesome scenarios. I glanced over at Clay's house, wondering how safe I was.

Last night Holly had demanded that I rearrange my priorities. She wanted to know what I had been doing looking for nests and collecting dead yellow jackets in plastic bags when I was close to becoming the most wanted woman in Moraine. Being wanted was not a good thing under these circumstances, but I didn't plan on letting it get that far. If only I could think of something to make this all go away.

I could go on forever with what-ifs and if-onlys. Life and death were filled with hard questions and elusive answers. I could have explained to Holly that since I couldn't bring back Manny or Faye, rescuing hundreds of live honeybees was the only way I could feel useful. But she would have poked holes in my dream.

To cheer myself, I walked through my garden, picking ripe vegetables. I'd planted the garden for my own use, not for the produce aisle at The Wild Clover. Every year I experimented with different plants. The early crops like lettuce, peas, arugula, and radishes were done for this year. My fall crop consisted of:

- Tomatoes—heritage pineapple tomatoes grown from saved seeds and Romas because I can throw them in the freezer right from the garden.

- Ground cherries—they form inside a husk and taste like a cross between a tomato, a cherry, and a pineapple. And they make an awesome pie.

- All my favorite things for making salsas—sweet green peppers, Anaheim and poblano peppers, onions, and tomatillos.

- Beets—both red and golden. I make the best beet soup in the Midwest.

- Squash—both summer and winter.

- Potatoes—fingerlings and red golds.

I set an armful of ripe garden veggies on the patio table, then drizzled some honey into a five-gallon bucket and set it out for my bees, the same way Manny had given his honeybees a treat, right before his death. I stared longingly at the spot where I'd kept my kayak, wondering when I'd get it back and if so, if I'd ever take it out again without seeing the image of Faye's lifeless body inside, not to mention Clay and Faye doing you-know-what in *my* kayak.

I was listening to the music of the bees buzzing when I heard human voices rising above the familiar hum. Lori Spandle's shrewish voice stood out above the din. She rounded my house wearing her bee veil, and she had a gang right behind her.

I had a feeling I was going to lose a few store customers this morning.

Clay came out of his house and watched from his porch. P. P. Patti Dwyre slipped through the cedars separating her house from mine. But to give her a teensy amount of credit for a change, she didn't join Lori's group. Instead she lingered near the shrubs within hearing range.

"What are you doing with *her*?" I said to Stanley Peck, using my head to indicate Lori. Stanley towered over the rest of Lori's bunch, making it hard for him to conceal himself. He looked embarrassed, as well he should be. I peered to the back, counting heads. Seven in all. The group seemed so much larger.

"I'm making sure things don't get out of hand," he said.

Lori turned to him. "Who went and made you sheriff?"

Stanley squirmed under her glare but didn't say anything more.

"You're either with us or against us," she added to her mob, mostly for Stanley's benefit, before turning her attention back to me. "Ray Goodwin was stung yesterday while he was making a delivery run."

"Since when does Ray work on Sundays?" I asked. Ray averaged two deliveries each week, sometimes more, showing up whenever it suited him. But he'd never come around on a Sunday.

"The economy is tough," someone said. "We all do what we have to."

"What's his route schedule got to do with anything?" Lori said impatiently. "The important thing is he was stung. Twice."

"Yellow jackets," I announced.

"Tell her, Stanley," Lori said, hands on her hips.

"He came to me afterward," Stanley said, unable to meet my eyes. "I know a little something about barbed stingers. I took the stingers out for him."

Jeez. I couldn't blame this one on yellow jackets if the stingers were left behind.

"Where did this happen?" I wanted to know.

"At Country Delight Farm," Lori said. "He was picking up apples for today's deliveries."

Country Delight Farm was less than two miles out of town and specialized in fall produce—apples, pumpkins, cider—along with autumn activities like corn mazes and hayrides. "I don't see Ray here with you." It figures that busybody Lori would interfere in Ray's business instead of worrying about her own! "If he had a problem, he should come to me," I said.

"We're representing him," she said. "Your bees are a danger to our community and to our lives."

"My bees don't roam as far as Country Delight Farm," I lied.

"Stanley says different," she said.

"Well, she asked," Stanley said with a faint whine when he saw the look I gave him. "So I looked it up. Bees can go farther than two miles if they want to."

"We are going to take care of this right now," Lori said, producing a spray can from out of nowhere.

People can be dumb as dirt, especially dopey, overly aggressive real estate agents named Lori. "You can't spray bees during the day," I said. "Not that I would let you do it at any time, day or night."

"Oh, yeah?" Lori moved forward, taking my statement as the challenge I meant it to be. If she sprayed my honeybees, some of them would die, but the rest would go on attack and we'd have to run for our lives. And if they didn't kill Lori, I would.

To end an already bad situation, I gave Lori a push backward, putting some muscle into it because she was moving forward fast, and I wanted to do more than stop her in her tracks. We were surrounded by spectators, everybody focused on Lori and me. I felt like a chicken in a ring.

Lori stumbled and flew back, looking like she would fall down if I so much as nudged her with my index finger, then she regained her footing and came up with her veil askew. She flung it off, and I noticed that her round face had turned the color of my ripe Roma tomatoes lying on the patio table. Her eyes shot daggers at me.

"Back off," I warned, when I saw that she was readjusting herself for another attack. "Somebody restrain her. Please."

Everybody looked stricken. Nobody moved.

Lori came directly at me, with the poisonous spray can pointed at my face. Was she insane? Would she really spray bee poison in my face? Finally her mob of "do-gooders" decided to react. Several hands clutched at her when they realized what she was up to.

"Clay!" I shouted. "Call the police!"

"That won't be necessary," Stanley yelled, as a shot exploded. Everyone froze. My ears rang like my head had been banged on both sides with cymbals. A few people dove for the ground. Some had their hands over their ears and stunned looks on their faces and round O's for mouths.

I blinked a few times and shook my head to clear it.

Stanley kept his loaded pistol raised in the air for effect. "Clear out!" he said. "Now! Especially you, Lori."

"We never would have come along," someone else grumbled, "if we'd known that Lori was going to get physical. We were just supposed to talk it out."

"You can't fire a weapon in town," Lori shouted at Stanley. "Are you crazy?" But she backed off and put the spray can away. Then she pointed at me. "Story Fischer attacked me, and you all saw it. I'm calling you as witnesses when I sue her butt for assault."

"Story was only protecting her property," Stanley said. By now the pistol had vanished to wherever he'd kept it hidden before. "You'll be lucky if Story doesn't file charges against *you*. Now, go! Get out of here."

My uninvited backyard guests cleared out, except for Stanley. P. P. Patti ducked back through the hedge; I was sure she was racing for her phone and the gossip freeway.

I saw Clay go back inside without lifting a finger to help. Another mark against him.

Lori's bee veil was still on the grass. She'd forgotten it in her hasty retreat. I picked it up and put it on the patio table.

"You just got added to Lori's list, too," I said to Stanley. "Once she goes after you, she never backs down. I'm finding that out the hard way."

"She doesn't bother me a bit. Let her start in on me. We'll see who's toughest."

At that, I opened my arms and rushed Stanley. While I was giving him a happy hug for saving the situation from escalating to who-knew-where, Hunter came around the side of the house with his dog, Ben, and stopped in his tracks. I still had Stanley in a bear hug. Looking over his shoulder, I saw Hunter take a step back as if he wanted to hustle back around the corner except that I'd spotted him already.

I let Stanley go. What did Hunter think? That he'd interrupted us in a romantic clench? Stanley was much older than me. And, more important, definitely not my type.

But Hunter and Ben weren't by themselves. I saw the rest of the C.I.T. squad behind him, and Johnny Jay creeping around the other side of the house, on the driveway that separated my house from Clay's.

This was it. The moment I'd feared. They were going to arrest me and throw me in jail, leaving my bees vulnerable to Lori's deadly spray can. Not to mention that my own pathetic life was in ruins.

"You don't need all this backup," I said quietly to Hunter, not moving a muscle. "There won't be a scene."

"It's standard procedure," Hunter said with a serious expression. I looked at the dog, who seemed ready for action. Maybe *too* ready. The last thing I wanted was that dog unleashed on me.

I put my hands up in the air, hoping that would calm the animal, praying he understood the universal gesture of surrender.

"Where did the shot come from?" Hunter said. I slid a look at Stanley, who put his hands in the air, too.

"It went off accidentally," Stanley said, prepared to own up and admit his illegal action.

"It didn't come from inside the house?"

"Of course not," Stanley said. He looked around at the rest of the law enforcement officials. "You didn't have to bring the entire team just because of one little shot."

Hunter shook his head, frowning, then ran his blue eyes along our raised arms, and said, "You need to wait inside your house, Story. You, too, Stanley."

Then I noticed that every member of C.I.T. had his attention focused, not on Stanley and me, but on Clay's house.

"What's going on?" I finally asked, lowering my arm.

"We're arresting your ex-husband," Hunter said. "Now please go inside."

Fourteen

Attitude is important. So is positive thinking. I was finding both mind-sets a little hard to master at the moment. My emotions were all over the place. First, I felt relieved that I wasn't going to prison for life. Fear peeled from my shoulders like the final stages of a bad sunburn when the healing starts. I wouldn't be hauled down to the station in handcuffs and accused of a crime I didn't commit. But my stomach knotted thinking about my ex and murder and how I could have been the one who popped out of the cattails with sightless eyes.

My ex-husband had killed his girlfriend. My feelings about his inability to physically harm another human being had been wrong, wrong, wrong.

I knew I was sentencing him prematurely but I couldn't help myself. In the United States of America the accused party is supposed to be innocent until proven guilty, but that wasn't really how it worked in people's minds. The reality was more like this: guilty until proven innocent, and good luck with that.

It took Johnny Jay and Hunter no time at all to haul Clay out of his house and send him off in a squad car. Then another team of professionals went inside, wearing gloves and carrying equipment boxes.

"They're searching for clues," Stanley said, watching from the window.

"Let's get out of here." I didn't want to give Johnny Jay any reason to turn his attention my way, remembering what Clay had said about the police chief thinking we were in it together. The only positive thought I could drum up was that Clay's arrest would be the hot topic of conversation today, not me or my bees. They were safe for now. No one was going to sneak into my backyard with all this action going on.

Deputies posted outside didn't stop me and Stanley from leaving; according to them, the danger had passed. But when we saw the crowd forming on the corner of Willow and Main, we did a quick U-turn and snuck through the back of Moraine Gardens. I went to the market, and Stanley got in his car and drove away.

I stood on the sidewalk, staring up at The Wild Clover's stained-glass windows, remembering the days when the building's congregation met inside to sing praise to God. I could almost hear the steeple bells ringing again.

Ray Goodwin's truck pulled in, and I quickly approached.

"There's nobody to help unload," I said, thinking my voice sounded a little shaky. "Except me. Do you need help?"

"No, that's okay," Ray said, swinging a crate of apples down from his delivery truck onto a dolly.

"If you would plan your deliveries for later in the day, after three, the twins are usually here."

"I said it's no problem. What's going on down the street?"

"My ex-husband was just arrested for murdering his girlfriend."

"No kidding." Ray didn't say anything for a few minutes. He was as speechless as the rest of us.

I noticed the swelling on the side of Ray's head, right next to his eye. "I heard you were stung. That's a nasty one. Did you put ice on it?"

Ray gingerly touched the spot with his fingers. "Of course," he said, but I doubted him.

"A paste of baking soda and water would have helped, too." Beekeepers had a variety of remedies for reducing the swelling of bee stings—meat tenderizer and water, raw onions, ammonia, even toothpaste could do the trick.

"The other bee got me on my finger," Ray said, showing me the spot. It wasn't nearly as swollen, but stings to the fingers really hurt, I knew from experience.

"How did Stanley take out the stingers?" I didn't really care one bit after what had just happened with Lori and then Clay's arrest, but I didn't want to be alone with my thoughts.

"How did you know he helped me? Doesn't this town have anything better to do than gossip all day?"

"Just tell me what he used."

"Tweezers," Ray said, going back to stacking boxes of apples.

"Well, *that's* your problem," I said. "When he squeezed the stingers, they were still loaded with poison. He pumped more venom into you by mistake. Next time, scrape the stinger out like this." I demonstrated by sliding my thumb along my hand. "Or use a credit card to scrape it out."

"I hope there isn't going to be a next time," Ray said.

"What were you doing to aggravate them?" I couldn't help asking, thinking he had to have provoked them the same way Lori had when she'd banged through my apiary en route to Clay's house that time.

"Nothing unusual. Quit defending them. Admit it, sometimes bees just sting for no reason that we can figure out."

I refused to respond, mostly because he had a legitimate point. Instead I said, "Have you talked to Lori Spandle lately?" I asked.

"No, why?"

"Your bee stings happened at a very convenient time for her. She's trying to turn the town against my bees."

"I don't have any problem with your bees," Ray said. "I'll talk to her and tell her that if it will help, tell her it's no big deal what happened."

I nodded. "That might help," I said, although truthfully, I didn't think anything could slow that woman down.

Ray and I went in the back door together. Carrie Ann was lounging against the cash register, talking on her cell. I heard her say, "See you tonight, then. And thanks, Hunter."

"Hey," I said, still feeling a lingering, foolish loss when I thought of Hunter, and how I should have caught his pass a while ago and run with it before he and my cousin hooked up.

"What are you doing here?" Carrie Ann asked, putting her cell in her back pocket. "I thought you were supposed to be off."

I inhaled discreetly but didn't detect even a whiff of tobacco smoke. "I have to work off some stress. Johnny Jay just arrested Clay."

"I heard already. Patti's making calls, spreading the news like hot butter on fresh popcorn." Carrie Ann had a nutty, desperate look in her eyes. "It's an awful situation. You poor thing!"

"How are you doing?" I asked.

"I'm not going to make it much longer without a smoke."

"Sure you are."

"As long as I stay busy, it's not so bad. Oh good, here come more customers."

I left her to her demons and made sure Ray put the cases where I wanted them. Then I went to work, placing apples in attractive piles, trying to keep my mind off everybody's troubles. September's harvest brings Cortland, Gala, McIntosh, and Jersey Mac apples to the market. Next month Ray will deliver Honey Crisps, Spartans, and Empires, to name just a few.

Milly came in looking for the bunches of wild grapes I'd promised to bring for her so she could work up a new recipe for the newsletter.

"I forgot," I said. "I'm sorry, but I have other things on my mind."

"I can imagine. I heard about Clay's arrest." Milly picked up a shopping basket and fingered the Cortlands. "I'm really sorry. Is there anything I can do to help?"

"I'm okay. It's not like we are still married." *Thank God!*

"These apples look good."

"Don't they? Hey, if you're going to be in the store for a little while, I'll go pick you some grapes right now."

"Sure, I'm planning on sticking around to hear the scuttlebutt about the arrest," she said, moving toward the cash register where Carrie Ann and a customer were swapping notes on the limited information they had to work with.

I selected a choice apple for a quick snack, got a plastic bag from the back room, and was walking out the front door when I heard Carrie Ann say something about Clay's womanizing.

"What was that you just said?" I took two steps back, noticing that the customer was Sally Maylor. She'd been the one in dispatch I'd talked to right after the interrogation by Johnny Jay. I thought about the comment she'd made about Johnny holding a grudge against me because I had turned him down for prom. I suspected it went deeper than that, but I could be wrong. Johnny Jay wasn't a deep kind of guy.

"I'm so sorry you overheard us," Carrie Ann said to me. "We try not to bring up unpleasant things about him when you're around."

"Besides," Sally said. "Carrie Ann knows I can't talk about official business. Johnny Jay would fire me on the spot. Have a nice day, you two."

I stuck around until the checkout counter cleared, then began to grill Carrie Ann. "If you know something I don't, you need to tell me," I said.

"I don't know what you know and what you don't, so how am I supposed to figure out what to tell you?"

"I know about Lori Spandle and Clay messing around when we were separated."

"So does everybody in town, except Gary, Lori's husband. That woman has been after your men since grade school."

Which was true. Lori had had enormous boobs from the age of twelve, and she'd pointed them at every one of my boyfriends.

"And I know about enough of the times Clay cheated on me." I was starting to regret my curiosity. "If it's past history, I guess I don't want to know after all."

"You were split up the time I'm thinking of."

Nothing like whetting my curiosity. "Who then?"

"Nobody. I'm sorry I brought it up."

"Come on."

"I said nobody."

"Clay was after every woman in Moraine. Nothing you say will come as a surprise."

"He hit on me once," Carrie Ann said, then instantly slapped her hand across her mouth. "See what withdrawal does to a woman," she said through her fingers. "But don't worry, I didn't do anything about it. You're my cousin. It wouldn't be right."

"Who else?" I gave her my best I-really-mean-it glare. Quit trying to spare my feelings. Clay never did."

"If you must know, the rumor is it's Grace Chapman."

"Grace and Clay?" I thought about quiet, plain Grace. "Really?"

Carrie Ann nodded. "That's what's going around. Don't look at me like that, I didn't start it and I don't know if it's true. Don't shoot the messenger."

"I don't believe it for one second," I declared.

But I did.

Fifteen

Clay and Grace! I tried to look at the issue from all sides instead of instantly believing that Grace had cheated on Manny. And what about her husband, my friend? Manny hadn't discussed their marriage much, but when he did, it was in a good light. He certainly never complained about Grace.

I could see, though, how Clay's charm—and he did have it if he put his mind to it—might entice some of the local women who didn't get much male attention. But Grace didn't seem like the fling type, and to my knowledge there wasn't a woman in the entire town who didn't have Clay's number by now.

Small town gossip can start with one tiny comment and balloon out into something entirely different. I knew that. Especially when it came to someone like my ex-husband, who had been giving big juicy grist to the gossip mill from the beginning.

The more I thought about it, the more I didn't want to believe it.

I decided to put it out of my mind, pretend I'd never heard it. Grace, with all her righteousness, would never do such a thing. She wouldn't hurt Manny that way.

Wild grapes grow on thick, woody perennial vines along the roadways and pasture edges, winding up trees and bearing their fruits in abundant clumps. I waded in behind my house and moved downstream to my secret picking spot tucked in along the edge of the river. There they were, growing up as high as twenty feet, mingling with the hardwoods and red sumac.

About wild grapes:

- They grow along fences, forest edges, roadsides, and waterways.

- Wild grapes look like very tiny purple-blue Concord grapes. Since they are so small, gather them in the clusters they grow in, not individually, or it will take all day.

- If eaten straight from the vine, they have been described as tart, tangy, sour, bitter, yucky. Not everyone's idea of a tasty raw snack.

- The leaves are edible; stuffed grape leaves (rolled with rice) are delicious.

- Wear gloves if you don't like purple stains on your fingers.

- Pick off any grapes that don't look good, then cook the rest, stems and all, for juice, jam, jelly, or wine.

- Raisins are dried grapes. It's amazing how many people don't know that.

After breaking off as many bunches as I thought Milly might need, I sat on a large rock on the riverbank with my feet swishing through the water, eating my apple, watching wildlife, and emptying my mind of all thoughts, which took some effort.

After idling away some more time, I remembered Milly was probably still waiting at The Wild Clover for me. So I tossed down my apple core as a treat for some lucky animal and headed back just in time to see Grams, Mom, and my sister enter the market. Rats! I wanted to hide. A visit from all of them together couldn't be a good thing.

"This is a family intervention," my mother said after I handed Milly the bag of grapes and Mom had ushered the family behind closed doors in the back room. "We are here to help you through this time of crisis."

I glanced at Holly. She kept her head down and her eyes averted. A slight shake of her head reassured me that the information about the tip from the library was still a secret.

"I can't believe that nice young man killed anybody," Grams said, always believing the best of everybody whether they had a good side or not.

"It's obvious that Clay *did* commit murder, Mother," Mom said with a hint of frustration. "Nice man, indeed! We have to do damage control, if that's even possible at this late date. The family's reputation is at stake. "

"Talk will die down," I said. "Clay was just arrested. Everyone's excited at the moment, but things will return to normal. You'll see." Eventually, that was, after all his indiscretions were exposed and analyzed every which way. After that, theories about his motive would fly through the air, and doubt would set into people's minds. "He isn't my worry anymore," I said.

"At a time like this we must appear united," Mom said matter-of-factly. "Holly is going to help you with the store." That was Mom's way of saying my sister had to keep tabs on me so that I wouldn't get into any more trouble that reflected poorly on our family's good name.

"I'm perfectly fine with things the way they are," I said. "I'm refusing Holly's help."

"You can't do that," Mom said with total authority. "She owns Clay's shares since she gave you the loan. I read the contract. Until the money is paid back, she can protect her investment as she sees fit. And she's exercising her option to become involved. Besides, your business here is expanding. It's too much for one person to handle."

"And what do you say about all this, Holly?" I waited for my sister to grow a spine. I also wondered where exactly the loan agreement was. Who reads all that tiny print?

"Mom's right about the contract," Holly said. "BC (*because*) Max is gone so much these days, I'd kind of like to work with you. Besides, you're going to need extra help when you buy Manny's beekeeping equipment and go into honey production."

She gave me a wink along with the bribe that spoke volumes. Holly would lend me more money to rescue the honey house, and I'd give her a reason to feel useful. My market was doing well, so I'd be able to pay off the loan at some point. After that, she and I would be back on equal footing and we'd see where things went from there. The unspoken plan wasn't half bad.

Besides, my sister needed something to keep her busy enough that she would stop with the text-speak.

"You two girls are so cute," Grams said. "Let's get Carrie Ann to take a family picture." She hauled out a small digital camera and away we went.

After that, we worked up a plan I could live with. I hated to admit defeat, but Mom was right. The business was growing and I needed at least two people at the market most of the time. We nailed down a weekday schedule. Carrie Ann and I would work mornings until eleven, since Holly hadn't seen the sunrise since she married Max. My sister and I would work until three, and the twins would take over from there. The weekend schedule was up in the air, but we'd polish it off in the next day or two.

Holly cheerfully followed along with Carrie Ann, learning how to use the register. As usual, Mom and Grams argued about who was going to drive home. Grams, emerging as the victor again and proving she's the only family member who can win a confrontation with Mom, pulled out into the street at her normal crawl. I heard someone honk at her, then an angry male voice call out something unprintable.

Holly came over to watch. "Grams is going to get killed one of these days," she said.

"But she'll go out happy."

"IK (*I know*). BTW (*by the way*), I didn't get any sleep last night worrying about you and that tip. I'm almost relieved they arrested Clay. But I'm not sure you are out of the proverbial woods yet. What about that e-mail? Do you think Clay did it? If he did, he better admit it."

"Holly, do you think Grace Chapman is capable of murder?"

"What are you thinking? That she killed Faye?"

I hadn't really thought about that. "I was thinking more along the lines of Manny."

"That's crazy talk. Why would Grace murder her husband?" Holly asked, looking surprised that I'd even suggest that. "And how?"

"What if she managed to catch a nest of yellow jackets and used the blower to direct them at Manny?" Okay, that was a stretch, even to my ears, but it was a new angle and had possibilities. "She could have locked him out of the house and out of his car, so he didn't have any place to hide. Yellow jackets don't give up until they chase you down."

"What about Grace during all this? Why didn't she get stung?"

A flash of insight. "She wore the bee suit."

"Is Grace still plain and mousy and righteous?"

"Yup. That's her."

"Well, when you work out her motive, please share it with me."

"Holly, I heard that Clay and Grace were having an affair."

"Noooo!"

I told Holly what I knew, which was totally unsubstantiated gossip.

"You can't believe everything you hear," Holly said, which was exactly what I had thought at first.

"You're right. I can't see Grace with Clay."

"Not in a million years. It's just nasty talk. And you're above that stuff."

"Right."

"Besides, you're supposed to be concentrating on staying out of trouble with the law."

"Right."

I drove my truck toward Holy Hill, searching for Hunter's place, hoping he was home. I passed the Holy Hill National Shrine of Mary, which was run by the Carmelites, towering above the countryside at the highest point in southeastern Wisconsin. Devout worshippers made pilgrimages to the sacred chapel, and on weekends hundreds of visitors picnicked on the grounds.

I passed the Shrine's entrance and turned onto Friess Lake Road, checking mailboxes on the side of the road as I drove, looking for the address Carrie Ann had scrawled for

me on the back of a napkin. Most of the homes were hidden
at the end of long, curving driveways, tucked back behind
pines and native shrubs. I turned in when I found numbers
that matched Carrie Ann's.

Hunter's truck and his Harley were parked next to a
small, log-hewed house, surrounded by woods.

Wisconsin is Harley country, since the motorcycles are
made here and they are such fine machines.

About Harleys:

• Hog fever affects people from all walks of life—
  professionals, skilled workers, white collar, blue collar,
  retirees, the unemployed, you name it.

• Some famous riders are Malcolm Forbes, Jay Leno,
  Elvis, and the duo Dennis Hopper and Peter Fonda in
  Easy Rider.

• Harley bikers have their own dating website.

• More and more women are riding their own bikes.

• The black leather outfits rock—jackets, boots, all the
  accessories.

The September afternoon sun ribboned through the tree
canopy as I walked up to the house, the smell of burning
firewood drifting on the air. Gleaming canine eyes watched
me from inside a screened door. Alert and ready.

"Hey, Ben," I said, thinking he'd relax if I said his
name. A tail wag would be nice. Maybe even a bark or two.
Instead, Ben watched me in silent anticipation.

"Hey, Story." Hunter came out of the house wearing
jeans, slung low on his hips, and pulling a shirt over his
head, giving me a glimpse of hard muscle and lean torso.
"What's up?"

"I'm glad I caught you home."

"I just now stopped home for a late lunch." Hunter placed a hand on my shoulder. "Come on in and join me?

"Sounds great," I said, realizing how hungry I was. "But why don't you come out here instead?"

"Come in. He won't hurt you." Hunter opened the screen door and waited for me to enter. Ben was right there, standing guard at the door, but he let me pass without licking his chops.

"I heard you went over to the county K-9 unit."

"Yep, it was the right move for me. Ben is my permanent canine partner, and we work as a team to train other dogs. I love it." Hunter led me to the kitchen. The inside of the house was all warm wood, soft leather, and outdoorsy male.

"Sit down." Hunter held up a deli package. "Is smoked turkey okay?"

I nodded and sat down while he built me a fabulous sandwich.

"There must have been a lot of evidence against Clay if Johnny Jay arrested him," I said, taking a bite of the sandwich.

Hunter nodded. "Enough. No alibi, and his fingerprints all over your kayak."

Because they had sex in my kayak, I wanted to say, but for all I knew that was a lie Clay had concocted to explain why his fingerprints would be found there. "Has he confessed?" I asked, taking another bite.

Hunter put away the sandwich makings and joined me at the table. "He isn't talking at all, other than to demand an attorney."

"Smart. That's what I'd do." Which was true, but that meant he hadn't admitted that he'd tried to frame me by lying.

Hunter grinned. "The only difference is, I'd get a confession out of you. All I'd have to do is tickle your feet."

"You remember." I had always been extremely sensitive when it came to my feet. Hunter had made me wet my pants more than once during a teenage tickling fight.

"I remember more than that," he reminded me. I tried not to blush and I think I pulled it off, even with him watching my reaction with a steady gaze.

"Did they find Faye's other earring?" I asked.

Hunter shook his head. "It wasn't in the brush along the shoreline, and the divers didn't have any luck."

"It wasn't in Clay's house?"

"No."

"Where are they holding Clay?"

"Waukesha jail." Hunter smiled. "You come out to pump me for information?"

"I came to ask for advice."

Since I didn't know where or how to begin, I just let the words fly without preamble. "Someone told Johnny Jay that I had a disagreement with Faye behind my house the night before we found her dead," I said. "Which was a lie. I didn't see her at all that night. But I *did* hear raised voices outside after dark. I didn't tell Johnny Jay what I heard when I had the chance, and if I tell him now, he'll think I'm making up a story to save myself. To make things worse, before Clay was arrested he told me the police chief thought my ex and I plotted to kill Faye Tilley together."

"Tell me everything, starting at the beginning."

So I did. At least everything I knew about Faye and Clay.

When I was through, Hunter stared into my eyes for the longest time. Then he looked down at his hands, which were folded on the table. He wasn't a happy camper. I chewed my lower lip until it almost bled. When he finally responded, he said, "You should have told me about the scream when we found her."

"I didn't even remember it until Johnny Jay told me about the tip, and then it was too late to tell the truth."

"She was killed late Friday night or early Saturday morning. The scream you heard helps establish the time that she was assaulted. That's important."

"I thought I was dreaming," I said lamely.

Another long silence. I used to like that about Hunter, those times when we could just be together without filling up all the space. Now I wasn't so sure.

"It's never too late to tell the truth," he finally said.

I wasn't sure I agreed, at least in certain cases.

"Do you think Clay tried to frame me?"

"I don't know what to think at this point," Hunter said.

"How did Faye die?" I asked. "I didn't see stab wounds or anything obvious."

"She was held under the water until she drowned. That's strictly confidential at this point."

How awful for Faye. I almost couldn't breathe, thinking about her struggling for air underneath all that river water.

"Wouldn't it have taken a strong man to hold her under?" I pointed out. "Clay isn't exactly a heavyweight."

"A head injury indicated she was struck with a flat object, possibly the kayak paddle. Then held under."

"Oh."

"Johnny Jay is going to be pissed when he finds out you withheld information," Hunter said.

"That's why I came to you. Can you help me?"

"I'm not a miracle worker, but I'll see what I can do. It would be best if you went to him voluntarily."

"I will, but at least soften him up a little?"

Hunter's eyes went smoky. "Let's get you out of the middle of this mess as soon as we can." He reached across the table and took my hand in his. I could definitely feel a connection through our fingers.

Then he touched my face, gently and caressing, and I knew exactly where this was heading. And at the last second, to my dismay, I remembered Carrie Ann.

I jumped up from the table. Part of me, the immature me, thought Hunter was a cute flirt. The other part thought he wasn't behaving much better than Clay had. He didn't have any excuse for coming on to me when he was involved with my cousin, in case he'd forgotten.

"Jerk," I said, spitting a little of my own kind of venom, just enough to sting.

The look on Hunter's face was one of stunned disbelief, but I didn't hang around to talk it out. Men! So dense! Were there any good ones left in this world?

I stormed out and almost hit his truck when I swung my car around. Not that that would have made a difference to my rusty truck, but it would have served Hunter right.

The Wild Clover came into sight before I calmed down enough to realize I had handled the situation badly. Apparently, my scars from Clay's infidelity were deeper than I thought.

Sixteen

Carrie Ann was sitting on a bench outside The Wild Clover with an unlit cigarette dangling between her lips. She quickly removed it and tried to hide it in her palm when she saw me coming.

"I wasn't going to light up," she said when she saw my eyes following her hand. "Honest. Search me if you want. I don't even have a lighter with me." She stood up in case I wanted to frisk her, but I had other things on my mind.

There were enough cars on the street to indicate that business was booming inside the market. "Did you leave Holly inside alone?"

Carrie Ann must have figured that I wasn't going to scold her for the cigarette because she stuck it back in the side of her mouth, unlit, and talked around it. "She's a whiz at the register. And I needed a break. I'm not used to working straight through without stopping for a few smokes."

"Looks like we're really busy," I said, looking at all the cars and spotting my grandmother's car parked close by. Then I remembered.

Every Monday afternoon a group of seniors played cards in the old choir loft. My original vision of the market had included community events like this one. It made me feel good to know the store was like a second home to them.

"What's today's game?" I asked.

"Sheepshead," Carrie Ann said. "As usual, all the old fogies drove themselves here, whether they lived two miles away or two doors down. Business has been steady, but not too much to handle."

Sheepshead is Wisconsin's state card game, brought over by all the Germans who settled here. If you live in Wisconsin, you know how to play sheepshead. That's the Monday group's favorite card game, with rummy coming in a close second.

Carrie Ann took the cigarette out of her mouth, looked at it longingly, and rearranged it in her mouth. "Are you ready for the showdown at the Town Council meeting tonight?" she asked.

"As ready as I'll ever be. Will you come for support? I need your vote."

"I'm really sorry, but I can't."

"You could bring Hunter along."

Carrie Ann's mouth dropped open and the cigarette hung on the edge of her lower lip for a moment before she tucked it back in with her tongue. If nothing else, my cousin was a professional cigarette juggler. "How did you know about that?"

"It's obvious," I said.

"It is?"

I nodded.

"Don't tell anybody, okay."

"'K," I said, sounding like my sister. "It's our secret. So are you coming tonight or not?"

"Not," Carrie Ann said.

I don't know what possessed me, it must have been all those emotions bouncing around inside my body, the anger and frustration, because I reached out and grabbed that stupid dangling cigarette from her mouth and broke it in two. Then I took her hand and jammed the pieces into it. "Suit yourself," I said before stomping inside.

I didn't look back but I could hear Carrie Ann sputtering behind me.

"Hey, sis," Holly said, grinning like she was very pleased with herself. "I'm getting the hang of the register. I'm a natural!"

I forced a smile in spite of the extremely bad day I was still trying to get through and greeted the customers in line, determined to rearrange my attitude as we exchanged pleasantries.

Laughter floated down from above. The sheepshead games were in full swing. The market was filled with beautiful light from all the stained glass. Milly's bouquets of flowers were right next to the checkout, where their fragrances wafted in the air and customers picked them up on impulse. Bins brimmed with corn, raspberries, and multicolored squashes, completing the picture of bliss and bountifulness.

"Story needs a waggle dance," Carrie Ann said, coming over to the register.

"Huh?" Holly said, waving good-bye to her last customer in line.

"That's what Story's bees do when they find a new pollen patch," Carrie Ann said. "Tell her, Story."

"Once a field bee discovers a new source of pollen," I explained, "she will fly home, crawl into the hive with the news, and do a dance in certain patterns, like a figure eight.

That tells the other bees the exact location of the newly discovered flower field."

"It's kind of done like this," Carrie Ann demonstrated to Holly by thrusting out her back end and shaking it. At first I was surprised that she knew about the waggle dance, then I remembered that she had been working the day I burst in with the exciting news that I'd actually seen a honeybee waggle dance and had gone on to demonstrate it. Carrie Ann remembered! How cool was that?

Holly mimicked Carrie Ann, shaking right along. The three of us must have looked ridiculous to anyone peering through the window and to the customers in the store, but we didn't care as we wiggled and waggled down the aisles until we were laughing and the world wasn't tilting quite so far into the shadows.

A few minutes later, I settled at my tiny desk in the storage room and prioritized. I was surprised when the very first item on my list turned out to be the very subject I didn't want to pursue. I guess my subconscious took over. My to-do list went like this:

- The current rumor about Grace and Clay was substantial. Had she really cheated on Manny? And if so, when and where?

- Prove that Manny was killed by yellow jackets, although that would be difficult without an official autopsy by the medical examiner.

- Find Gerald Smith, the bee association member who took Manny's beehives, and convince him to return the honeybee hives to me.

- Once that was accomplished, figure out how to transport eighty-one hives and where to stash them if everybody in town remained hostile toward honeybees.

- Convince Grace to sell Manny's equipment to me, all of it, including the honey house, now that Holly would loan me the funds.

- Calculate how long it would take to pay my sister back, so I could get out from under my family's thumb.

- Respect Grace by waiting until after tomorrow's funeral to begin negotiations for the equipment.

I started with bullet point number three, since that seemed easier than one and two—find the beekeeper who had made off with Manny's honeybees. I picked up the phone and called Eric Hanson, the president of the county bee association.

"Hi, Story, long time no talk," said Eric. "It's such a shame about Manny Chapman."

"I can't believe he's gone. It's like a bad dream," I agreed. "Listen, Eric, I'm actually calling about Manny. I heard that someone from the association named Gerald Smith took all his hives, and I'm trying to find the guy. Can you get me his contact information?"

"Don't know that name, but we have a lot of inactive members. Let me check and get back to you in about ten minutes."

While I waited, I wandered upstairs into the choir loft. Most of the seniors were wearing shirts with playing cards on the front of them.

Grams gave me a wink. She had her trademark daisy in her hair and a fistful of queens, a very good place to be.

Sheepshead is an intense game. The players don't chit-chat much while they're wheeling and dealing, so I was spared all the questions that might have come up about Clay's arrest or his girlfriend's murder. I made a mental note to disappear by the time the games broke up to avoid a lot of awkward questions.

Five minutes later, I went back down to the storage room and paged through the phone book. Smiths. Lots of Smiths. No Geralds. Several G. Smiths, though.

I drummed my fingers on the desk, wondering what I would say to Gerald Smith to talk him into returning the bees. That might be a trick in itself, getting them back. I'd have to come up with a spiel to convince him.

Holly came in, closing the door tightly behind her, and informed me that the police chief was in the building. Great.

"He's asking for you," she said.

The phone rang and I held up a finger to indicate that I needed a second to take the call.

"Eric, here," the president of the county bee association said. "You must have that name wrong."

"Gerald Smith," I said, pronouncing the name slowly, but I knew the truth before I spelled it out.

Eric said exactly what I thought he would. "No one in the association by that name."

"Anything close? Maybe I *did* get it wrong."

"Nothing. Sorry."

I hung up.

"What should I do with Johnny Jay?" Holly asked. "I gave you an out by telling him I didn't know whether you were here or not. Want me to cover for you? I'll tell him you're on a CB."

"CB?" I didn't know that one.

"Coffee break," Holly translated.

"I can hear you two talking about me right through the door," the police chief called out, coming in without an invitation. "In case you don't know, it's against the law to obstruct justice." He glared at Holly.

"Johnny Jay," I said brightly, "I was just going to call you."

"It's Police Chief Jay to you. How many times do I have to tell you that? A little respect wouldn't kill you."

Johnny Jay looked angry.

"Holly, you need to stay as a witness," I said, implying that I thought the police chief capable of using his position in a negative manner. Which was true, especially when he was mad.

I stood up, not wanting to give Johnny more of an advantage than he already had. We stood almost eye to eye when I stretched out tall.

"So you heard a scream, did you? Either you withheld important information," he said, puffy-faced with temper, "or you're lying to cover up. A bald-faced lie to a law-enforcement official could buy you time in jail, Missy Fischer."

"I didn't lie. And you're threatening me. Did you hear that, Holly?"

Holly was out of my sight range, but I'm sure she nodded. The police chief and I were locked in a stare-down. He didn't know it, but I always won stare-downs.

He poked a finger at my face.

I didn't blink as I said, "Don't touch me." I refrained from any emotional display since bullies enjoy getting reactions. The best course of action was to stay calm but firm. "Or I'll file a complaint. Police brutality."

Johnny Jay removed his finger and glanced at Holly, breaking the stare-down before we got far into it. "I need a moment alone with your sister."

"No way. I'm staying," Holly said. She leaned against a storage shelf and folded her arms. She knew the bully rules as well as I did. Keep close to a friend.

In school, Johnny Jay used to go after the weak kids, the ones who wouldn't stand up to him and didn't tell. Or the kids who had the shortest fuses. With them, he'd swoop in and attack, then stand back all innocent when the other kid lost his cool. Most of the time his victim was the one who got in trouble.

I hadn't belonged to either of those groups. Not the weak ones or the short fuses.

"You two could have used a little discipline growing up," he said.

Johnny Jay was a serial bully. He had to have someone to pick on at all times. I was his current target for some unknown reason. But saying we didn't have any discipline as kids was a big joke. Mom wasn't exactly a lenient parent, and Dad had worked all the time and never really tried to cross over her strict line of authority to help me out.

"No sense lying anymore. It'll only make matters worse for you." The police chief was on a roll. "You heard a scream all right, didn't you? Only you weren't in your bed, dreaming, were you? Come on, admit it. You and Clay Lane were in it together. She was in the way, but why? Why did you have to kill her?"

Holly let out a little gasp. I slipped her a look. She covered her mouth.

Then I said something really stupid. I said, "You've known me my whole life. Do you actually think I could hit another person over the head and hold them under water while they drowned?"

Johnny Jay's eyes narrowed and I realized my mistake. I shouldn't know how Faye had died. Hunter had said it was confidential police information.

"Did Hunter Wallace tell you that?"

What would happen to Hunter's law-enforcement career if I told the truth? "No," I said, unable to betray his confidence even if I suffered for it.

"Come on, let's go," the police chief said.

"Go where?"

And that's how I found myself, once again, in the interrogation room.

Seventeen

Johnny Jay left me alone for what seemed like hours in the exact same room I'd been in last time, while I "stewed in my own juices." That was one of my mother's phrases. I had to get out of here in time for the seven o'clock meeting tonight or there would be no one to defend my bees against Lori Spandle. She'd work everyone into a frenzy and mob my house again, this time after dark when she'd be more effective.

Five o'clock came and went. Still no police chief. I tried to use my cell phone to call Holly, but there was no signal in the room. I hadn't gotten any mandatory one phone call, either. Was that a good thing or a bad thing? The only good thing so far was that Johnny Jay hadn't read me my rights.

I had to count on Holly to do damage control with our mother. If only Johnny Jay hadn't made such a big deal of putting me in the back of his squad car like a caged animal.

And right in front of all the sheepshead players, the old-timers, Grams and all her friends.

I continued to wait for something to happen while staring at the eagle picture on the wall and thought about Clay sitting in a cell in the Waukesha jail and whether or not I was about to join him. What a mess! And since I was innocent of any crime but sinking in quicksand in spite of that, what did that say about Clay's situation? What if he was innocent, too?

At one point, I thought I heard Hunter's voice out in the hall, but I couldn't be sure.

From time to time, I smiled at the two-way mirror in case someone was on the other side, to let whoever it was see that I was calm and cool and innocent.

Sure.

Finally, Johnny Jay strolled in.

"I have to leave now," I said, trying to keep my voice even and businesslike. "I have a meeting tonight that I can't miss. Why don't we get together for a talk around"—I checked the time—"nine or ten tonight. Although, tomorrow morning would be better for me. Does that work for you?"

That got him laughing. "The only way you have a remote chance of getting out of here at all," he said, "is if you start telling the truth."

So I did. With only a few modifications.

- Yes, I'd heard something that sounded like an argument and then a scream (truth).

- But I hadn't realized it was anything other than a dream until right before I asked Hunter to relay the information to the police chief (modified slightly).

- Everybody in town knew how Faye had been killed. The store was a hotbed of intrigue (last sentence totally true).

- I couldn't remember exactly who told me (major modification).

- And yes, I was perfectly willing to take a lie detector test if the police chief felt it was necessary (yikes).

- If I'd had any idea how important what I'd heard was, I would have rushed right in to inform Police Chief Jay (major modification).

I even addressed Johnny Jay by his professional name for the first time ever. Call me desperate.

"Hunter Wallace has been in here for hours trying to get you released," the police chief finally said. "And I know he told you how Faye Tilley died, so you can stop protecting him."

Johnny Jay tipped back in his chair and thought things over. "I'm a reasonable man," he said. I choked back a retort. "But I wasn't born in a barn. People outsmart lie detectors, although I doubt that you could. At some point we might have the chance to test you. In the meantime, you're living free on borrowed time because if Clay Lane sent that e-mail, I'm going to get a confession, and if he didn't, I'm going to find the person who did and we're going to have an honest to goodness witness. Trust me on that."

Yay! I wasn't going to jail!

Johnny Jay continued, "Who knows? Maybe your ex-husband really was trying to frame you."

"That's what I believe, Police Chief Jay," I agreed, politely.

"Then again, you could be his accomplice and he turned on you."

The clock hands kept moving. The Town Council meeting would begin in ten minutes.

I shook my head. "If I was planning a murder," I said, "the dead person would be Clay."

"So you're capable of murder. Is that what you want to tell me? On the record?"

Johnny Jay dinked around, playing semantics games until I wanted to deck him. Finally, he let me go. I half expected to find Hunter waiting for me outside, but he wasn't there. Just when I was about to give up on getting to the meeting, Grams pulled up next to me, slid the passenger's window down, and offered me a ride.

"How's Mom taking . . . this?" I asked.

"You don't want to know, sweetie. I'd come into the meeting and help you out, but it's getting late for me to be driving around. My eyes aren't what they used to be, and it's almost my bedtime.

"That's okay. I can handle it."

We cruised along on the incredibly slow and jerky ride. My only hope of making it in time to state my case was if the meeting started late, which it almost always did.

This time was no exception.

Eighteen

After shouting a big, heartfelt thank-you to my grand-mother, I bolted through the library doors as the last of the board members were taking their official positions. Now that I was present, the meeting couldn't get under way quick enough for me. I had a stream of adrenaline built up and was in fast forward after all the waiting and worrying.

"I have something to say," I blurted.

"You always do," Tom Peterson, one of the town super-visors, said. He poured himself a cup of coffee from the service tray and made his way up to take a seat with the other town supervisors. "You have to follow procedure just like everybody else."

Town hall meetings are not well-attended events. Every two years we make a big deal of elections for the volunteer, yet highly coveted, positions of town supervisor. Campaign signs line our lawns, the local newspaper covers all sides, then we vote and hang out at Stu's Bar and Grill waiting for the results. The old-timers almost always win, but that doesn't stop newcomers from trying. Once in a while, one of the old guard will keel over dead from extreme old age, making room for a younger member, almost always related to the deceased. We still haven't elected any women yet, but that had to change one of these days soon.

Then, after the residents of Moraine make such a big fuss about the election, we disappear back to our own lives and expect our officials to handle things for us the right way. Sometimes that's a big mistake.

At the moment, Grant Spandle, Lori's henpecked husband and poor excuse for a town chairman, sat in the middle of a table at the front of the room. Two town supervisors sat on either side of him with little nameplates in front of each of them in case we forgot who they were.

The town board consisted of:

- Grant Spandle—chairman of the board and local land developer.

- Tom Peterson—supervisor and long-time dairy farmer.

- Bud Craig—supervisor, Waukesha firefighter, and father of my part-time helpers, the twins Brent and Trent.

- Stanley Peck—supervisor and retired farmer.

- Bruce Cook—third-grade teacher, and our newest supervisor, after the unexpected death of his father, our previous supervisor.

Others present were:

- Aurora Tyler—owner of Moraine Gardens, across from my house.

- Emily Nolan—library director.

- Karin Nolan—librarian and Emily's daughter.

- Larry Koon—frozen custard maker and owner of Koon's Custard Shop.

- Milly Hopticourt—recipe tester and gifted flower arranger.

- P. P. Patti Dwyre—my neighbor and main town gossip.

- Several others I knew by sight, but not by name. They had paperwork with them, so I guessed they were on the agenda.

Note: My nemesis, Lori Spandle, was MIA. And after all that threatening!

Impatient as I was, I listened to the minutes from the last meeting and the other *blah, blah, blah* regarding old business. The summaries probably didn't take as long as they seemed to me. New business was next, but I was last on the agenda, after some issues regarding bike paths and conditional use permits, I couldn't wait another second, so I pushed off from my position against the back wall and stomped up, hoping I looked confident and firm. No one tried to stop me. Usually the meetings follow an orderly agenda, but this one promised to become a free-for-all.

"You're out of turn," Grant said to me.

"For those of you waiting for your turn, do any of you object to me going first?" I glanced around the room. Nobody objected.

"Then say your piece," Grant said, giving up.

I plowed ahead. "As everyone in this room knows, Manny Chapman died recently—stung to death—and since then, a certain individual has been on a campaign to wipe out all our local honeybees. I'm here to explain why that's absolutely ridiculous, not to mention against the town's best interest."

I began with bullet points.

"Number one," I said to the handful of concerned citizens and board members, "Manny was stung by yellow jackets, which are wasps, not bees. Number two, since Manny's honeybees didn't kill him, why would anyone want to destroy them? Number three, the honey business has benefited our community, and every single one of you has enjoyed having access to local honey products. Number four, why can't anyone seem to understand that honeybees and yellow jackets aren't the same thing? If you want, I can explain the difference between bees and yellow jackets right now."

The board members glanced at each other to see if any of them cared to hear me out.

"We'd all enjoy hearing a biology lesson," Grant decided for them, "but that won't be necessary. We have us a teacher right up at this table if we need anybody to explain the birds and bees."

That brought some chuckles.

"The main point is, I don't want anyone messing around with my bees," I said. "Is that understood?"

"Perfectly," Stanley said. "Nobody's going to bother you."

"I'm not worried about me, Stanley. It's my bees."

I still had a bunch of bullet points, like the importance of pollination and how weak crops could create financial hardship for all the local producers.

Before I got back to my pro-bee argument, Grant piped up, "Let's vote on this thing and get it over with. If your bees are a threat to our community, they have to be dealt with." He glanced toward the back door. "Wonder where Lori is? She should be here to make her case. We need to wait for her."

"That doesn't seem right," Bruce Cook said. "She knew about the meeting and she chose to miss it. Besides, most of us know how we're going to vote."

Nods around the room indicated Bruce was right about minds already being made up. Other than Milly and maybe Bruce, since his class had visited without incident, I wasn't sure who else was in my court. I could be in serious trouble if enough votes came in for annihilation.

I would have tried to sneak my sister, Holly, in, but everybody knew she wasn't a resident of Moraine and didn't qualify. Same with Hunter, who lived outside the town's limits. Too bad Carrie Ann hadn't shown up to give me her support.

Just when everybody was getting ready to cast their votes, the siren went off at the fire department south of town. That wail meant we had an emergency situation and all available volunteers better get down there pronto.

At that point, the meeting fell apart, since we lost two of our elected officials, Tom and Bud. Bud was a paid fire-fighter in the city of Waukesha, but he also volunteered in Moraine. I have to give them credit; Tom and Bud took their emergency response positions seriously, and they disappeared like the last clap of thunder in an electric storm, leaving the room so quiet I could hear Grant Spandle recap his pen.

The meeting over, the rest of us began filing out of the library and into that moment between dark and light right before the streetlights go on. We gathered in front of the library, wondering what emergency had happened.

"Where's Lori?" Milly asked.

"Here she comes," I said.

Lori Spandle came down the sidewalk, traveling fast. Under the streetlights that had popped on that very moment, I could see she was wearing her bee veil, the one she had left at my house. Unless she had more than one, that meant she'd been trespassing on my property again. Were my bees safe? Had she used the meeting as an opportunity to kill them? I fought an urge to rip the veil off her face and tear it to shreds.

"Meeting's over," I said to her, refusing to show panic over my bees' safety. "Your side lost. No more talk of killing."

"That's not true," her husband told her. "The vote's been postponed, that's all. Sorry, Sweety-poo, I know how important it was to you. Where have you been anyway?"

"I misplaced my car keys," Sweety-poo said. "Then my sister called with another one of her dramas, and I couldn't get off the phone."

"Why don't we adjourn to the custard shop," Larry said, always one to make a sale if he saw an opportunity.

"Let me close up the library first," Emily said. "Are you buying, Larry?"

"Now, Emily," Larry said. "You wouldn't begrudge a man his livelihood, would you?"

"I'm allergic to ice cream," P. P. Patti announced. "My stomach starts rolling around and sometimes I upchuck."

"Thank you for sharing that, Patti," Stanley said. "I think I'll stick to beer just in case. I'm going to Stu's Bar and Grill once we find out what the emergency is all about."

Before the crowd could break off into the beer guzzlers and the custard lickers, we collectively paused to listen to the sirens coming our way. I started toward home to check on my bees. If Lori had harmed a single one while I was at the meeting trying to save them, the police chief would have another murder suspect in custody before the night was over.

The rest of them stood on the sidewalk, watching a fire engine as it passed The Wild Clover. An ambulance and Johnny Jay's official police vehicle followed close behind, turning onto Willow Street ahead of me. Onto *my* street.

I broke into a run, rounding the corner. The vehicles had

stopped in front of my house; Clay's place and mine were the only buildings there other than Moraine Gardens and Patti's house on the corner, which they passed right by.

The garden owner, Aurora Tyler, was right on my heels, breathing hard. We both stopped in the middle of the street. In which direction would the firefighters head when they poured out of the fire truck? Emergency vehicles continued to turn onto Willow. Any situation in our area brings out every single fire and police unit in the surrounding towns. This time was no exception.

Aurora clutched my arm when the first responders headed for her flower nursery. I felt guilty about the wave of relief that swept through me, but it was immediately replaced with concern for Aurora.

I'd never seen so many axes in my life. The firefighters all carried axes and wore helmets and boots ready to fight whatever they encountered. According to residents unfortunate enough to have had small electrical fires, those guys can do some major damage. They have been described by many as overzealous.

They have also saved plenty of lives.

"Where's the fire?" one of them said to Aurora. In the dusk and with them wearing suits that covered their entire bodies, I couldn't tell one from the other.

"I don't know. I didn't call you about any fire," she said.

"Well, somebody did. Let's take a look."

Aurora ran ahead, unlocked the door to her shop and the firefighters poured in, axes at the ready. By now, most of the town watched from across the street, shooed there by Johnny Jay. I saw lights go on in the main building, then in the greenhouse and supply shed. Voices called out.

I took a moment to hustle around the back of my house and check on my bees, confirming that the veil was gone from the patio table, so Lori must have been here. Not a good sign. The flashlight I kept near the hives lighted the way. Nothing unusual stood out, but my heart was beating an irregular pattern as I lifted a frame from the box.

Bees! Thank goodness they were all still here. And they were crawling around, seemingly unharmed. I checked more frames. Everybody was safe for now.

As I returned to the front sidewalk, Grams pulled up, almost swiping the police chief's side mirror off his squad car, and either ignoring or not seeing him as he frantically waved his arms to get her attention. This was serious stuff to get Grams out this late.

"You can't leave that car there," Johnny called to Grams. She didn't pay any attention. Grams, Holly, and Mom all got out, spotted me, and came over.

"Is the greenhouse burning?" Mom asked.

"I don't see flames or smoke," I answered.

"False alarm," we heard, coming from the back of the greenhouse.

"Who the hell called it in?" asked another voice that sounded like Bud's.

"Pranksters," Mom said to anyone who wanted to listen, shaking her head in disgust. People began wandering away.

Johnny Jay came stomping over to us.

"Quite a coincidence," he said, looking right at me. "Tell me, how did the town meeting go?"

"It broke up almost before it got started," Grant Spandle said from close by. "Half the board members are fire volunteers. Can't vote without them."

"My point exactly," the police chief said, still staring at me. "Let's see your cell phone."

I rolled my eyes. Johnny Jay actually thought I would call in a false fire report just to disrupt the meeting? How pathetic was that? If anyone should be under suspicion, it should be Lori. She'd been late to the meeting and I had evidence that she'd been on my property without my permission. I couldn't think of any reason why she would call in a false fire alarm, but the woman was nuts. Did she need a reason?

"I'm refusing to show you my cell phone," I said to Johnny Jay. "If you'd think this through, you'd realize I couldn't have called it in because I was making my case to the town board."

Grams was firing on all cylinders, sharp as a filet knife in spite of the fact that it was now way past her bedtime. "Are you suggesting that one of my own did something unscrupulous?" she asked him, in her sweet little voice. "Because my granddaughter is a real peach."

"I'm sure she is, ma'am," Johnny Jay said. He dropped the subject for the moment; he'd never go up against Grams because she might round up the rest of the locals and go after him. In Moraine, you showed respect for the old-timers, or you paid the price.

"Let's get a nice picture of the two of you together," Grams said. "Story, come over here next to the police chief."

"Oh for cripes' sake," Mom blurted. "No more pictures."

Grams flashed one in Johnny Jay's face anyway.

Even though there was no sign of a fire, the firefighters stuck around to make sure there wasn't a spark smoldering somewhere in an overlooked corner. Brent and Trent Craig arrived, reassuring me that the market was locked down tight for the night and that sales had been good for a Monday evening. At that moment, I really missed the store—the banter, the smells, the whole atmosphere. It was the only place where things seemed normal lately.

Hunter and Carrie Ann roared up on his Harley Davidson. Too bad it was Carrie Ann with her arms wrapped around Hunter's tight abs.

Hunter gave me a friendly wink, but kept his distance. I didn't blame him. I'd have done the same if he'd been the one who'd called me names. Carrie Ann joined us while Hunter headed for the cops doing crowd control.

"False alarm," I said to my cousin.

"Thank God," she said. "I thought it might be your place." Grams took another picture.

After that, the excitement died down.

"We need to talk," Mom hissed at me when we had a private moment. "Alone."

"It's been a hard day," I replied. "Lori Spandle tried to kill my bees, Clay was arrested for murder, the police chief invited me down for a consultation, and for a brief second I thought my house was on fire." I wasn't telling her anything that she didn't already know. "I'm beat."

"I feel bad for you, but this time you're going to sit down and listen to me, and that's final. Holly, take your grandmother to the frozen custard shop."

I watched in dismay as Grams and Holly did what Mom said, leaving me without a defensive line to back me up.

Mom and I sat in my Adirondack chairs on the front porch, watching the last of the spectators leave. I lit a lantern and turned on a small heater I kept on the porch so I could enjoy the outdoors well into late fall. The temperature had dropped to the low fifties, but by tomorrow it would climb to the high seventies as long as the sun came out.

Mom had never been an overly affectionate mother. I couldn't recall more than a handful of times that she'd told me she loved me, and none of those times were recent. And she was never any good with timing. A thought would hit her brain and come out her mouth seconds later. This time she surprised me.

"Have you heard any more about Clay?" she asked and for once she didn't sound angry or disgusted.

"Only that he's in jail and not talking."

She nodded. "And the town meeting? It was postponed?"

"Yes. I could almost feel the hostility in the room. No one wants to listen to the facts."

"Mob mentality. They can be like a pack of wild dogs." Her voice was gentle when she said, "You know you're killing me, right? I've spent my life living up to the standards of this community. Appearances are important with my generation. Yours doesn't seem to care what people say or think."

In the soft light from the lantern, I could see her eyes tearing up. This was tons worse than being yelled at. Now I felt bad for coming back to Moraine two years ago and dropping my personal problems and Clay's bad behavior into Mom's perfect world.

"I'm sorry," I said, "I've really tried to measure up."

Which wasn't exactly a lie. I loved Moraine and wanted to be accepted, but circumstances kept dragging me into the limelight and not in a good way.

"Lie low for a while," Mom said. "Tend your store, get into a routine. Promise me you'll stay out of trouble."

"I promise."

Well, what else could I say? She wanted to hear it. And I promised with total sincerity.

"Whether your honeybees are dangerous or not is beside the point," she went on. "They've caused too much division among our residents. Promise me you'll get rid of them."

I was silent for a minute.

"Promise me?"

"Okay, I promise."

And I said it with the exact same sincerity.

Nineteen

I'd found five G. Smiths in the phone directory, and I decided to call every one of them. Four were women. The last one turned out to be male, but his name was Gary, not Gerald, and he knew nothing about bees.

If Gerald Smith didn't exist, and I had a bad feeling that he didn't, where were Manny's honeybees and the hives? Had Grace lied to me about the name because she didn't want me to know where Manny's bees went? Or had someone lied to Grace? I'd have to try to find the right moment to broach the subject of the missing bees after the funeral tomorrow.

Putting that problem aside for the light of day, I went to work making good on my promise to Mom as soon as I was sure it was dark enough to cover my tracks.

September nights are cool in Wisconsin, perfect weather

to move bees, although rain would have been even better for keeping the colonies snug inside their hives. I'd helped Manny move these two hives from his place to mine. I could do this alone.

I'd thought long and hard about where to stash the hives. Most homeowners don't mind a few bees wandering into their yards as long as the busy workers didn't disrupt their lives. But two entire hives, with thousands of workers in each, tended to make people nervous.

Stanley Peck's place was an option. He had plenty of farmland and he seemed to have some bee knowledge based on the information he imparted to the mob about my bees and the distances they could fly. And he'd defended me against Lori. But I didn't entirely trust him. He'd been part of her original group, and I hadn't forgotten that.

Holly's lake home was another possibility. But she had one of those totally pristine yards with everything in place, manicured, pruned, etc. My two box hives would stand out like warts on a baby's bottom.

That left only one place. Grams's house. The location was perfect—only a mile and a half from my house, so the bees would still be within their home flying area. I certainly couldn't let her or Mom know what I was up to because then Mom would launch into one of her long-winded lectures intended to force me to toe her line, which happened to be covered with barbed wire. She'd made me promise to get rid of my bees because of politics, but she hadn't approved of them from the very beginning. Although, come to think of it, I'm not sure she had ever approved of anything I'd ever done, past or present. Or future. That first-daughter syndrome again. I could spend the rest of my life trying to get her approval without any success.

How a sweet woman like Grams could have a cranky daughter like Mom amazed me.

Yes, Grams's house was the answer. It would be easy to slip in undercover with the hives, without Grams or Mom even knowing. Here's why:

- They both go to bed incredibly early.

- Mom uses earplugs because Grams can take down the roof with her snoring.

- Grams has refused to give up any of the family's old farmland to developers, thus I had a significant area on which to hide the hives.

- She rents out some of the land to a farmer who planted corn this year (next year will be alfalfa), and he wouldn't be out in the fields again until harvest time next month. Even if he *did* see them, he wouldn't think anything of them.

- The green corn stalks had ripened to a beautiful fall yellow and would effectively camouflage the hives, since I had painted them yellow to match my house. Yellow corn, yellow stalks, yellow hive boxes.

I backed my truck into my driveway, and then dressed in coveralls, boots, a veil, and gloves, taking care to tuck in all my loose ends where a bee might wander in. Tight pant cuffs and sleeves work best when dealing with bees, so I rubber-banded myself. I even pulled my hair up into a ponytail to keep it out of my face. Then I closed off the entrances to both hives with wire mesh, gave them a few puffs of smoke from the smoker, which worked wonders in keeping them calm, started the truck engine because vibrations also help quiet bees for some unknown reason, and began trying to load the boxes into the back of my truck. That turned out to be harder than I thought. The hives were incredibly heavy.

Impossible to lift, in fact.

I gave up and called Holly. "I need you to help me lift something," I said into the phone.

"Do you know what time it is?"

"So? You sleep all morning. I assume you stay up all night."

"K, K (*okay, okay*). Where and when?"

"My house. Now."

Good thing my sister didn't ask *what* she was going to lift or she never would have shown up.

"You've got to be kidding," she said when I handed her the proper attire. "I'm afraid of bees. I might be allergic."

"Bee allergies are hereditary," I said, pulling that scientific fact out of thin air. "We don't have it in our family."

Holly sighed, one of those big, noisy, disgusted, why-me air releases that might cause a lesser woman to excuse her from the task at hand. After she realized I wasn't going to back down, she got herself dressed in the protective clothing.

Getting her to take a position at the side of a hive was another thing. "They can't get out of the hives," I reassured her. "See the wire mesh? It's literally impossible for them to get at you."

With further coaxing, we got to work, gingerly loading the hives into the truck, being as careful as we could not to jar them.

The bees weren't too happy. They fanned inside the hive boxes, causing a wild vibration and scaring Holly into a few dashes toward the house before we completed the task.

After tying everything down and shutting the truck doors softly, we were on our way.

Suddenly I felt the stress draining from my body. The farther we got from my house, the better I felt. Enough bad things had happened in the last few days without the added worry of Lori Spandle killing my last two hives of honeybees. The back of my neck and my shoulders ached from carrying around that fear. Tomorrow couldn't come fast enough. My bees would be safe, no more stressing over them.

I checked my rearview mirror to make sure we weren't followed. We weren't.

"Where are we going?" Holly wanted to know.

"You'll see," I answered.

I cut the truck lights a quarter mile from the house, right after Holly figured out where we were going. I eased along with the windows rolled down, smelling earth and green growth. Crickets sang and bullfrogs croaked. The ground leading into the field was rough, causing the truck to bounce. I slowed down to a crawl for the hives' sake.

I headed to the far side of the cornfield, where the early-morning sun would warm the hives. The boxes were just as heavy as they'd been when we loaded them up, but getting them down was definitely easier. I picked the most level spot I could find, we finished placing the hives, then we both got back into the truck and I moved it a distance away.

"Stay in the truck," I said to my sister. "They are going to be angry once I open up the hives."

"Great. Just great," Holly said, hunkering down.

The wire mesh across the entrances came away easily.

I ran like crazy when I saw bees crawling out of the hives. Their collective hum was loud and angry, just as I'd predicted.

Honeybees navigate by the UV patterns of the sun, but that doesn't mean they can't fly at night. They will fly toward light. So when I opened the truck door and realized I had forgotten to disable the interior light, they flew right in after me.

Not to mention that I'd left my window down.

I slammed the door shut. The guard bees stayed with me. Holly screamed as though her life was ending. The bees unanimously decided that we were the bad guys. They went to town on my hands. One stung me right through the gloves that were guaranteed to be sting-proof. At least the veil protected my head and eyes. Who knew what kind of attack they were mounting on my sister; I was too busy to look.

Holly and I jumped out of the truck and ran in different directions, leaving the doors wide open.

Then we met up and sat in a ditch for a long time. Holly, in spite of all her screaming, hadn't been stung at all. Not once. I had six or seven throbbing areas. Before returning to the truck, Holly took the opportunity to get what was bothering her off her chest.

"Don't ever, ever ask me for a favor again," she said. "You owe me big-time for this one."

"I know," I said. We crept back to find the truck empty of bees.

"I have to check on them one more time," I said.

"Please, let's get out of here," Holly begged. I could hear panic rising in her voice.

"Relax," I said. "I have it down pat this time. I just want to make sure they're settled down and that I haven't forgotten anything important, like removing all the wire mesh."

"Trust me, you removed all of it."

"I wouldn't be able to sleep tonight without double-checking."

"Take me home first. Please."

"It'll only take a minute."

I adjusted the truck's interior lights so they wouldn't come on this time, made sure all the windows were closed, shushed Holly's whimpers, and stumbled through the dark, listening. Sure enough, the honeybees were still riled up.

And they already had a visitor.

Did I mention that skunks like to position their bodies near beehive entrances and lap up as many guard bees as they can? Why the stings don't deter them is anybody's guess. Manny had had an ongoing war with skunks, and he'd taught me what he knew, a lesson that was about to be wasted on the current situation. I might have heard the skunk's warning stomp if the bees hadn't been making so much noise. And I might have seen the skunk raise its tail if the moon had been shining, instead of the pitch-black darkness I stumbled through.

I'd never been skunked before. Trust me, it's the nastiest thing imaginable. At least the musk didn't hit me in my eyes, thanks to the bee veil I still wore. But the fumes came close enough that I felt the burn. And my stomach churned. I didn't feel too good.

On top of that, Holly must have smelled me staggering back toward the truck, or her night vision was better than mine, because she locked me out. I peeled off as many of my clothes as possible—the veil, gloves, and overalls—and threw them into the back of the truck. Everything reeked of skunk musk. And I mean everything. Including my jeans and top, which should have been protected by the overalls.

"Let me in." I banged on the window on her side. "I don't smell now that I took off the overalls."

What a lie, but I was desperate.

In answer, Holly scooted over into the driver's seat, started the truck, and drove away.

I gaped at my disappearing taillights.

As much as I didn't want to do it, I stumbled over to Grams's house and rang the doorbell. After I rang several times, a light came on and Grams opened the door in her nightclothes.

"Oh, my," she said, closing the door to a tiny crack. "You've been skunked."

"What should I do?" *Don't cry,* I warned myself. Remember, big girls don't cry.

"I'll be right back." The kitchen light went on. Through the window, I could see her preparing a wash with hydrogen peroxide and soap and some other things. Mom walked into the kitchen. Their mouths moved. Mom glared at the window. I ducked back where she couldn't see me.

When Grams opened the door, I could hear Mom. "Story, this is completely inappropriate. The next time you do something this foolish, don't come to me."

I hadn't come to her, just to keep the record straight. I'd come to Grams, who shoved her concoction through the door. "Soap up with this," she said. "Make sure you get it all over. Then use the hose to rinse off."

"I have to do it outside?"

Mom answered by calling out, "You bet you do. What? We're supposed to let you inside smelling like that?"

"What happened to all the family intervention? Aren't you supposed to be helping me?"

Nobody answered.

I went behind the barn and striped down, lathered up, rinsed, and did it again until my skin was raw. Then I realized I didn't have any other clothes to wear besides the smelly jeans and top. I couldn't bring myself to put on the skunked clothes. I'd rather run naked through downtown Moraine.

Which might happen if Holly didn't come back.

Since I come from an overall type of family, I found a dirty pair hanging in the barn and put them on, adjusting the buckles so my private parts stayed private. Then I rummaged around until I found what I needed.

That skunk would be back, if not tonight, then tomorrow. He'd scratch on the hive entrance until the guard bees came out to investigate. He could wipe out both colonies if I didn't do something fast. I dug out two pieces of plywood and drove nails through them, setting the nails in an inch apart all over the boards. Then I walked back, hauling my masterpieces to the hives and adjusted the boards, nails up, in front of the entrances. If the skunk wanted bees, he'd have to walk over nails.

I heard a motor and turned to see my truck idling a short distance away.

The drive home was quieter that the ride over. In fact, I was pretty sure my sister wasn't speaking to me.

I went to bed for the night, what was left of it, and decided this day was way up there on my list of worst ones ever.

Twenty

Tuesday morning the air was thick and heavy, as though a major storm was gathering, although there wasn't a cloud in the sky. The small world of Moraine had the same storm-brewing quietness and anticipation to it that I've sensed before on funeral days.

My friend and mentor would be buried today, and I didn't want to accept it. For me, the worst part of a funeral service was when the casket was closed up. Every time, the finality of it hit home like a blow to my body.

I wondered about Faye, if her body had been released, and whether her family had made arrangements. And whether Clay was really guilty and how it must feel to be behind bars, locked up like an animal.

As I was getting ready to go to the market, Ray Goodwin knocked on my back door. I felt awful from lack of sleep and, I swear, I could still smell skunk. It had permeated my skin and was running rampant through my blood system. The good news was the effects of the bee stings had almost disappeared.

I went outside to greet him rather than let him inside my home.

"I heard talk about a meeting to destroy your bees," he said, his head cranked in every direction but mine. "I don't see 'em—did they get them after all?"

"Nobody got my bees, Ray. I moved them, since Lori was determined to get her way."

"That's a relief. I hope my bee stings didn't make things worse for you?"

"The situation couldn't have gotten any worse, but that's Lori's fault, not yours. Don't worry about it."

"Bet you're wondering why I stopped by."

"A little, yes."

"Just to see how you're doing. I know you and Manny Chapman were real close."

"That's nice of you. Actually, you're just the person I need to talk to." Ray might know something about Manny's bees that I didn't. He was on the road, traveling the county most of the time, and people talked at his stops. "Have a seat." I gestured to the patio table and chairs.

Ray took a seat without sniffing the air or backing his chair away from me, so I hoped that the skunk odor was a figment of my imagination. "I said I was sorry for what I did with Kenny's Bees," he said. "You aren't going to bust my chops over it again, are you?"

"No, no, I'm not still mad about finding out you were selling honey for Kenny's Bees as long as you quit." I didn't mention that Queen Bee Honey might not even exist in the future.

"I haven't been over there since our conversation."

"Good. I need to talk to you about Manny's bees. They're missing, and I'm trying to locate them."

"Did you ask Grace where they went?" Ray readjusted his ball cap.

"She said somebody named Gerald Smith picked them up."

"Well, there you are."

"I can't find him in the directory, and the association never heard of him."

"Maybe he's from someplace else."

"Grace said specifically he was from Manny's bee association. Have you heard anything on your route?"

Ray looked out over my backyard toward the river, thinking. "I'd heard that Manny had extra-strong colonies and that he wasn't plagued with colony collapse like a lot of the beekeepers."

"That's right," I said. "He was working on selective breeding, but it was his big secret. That's all I know. His research was all 'top secret.'" I used finger quotes to show how top secret it really was. According to Manny, if he came up with a cure for a bee disease or condition, he'd let everyone else know. Other than that, his honey secrets were his private business.

Talking about Manny's experiments reminded me of his bee journal. I'd have to see if Grace had come across it and ask her again if I could have it.

"Too bad he didn't tell you more about what he was working on," Ray said. "There's money in strong hives."

"I had my hands full just learning Beekeeping 101 without understanding the financial side of beekeeping." Which wasn't exactly true, but it wasn't any of Ray's business. Manny's honey business was a lot of work, but he knew how to turn a profit. "I better get going," I said. "I'm opening up the store this morning."

"I have gallons of fresh apple cider from Country Delight Farm," Ray said. "Want me to drop some off at the market?"

"Sure. By the way, any more trouble with bee stings?"

"No," he said. "I'm a quick learner."

I locked up, walked down to The Wild Clover, and went through the routine of opening the store while Ray added gallons of apple cider to my inventory. The phone rang. It was Carrie Ann.

"I can't make it in today," she said, sounding like her old, hungover self. "I'm sick."

How disappointing! I had been rooting for her. At least she'd called in. The old Carrie Ann never even bothered.

"Anything I can do to help?"

"Thanks for the offer. But I just need to sleep it off, I mean, you know, sleep is good for you when you're sick."

"Right."

I heard a voice in the background. "Is that Hunter I hear?"

"That's him."

"Tell him I'm sorry I called him a jerk."

"Tell him yourself." There were sounds of Carrie Ann passing the phone over.

Jeez. I wasn't ready for a face-to-face apology, or even a voice-to-voice one. I still didn't like what he had done, coming on to me while having a relationship with Carrie Ann.

"Hello?" Hunter said innocently.

"I'd like to apologize for calling you names," I said.

There was a pause. "You only called me one," he said.

"But I thought more of them in my head."

"Oh." Another pause, then, "We should talk."

"Yes, soon."

I hung up wondering if I still had to honor my promise to Hunter to give Carrie Ann another chance. He'd continue to push for it, I was sure, and she had been good for a few days. But I didn't have time to think on the cousin problem any longer because the store got jumping with business.

Stu Trembly came through on his way to the bar. He bought a newspaper and a bag of small chocolate bars.

"Has Carrie Ann been hanging at the bar?" I asked him.

"Last night was the first time this week."

Confirming my suspicions. "It's only Tuesday, Stu."

Aurora Tyler from Moraine Gardens came in for yogurt.

"Any idea who called in that fire alarm?" she still wanted to know.

"Not a hint," I said. "All I'm sure of is that it wasn't anybody who was at the meeting."

"Kids, you think?"

"Probably," I agreed.

Next, Lori Spandle came in without her headgear, looking for eggs—and trouble.

"My bees are gone," I told her.

"Good riddance. Mind if I check that out for myself?"

"Go ahead, just don't put one foot in my yard."

"Then how can I verify whether you are telling the truth or not?"

"Stu has a canoe. Use the river like the Indians did."

Lori smirked. "No way. I heard what happens on that river when you're around."

I overcharged her on the eggs. She didn't notice.

Her husband, Grant, showed up ten minutes later.

"My Sweetie-poo is seriously upset," he said.

I picked up a honey stick and held it out. "This should help with her condition. And a case of them might make a dent in sweetening her tart disposition." *Tart* having two meanings in this case.

"Why can't you be friends with her?" he asked. "That's all she wants."

Oh yeah, right. The poor mistreated schemer just wants to be friends.

Milly Hopticourt arrived with fresh bouquets for the

flower bin, followed by P. P. Patti Dwyre, just the woman I needed.

"Patti, I've been hearing rumors," I said. If anyone knew the gossip, Patti would, that is if there was gossip to know.

That perked her up. "Really!"

"About my ex."

She flapped a wrist at me. "Common knowledge. Yesterday's news."

"About him and Grace Chapman."

Patti's eyes lit up. "What do you know? Let's compare."

"All I heard was that she and Clay had . . . you know . . . something going."

Milly, still arranging bouquets, clucked in disapproval. "Grace is burying her husband this afternoon."

"You're right," I said. "How tacky of me."

Which it was.

Milly went on arranging the bouquets, tucking one here, moving one there, standing back and eyeing her work. Patti wandered off with a wink that said as soon as Milly left, we'd trade info.

She had to wait awhile because business stayed strong. When I had a chance, I opened a jug of the cider Ray had brought and set it out with little paper cups for customers to sample.

The phone rang a few times, and I had to let the answering machine pick it up. I needed to grow extra hands, or find more reliable help. Patti went outside and sat on a bench, determined to continue our conversation if she had to wait all day.

Some of the seniors who had been in the choir loft playing cards when the police chief took me away wanted to know the scoop.

"Vindicated," I said. "The police chief was overreacting."

"What do you think about that ex-husband of yours? Did he do it?"

"He'll get his day in court."

I should have gone into politics, I was so smooth at saying nothing. Not that I knew much. I hadn't heard any updates on Clay's situation or on the investigation into Faye's murder, which I assumed would be ongoing. Johnny Jay had a suspect in custody but he still had to prove Clay did it.

Milly rounded up the seniors to all go out for corn on the cob, and they set off up the street—corn on the cob drenched in butter and salt sounded good, but I couldn't leave the store. Instead I downed a handful of almonds.

My sister, Holly, finally arrived to help me. I let out a sigh of relief. "Eleven o'clock already?" I couldn't believe where the morning had gone. My sister wore a white, low-cut V-neck tee with jeans, and rings the size of rocks on her fingers. Expensive-looking ones, too, compared to the sterling silver, twelve-dollar Celtic knot ring I wore on my right hand. I always noticed these things about Holly, and it annoyed me that I had such a jealous streak. I wasn't exactly perfect, but I vowed on the spot to be a better sister and friend.

Holly sniffed. Either she was still angry, or I had left-over skunk smell on me.

"Can you smell skunk? You can, can't you?"

"Only if I try." Then she started laughing and wouldn't stop.

"I don't see any humor in the situation." I bristled. "And you didn't, either, last night."

"You should have heard what Mom said on the phone to me this morning." Holly wiped away tears. I was pleased to see that her mascara streaked—and I wasn't going to tell her.

"I don't want to know what she said."

"K. It would only make you mad," Holly agreed. "What should I do first here?"

"You have the hang of the cash register?"

"Like it's my own."

Which it sort of was, considering the fine print and the line I'd signed on.

"Then I'm going to sit outside for a few minutes. Get off my feet."

Outside, Patti slid over and patted the bench.

"Milly's right," I said. "Today isn't the day to dis Grace."

"Funeral days are the biggest gossip days of the year," Patti said. "That's when the family's past comes up for review. Haven't you ever noticed that?"

Now that she mentioned it, I had. People liked to tell stories about the deceased and that involved stories that included the loved ones left behind. Some of the stories were told in groups, some during eulogies, and some in quiet corners where the main focus of the story couldn't be overheard.

"I still think we should wait."

"Okay." Patti shrugged like it didn't matter. "But I have inside information and I might think it over and decide to keep it to myself."

She was making it hard on me.

"Who around here found out about them first?" I asked.

"Me, of course. I saw them together."

Right then, DeeDee Becker, Lori Spandle's little sister, walked past and entered The Wild Clover without a glance in our direction. DeeDee was into lots of pierced flesh, loud clashing colors, and carrying a purse the size of a suitcase. I was sure she'd been shoplifting from my store, but I hadn't been able to prove it. Then I realized I hadn't warned my sister to keep an eye on her.

"Sorry, Patti, I've got to get back inside," I said, deciding on the spot to speak only kindness about surviving loved ones. At least for one day.

Twenty-one

I went back inside and shared my suspicions with Holly. Then I followed DeeDee around the store for a while without any red-handed results and was about to call it a day when I heard commotion at the front door. Holly had busted DeeDee with a bag of potato chips in her purse and four packs of gum in her jeans' back pockets.

My sister had tackled DeeDee right on the sidewalk, pinned her to the pavement, and still had a hand free to use her cell phone to report the crime. Talk about multitasking.

"Since when did you learn wrestling holds?" I asked my sister.

"Let me up," DeeDee wailed. "I didn't do anything."

After a little more scuffling, Holly produced the evidence.

I couldn't believe my eyes. "Gum and chips? How damn

dumb can you get, DeeDee? I know you have enough money to pay for that!"

"I'll never do it again," DeeDee said, crying full-out. "I've learned my lesson."

Yeah, sure. Owning a store had taught me a few things I wished I didn't have to deal with. Shoplifting was the biggie. I'd learned a little bit about shoplifters:

- Most shoplifting crimes aren't need-based.

- A lot of shoplifters get some kind of high out of it.

- It can be as addictive as drugs.

- Many of them keep doing it even after they are caught.

In my opinion, DeeDee was a classic case.

Holly still had her in some sort of professional power hold.

Sirens in the distance were coming our way. DeeDee looked at me like a trapped wild animal.

"Maybe we shouldn't press charges," I said to Holly. My sister, though, wasn't about to catch and release this bottom-feeder. If it had been up to me, I would have let her go with a warning. "She feels bad enough," I argued, "and she doesn't need a criminal record. But I really do want to know where you learned those moves."

"Self-defense class," my sister said. "I modified just now, added a little offense."

I asked Johnny Jay not to call any more attention to us than we'd already attracted by Holly's sidewalk tackle, but he still left the lights flashing on his squad car while we all piled back into the store to find a private corner. All the while, DeeDee was denying any wrongdoing and begging to be released, but Johnny Jay kept a firm grip on her arm while he walked her to the back of the store.

I ended up working the cash register while Holly gave her report from the storage room. I tried to listen in, but it was hopeless. The squad lights had the locals all coming in for "forgotten" items, and I was stuck up front. It appeared that DeeDee had rounded up a little extra business for me while she worked on ruining her own life.

"The police chief locked himself out of his squad car with the lights going," I replied to everyone's inquiries, although they'd have the facts straight soon enough. Nothing was a secret around here for long. "He went looking for someone to bring a spare key. No big deal."

After a while, the three of them came out of the back. DeeDee wasn't wearing handcuffs, which was a good thing. Chatter in the store ceased. You could have heard a single corn silk hit the polished wood floor.

"It's your call," Johnny Jay said to me. "You own the store. She stole from you. What do you want to do?"

I didn't know what I wanted. Lori was my sworn enemy, and this was her sister. On the other hand, I couldn't blame DeeDee for having a rotten sibling. Although she wasn't much of a gem herself.

"I don't have all day, Missy Fischer," the police chief said.

"Let her go, but I don't want her in my store anymore."

"I can go along with that," Holly, the female all-star, said, nodding in agreement.

A few customers applauded. I heard one boo.

DeeDee was out the door and gone before we realized that the packs of gum were still missing. I hate it when I'm outsmarted.

But I had bigger robberies to worry about.

"I want to report a theft," I told the police chief after Holly went up front and I had pulled him into a corner. I explained how Manny's bees had vanished. "You're all over the county looking for trouble," I finished. "I'm just giving you a heads-up in case you see beehives where there weren't any before." Then I remembered that I'd moved my bees to Grams's back field, which would constitute a bee change of venue in the picture I was painting. "Except if you spot any near my Grams's house."

"Is this some kind of joke?" Johnny Jay said. "You can't file a report for something that doesn't belong to you in the first place."

"I'm just keeping you in the loop, then."

"What makes you think I care about your loop?"

"Fine, forget it."

Johnny Jay looked pleased, like he'd won a round, and I remembered what Sally the dispatcher had said about the consequences of turning down Johnny Jay's prom invitation. I'd suffer for the rest of my life for that one.

Then he said, "Maybe you have something after all. Where could those bees have gone? And do they figure into the break-in?"

"What break-in?"

"Manny must have told you."

"I didn't hear anything about it." Not too surprising. Manny wasn't a man of many words. Unless it had to do with his bees. Then he could go on for hours.

"I thought you two were such good *friends*." He said *friends* in a suggestive way that I didn't like, but that's Johnny Jay. Always nasty. "The robbery happened about a week ago," he continued. "Somebody broke a window in his kitchen and crawled through. Stole a camera and a few dollars out of the bureau. I chalked it up to an inexperienced burglar, kids probably. Whoever it was left behind things that were more valuable than what they took. Amateurs for sure."

"Maybe the robbery has something to do with the missing bees." I said that last part out loud instead of thinking it, like I planned.

"Well, Missy Fischer, you gave me a reason to think I

might have been wrong about it being kids who broke in. Now I think bees were involved. The bees could have been looking for something special inside the house. When they didn't find it, they must have tortured Manny to get it out of him and finished him off. Then they took whatever it was and disappeared."

"Very funny."

When the police chief strutted out, I knew he wasn't going to help at all.

Twenty-two

The visitation and funeral for Manny Chapman was held at the new Lutheran church on the southern end of Moraine. At four o'clock we began arriving for the viewing. It was our last chance to see Manny in a state as close as possible to the one we saw him in when he was still alive.

A poster board with pictures of Manny doing what he loved best, hanging around in his beeyard and spinning honey in his honey house greeted me as I entered, which surprised me, since Grace seemed to hate his bees so much. In one photo Ray and Manny were loading honey into the back of Ray's truck for distribution. I distinctly remembered being there when Manny asked Grace to take that picture. In fact, my smiling mug should have been in the picture. I spotted more photographs that I should have been in, but wasn't. I had a growing suspicion that Grace had used a software editing program to eliminate me. Delving into other people's minds wasn't my forte, however, so I focused on the open casket on the other side of the room rather than on Grace Chapman's motives for cropping me into nonexistence.

"Nice pictures," I said to Grace's brother, Carl.

"Thanks. I put them together myself. Grace didn't want me to include the bees, but they were Manny's whole life, so I managed to talk her into it."

"She didn't help with the photographs at all?" I was pretty sure she had sliced me out, but wanted to confirm it.

"Grace made a few . . . uh . . . changes." He had the decency to look embarrassed.

Grams and Mom arrived and agreed that Manny looked good in death, an observation they made at every funeral they attended. He certainly looked much better than the last time I'd seen him, when he'd been lying in the beeyard, swollen and red.

But the fact that I'd never see him again hit hard as I stood in line to offer my condolences. When my turn came, I extended my sympathies and gave Grace a hug. She stayed stiff like she couldn't bear the thought of being touched by me.

"Did Grace hug you back?" I said to Mom a little later when she and Grams had gone through the line.

"Of course," Mom said, then gave me a stern scowl and offered a tissue. "Get a grip, Story. Pull yourself together."

"Here," Grams said, digging in her purse, removing the cap from a medicine bottle and shaking out a little white pill. "Take this. You'll feel better."

Mom intercepted it. "She doesn't need a Valium. And where on earth did you get your hands on those?"

"I keep a few for emergencies," Grams said. "Times like now."

She slipped one to me when Mom wasn't looking. I wasn't much of a drug user, preferring to stay away from even the basics such as cold meds and common pain relievers like ibuprofen. This time, though, under the circumstances, I popped the pill. After all, it came from my grandmother. How harmful could it be?

Fifteen minutes later, I was standing with Stanley Peck and Emily Nolan from the library, feeling much better. I wore a silly little grin. In spite of my efforts, it wouldn't go away.

"How are you doing?" Stanley said, putting one arm around me and squeezing. "You spent more time with Manny than most of us did. This whole thing must be rough on you."

I nodded, forcing the corners of my lips down. "Life seems upside down without him," I agreed, briefly imagining a tilted universe.

"Nobody's been bothering you or your bees lately, have they?"

I shook my head.

"Speaking of bees," Emily said, looking at Stanley. "Are you enjoying the beekeeping book you checked out of the library? Sorry we only had one, but we're so small I have to be very careful what I order. Maybe I could do a search for you with other libraries if you want more."

Odd, I thought. This news seemed relatively important considering all the missing bees, but I couldn't seem to keep my focus.

"I didn't know you were interested in raising honeybees," I said to Stanley, who had the same trapped-animal look I'd seen on DeeDee Becker only a few hours earlier.

"I like learning about all kinds of things, is all," he said. "No big deal."

"Well," Emily said, "let me know if you want a few more."

"One is plenty," Stanley said.

The church filled up for the viewing. Based on past funerals in our community, most everybody would stay for the funeral service, then head to Stu's. Except Manny's family. They'd have a sit-down dinner someplace else.

Hunter Wallace came up to me. Looking around, I didn't see Carrie Ann.

"Where's your new friend?" I wanted to know.

"In the truck."

"You left her in the truck?"

"Him," Hunter said. "Ben's a him."

I stared at him blankly.

"You're asking about my dog, right?"

Oh, right.

"Sure," I said. The pill Grams had given me was doing a fine job of keeping me composed. The problem was, it couldn't determine which parts of my brain to shut down and which ones to keep in operation. So it shut down everything. And I noticed that concentrating on any one thing was impossible.

I was trying to remember something about Stanley. What was it?

I noticed that people had started to look away when I met their gaze. Or they were whispering but stopped when I wandered by. What was up with that?

This wasn't the first time I'd encountered this behavior. Live and let live was my new philosophy. If they knew something about me that I didn't, someone would eventually clue me in. Or . . . oh, well, who cared? The paranoid thought escaped into the vast emptiness of my drugged mind.

I kind of liked shutting down. I should do this more often.

Grace came up to me. "Did you run across Manny's bee journal?" she asked.

"Nope. I looked for it last time I was in the honey house, but it wasn't there. I assumed it was in your house."

"You're sure it's not out there?"

"Positive. Why don't you look for yourself?"

"You know I don't go near that place. The journal must be around someplace."

"Why do you want it?" For the life of me, I couldn't see Grace caring about Manny's bee journal. She'd never shown any interest.

"*I* don't want it," she said. "But Gerald Smith called and asked about any notes Manny made concerning his bees. That's when I remembered his journal. Gerald said it would be helpful to have it, since he will be working with the same bees. Manny wrote notes about the bees, you know, or whatever else beekeepers do."

"Interesting," I said, losing interest.

At that moment, ushers asked us to take our seats, and the funeral service began. Grams gave me a conspiratorial wink. I grinned. Hunter sat next to me, smelling fresh, like the outdoors with a faint hint of burning logs clinging to him. Nice.

Tears tried to form in my eyes as the funeral progressed, especially when they closed the casket, but something in that little pill refused to let them leak. The service was perfectly traditional, just like Grace, without any surprises or unscheduled oratories. Manny would have been pleased at the turnout.

Afterward, the family followed the hearse to the cemetery. The rest of us had a funeral procession to Stu's Bar and Grill to send Manny off properly. I'd finished off my second beer when Grams came rushing in to find me.

"Don't drink anything," she said. "I forgot to tell you not to mix alcohol with the drug."

"Okay," I said, trying not to slur my words. "Thanks for the warning."

"I didn't remember until I was home, then it dawned on me. You didn't have any alcohol, did you?"

"Nope," I lied, leaning against Hunter for support.

"What's going on?" he said to Grams.

"I gave Story a Valium at the funeral."

"And it really worked," I said.

"She doesn't usually take medications," Grams explained. "So it might affect her more than it would someone else. As long as she doesn't drink alcohol she should be okay. How do you feel, Sweetie?"

"Great," I said.

"That's not your beer, is it?" Grams pointed at a beer bottle on the bar, the one I'd just finished off.

"Nope."

"Let's get a picture of you two kids," Grams said. "You make a cute couple."

"Okay." I put on my best smile and stepped in closer to Hunter while Grams clicked away. She disappeared as quickly as she'd come.

"Let's get out of here," Hunter said. "The party's over."

"No, it's not," I said with nice relaxed muscles and not an anxious bone in my body. "It's only beginning."

Smiling, I threw him a question that would never have left my lips under normal circumstances. While he guided me to the door, I said, "Your place or mine?"

Twenty-three

The next morning, I remembered everything. Absolutely everything. In the light of a new day, with the effects of the drug and alcohol fading, I was shocked by my suggestive—okay, maybe more than merely suggestive—proposal to Hunter. I was equally embarrassed that he'd driven me home, helped me into bed, clothes intact, and then had left without one single inappropriate move.

He could have tried at least, and allowed me a proper moment of rebuff.

I'd like to believe I would have proved that my principles were sound, but frankly I'd been overly agreeable last night and anything could have happened if Hunter hadn't been in control of the situation.

I'd called Hunter a jerk the last time he'd shown affection. Then, when he was behaving himself, I'd propositioned him. If I was confused, imagine where that left Hunter. Talk about sending mixed signals.

In my fantasies, which I was quickly realizing weren't so spectacular in real life, Hunter would have undressed me for bed. I would have been wearing silky undies and my makeup would have been just as fresh as my shorts. But in reality, the only fresh part of me had been my offer.

And what about my disloyalty to my cousin Carrie Ann? When my ex-husband hit on her, she hadn't stabbed me in the back. Jeez. One little pill and a few beers and I had been ready to become as sleazy as Lori Spandle. Or Clay.

Where had Carrie Ann been, anyway? Sure she'd called in sick for her shift yesterday morning, but she must have really felt horrible. Otherwise she'd have been at the bar for Manny's going away party, even if she'd skipped the funeral.

My cousin arrived at the market at the same time I did. She still didn't know that I knew about her alcohol problem, and I wasn't about to tell her. She looked perky this morning, smelled fine, no cigarette smoke smell at all, and she didn't have hangover breath.

"Big night?" she asked, looking me over.

"I look that bad?"

Carrie Ann shrugged. "I've seen you better."

The morning's business started slow. I had plenty of spare time to putter with displays. And to think. My ex-husband, Clay, had been on my mind way too much lately. When I saw him, I'd been convinced he hadn't killed Faye, but now I wondered if it was possible. Emotionally, I was a confused mess.

"Everybody's home nursing hangovers," Carrie Ann said at one point, sounding slightly wistful that she hadn't participated in the morning-after headaches and stomach churns. "Should I leave? I could really use the money, though."

"Stay," I told her. It was the least I could do for her after my disgraceful behavior with her boyfriend. "I have to follow up on some things. This is a good time to take care of them."

I needed to know why Stanley Peck had a bee reference book from the library. And why the nonexistent Gerald Smith was searching for Manny Chapman's journal. Not to mention the rumors surfacing about Clay and Grace.

I drove my truck into Waukesha and used my driver's license to get into the jail.

"I'm Clay Lane's wife," I said, showing them my ID, which still said "Melissa Lane." I made a note to myself to hold off changing the last name on my license until some time when I didn't need to pump my ex for information while he was incarcerated. Although claiming that I was Clay's wife made me almost physically ill.

"We buried Manny Chapman yesterday," I told Clay from the free side of the Plexiglas. "Grace took it hard." Clay's expression didn't give anything away. If he had a secret affair going with Manny's wife, he didn't show it.

Clay looked out of place in a jumpsuit, a sad fashion statement coming from a man who wore a diamond earring. "Aren't you here to get me out, honey?" he said.

"Quit calling me honey. And I can't get you out. Why would you think that?"

"I thought, when they said you were here, that . . ."

"Bail's been set, then?"

"This morning."

"I'm not here to bail you out." Did he really think I would bail him out even if I could? "How's the food?" I asked, not sure what to say. This was my first experience visiting someone in jail. Should we move to small talk? The weather? The comings and goings of mutual acquaintances?

Clay took the lead. "You didn't come to ask about my jail diet. You came to hear me say I killed my girlfriend so you can go back to Moraine and spread it around. Well, I didn't do it," he said. "I didn't kill Faye."

"That's not why I'm here. I want you to talk to Johnny Jay, admit that you tried to frame me."

"What are you talking about?"

"You went to the library." I added an accusatory tone to my voice for maximum effect.

"Is that a crime now, too?"

If Clay was playing dumb, he was doing a good job of it. But then, he'd had plenty of practice.

"You tried to set me up, to make it look like I killed Faye," I said. "You used the library computer to send an e-mail to the police chief, lying about seeing me arguing with Faye."

"Why would I do that?" he asked.

"So Johnny Jay would lock me up instead of you. But it backfired on you."

Clay stared at me. "You've finally gone over the edge."

"Not me. Nope. If anyone went over the edge, it was you. Did you snap? Because the man I knew, the man I remember, was a rotten husband and a womanizer, but I never thought he was a killer. Or that he'd stoop so low as to try to blame me."

I was getting worked up, hot and flushed at the thought of what he'd tried to do to me after all the stuff I'd already endured because of him. "You deserve to rot here," I said.

"Guard?" Clay looked around wildly, but he was locked in a cubicle-sized room with no way out. For once, he couldn't run away from me. "Can someone take me back to my cell? Please?"

No one responded.

"And another thing," I continued, "you slept with Grace Chapman. How could you?"

"Oh, please." Clay tried to do a snorty, jokey laugh. "And thanks for visiting. It's been a real trip. I tell you, once I'm out of jail, I'm going to seriously consider leaving Moraine. I'm sick to death of all the talking behind everybody's back. I should have known you'd turn everybody against me."

"Me, turn everyone against you? Ha!" I said. "Maybe, if you didn't give the people I've known my whole life so much to talk about, they would have accepted you."

"Look who's talking!" He should have shut up and left it right there, but Clay never did know when to quit. He continued. "*You're* the one who made a mockery of our marriage. *You're* the one who broke our sacred wedding vows by divorcing me."

My turn. I really tried not to resort to name-calling. I really, really tried—for about ten seconds. It didn't work.

Painful and unpleasant memories from our toxic marital past were coming back to me, fast and furious. As though we had any other kind. Like all the times we'd argued about other women and where he had been all night and how he'd refused to confess his indiscretions even when I had concrete, indisputable evidence against him. And how I'd become spitting mad and start calling him names. No one in the world, not even my mother, could make me so hopping angry and frustrated.

"You sleaze-bucket," I said. "You #@!!%."

"Oh, that's really mature," Clay said before raising his voice. "Guard! Guard!"

"Okay," I said, taking a deep, calming breath and wishing for another of Grams's magic pills. "I'm all right now. I didn't mean to go off. It's just that when I heard about you and Grace . . ."

"I hardly even know the woman. She came to my place one time. Just one time."

Clay was a one-time type of guy. One time was all he really wanted. Pursue, conquer, move on to the next woman. Classic sex addiction. And I couldn't help noticing he didn't flat-out deny my accusation. The creep.

"I still can't figure out why you would kill Faye," I said. "You could have just dumped her like all the others. Wouldn't that have been the easiest way to break up?"

"Exactly right," Clay agreed. "If anyone's an expert at break-ups, it's me." He grinned, that little-boy impishness I used to find so cute. "When I get out, I'd like to spend time with you again. You know." He raked me with his eyes. I gagged.

I could barely sputter my outrage. "You have got to be *kidding*."

Was there a way to get to Clay so I could strangle him? There wasn't a door on my side or I might have tried.

"Patron privacy," Emily said, shaking her head when I asked her about Stanley's bee book checkout. "We can't discuss our patrons or their individual selections."

"Okay, then. Can you tell me when the book will be available for another patron to check out?"

All I wanted to know was when Stanley had checked out the book, either before or after Manny died and his bees had disappeared. How hard was that?

"You can use the computer over there to place a hold." She pointed at a row of computers against the wall.

I refrained from rolling my eyeballs skyward, although the temptation was almost irresistible.

"Emily, you're taking the privacy act way beyond its original intention. You know the computer program won't tell me when I can expect to get the book because I already tried looking that information up. When will it be available? That's all I want to know. If you can't get it for me soon, I'll have to try to get it from another library."

I hoped the threat of visiting another library would change her mind. Emily hated when her patrons went astray.

"I can get another one for you," she offered. "I can reserve one from a consortium library and have it sent over."

Frustrated, I tried another tack. "I hear that my ex-husband was in here the night of the bluegrass jam."

Emily brightened. Library events were her favorite topic. "I'm planning more like that. One every month, I'm thinking, to develop continuity and big audiences. Do you have any recommendations? Something you think will go over well?"

"I'll think on it. But getting back to that particular occasion. Remember, that's the day we found Faye Tilley in my kayak? What I want to know is, did Clay use one of your computers while he was here?"

"Again, patron privacy."

Just then, Stanley Peck walked in the door, or rather rushed in, threw a book on the counter, waved a hurried hello in our general direction, and disappeared out the door. I heard a sputtered word that sounded like "late."

"Wonderful," Emily said with glee after glancing at the front cover. "Now you can check it out."

My only regret was that I wasn't more discreet when I raced away without the bee book. But I didn't have time to dally and make excuses. And I didn't really care about the book at this point. I wanted to check out Stanley, not the book.

I was on his tail before he made a right turn out of the library's driveway.

He headed north on Main Street, passed through town, then turned right and followed the rustic road with open pastures on one side and woodlands on the other. The country air smelled like freshly mowed lawn. As I drove, I rolled down my window and inhaled some of the fresh fragrance, trying to stay back far enough that he wouldn't notice me. My truck wasn't exactly camo-colored. I didn't blend in well with the landscape in a bright blue vehicle. And I had to constantly remind myself to remain calm and to ease up on the accelerator each time I became over-eager. I'd start catching up in my excitement, then have to slow down when I realized the gap between us was closing.

If my hunch was right, I'd have Manny's bees back today.

Because I was convinced Stanley was leading me right to them.

Twenty-four

Facts about Wisconsin's rustic roads:

- They are part of a special state protection project aimed at preserving outstanding rural roads.

- The state has approximately one hundred of them.

- To qualify, they must be lightly traveled back roads with special natural features like rugged terrain or an abundance of native plants and wildlife.

- The town of Moraine's economic health is due in part to its location near a rustic road that is popular with tourists.

- The speed limit cannot be higher than forty-five miles per hour and many have lower postings.

Like this one, which was thirty-five miles per hour because of the winding, hilly route.

Did I mention winding?

The road curved one way then the other and before long I had a sneaky suspicion I'd lost Stanley. Worse yet, I wasn't sure how far back he'd slipped my loose noose, since the road had been twisting for the last mile or so. It hadn't intersected with any other roads, so he'd either pulled off into one of the driveways along the way or he'd sped up and outrun me, which wouldn't be hard to do. My truck was reliable, but I never said it was fast.

The first scenario, turning into a driveway, was the most likely. Only someone with a death wish would take these hills and curves at high speeds.

I turned around and retraced my route, counting seven driveways in the area where I thought I'd lost him. None of the houses were visible from the road, one of the reasons this qualified as a rustic road. But it was an incredibly annoying designation at the moment.

I tried one of the driveways, following it in. Then I tried another and another until I'd checked out every single driveway Stanley might have ducked down.

He had simply vanished.

Not letting my failure get me down, I rerouted toward Grams's field to check on my girls and whatever boys hadn't been kicked out of the hives.

Grams's car was in her driveway, and I saw Mom getting out of the passenger's side. I blew by, slouching down, hoping they wouldn't see me. As though slinking down in my seat would help conceal my truck.

I really, really wasn't in the mood for a lecture.

Pretty sure I'd slipped under Mom's radar, I bounced along the edge of the cornfield and parked close to the hives. All was in order. The nail bed had worked perfectly to convince the skunk to find a snack alternative, one more healthful to his paws. On routine inspection, my little workers were coming and going as though nothing had happened the night before.

I had washed my skunked clothing and beekeeping equipment in soap, water, and ammonia, but I'd forgotten to bring them along. After all, I'd had other ideas for the day, ideas that hadn't gone exactly as I'd expected. My original plan had me visiting my bees later in the day.

No big deal, I decided. I'd seen Manny work with his bees numerous times without protective gear of any kind. No veil or hat or gloves. He had gone among his honeybees with gentle bare hands and slow movements. I could handle that, too. Besides, didn't my bees know me by now?

After pulling a bucket of bee syrup from the bed of my truck, I opened one of the hives and poured some into a feeder. As I said, bees are hungry at this time of year when the flowers are still blooming but pollen is getting scarce. To preserve their stores of honey until they really need them the most, Manny always supplemented their diet with sugar syrup. I intended to follow his lead.

The tricky part when dealing with so many honeybees is making sure they aren't underneath your fingers.

"Ouch!" I quickly scraped off a stinger embedded in my thumb, closed up the top of the hive, and moved on to the next one, repeating the process over again.

"Ouch, jeez, that one really hurt." This time the target was my neck.

Did I mention that bee stings emit an odor that riles up the other bees? Once stung, my only recourse was to cover up any exposed body parts. That is, if I had anything to cover up with. Otherwise, they'll keep it up.

In my semi-panic, I stepped sideways, forgetting about the nails. Flip flops are *not* the proper foot gear for walking on nails.

By the time I returned to The Wild Clover, my neck was

red and throbbing, I had a pronounced limp, and I'd ruined one of my favorite pairs of flip flops.

"What happened to you?" Carrie Ann asked.

"Nothing. Never mind."

Before I could gimp to my storage room office, Holly came into the market.

"Your sister is up to something," Carrie Ann said to Holly, talking over my head as though I didn't exist. "She's been overly nice to me since I arrived this morning, then she informed me of errands but wouldn't share what they were, and finally she came back a few minutes ago all banged up."

"I wouldn't ask any questions if I were you," Holly replied. "You're better off not knowing."

"Isn't that the truth," Carrie Ann said.

"Story has a problem with physical coordination," Holly continued.

"Two left feet?" Carrie Ann chuckled. "Now that you mention it, I've noticed that, too."

"Since as far back as I can remember," Holly added.

"How's business been?" I asked, diverting them before they could start in on examples of my klutziness. I also was wondering if I should go to the emergency room with my bloody feet. When did I get my last tetanus shot?

"Still slow," Carrie Ann said. "A few tourists came through town, antiquing in the area. Lori Spandle stopped by and pumped me for information about your bees. I didn't tell her a thing, not that I actually know anything to tell her. Stu came for his paper. You know, the usual."

"Holly," I said, "can you handle the store while I have a word with Carrie Ann?"

"Sure."

"You're firing me, aren't you? I can hear it in your voice." My cousin stuck her fingers in her ears and started making some *la-la-la* noise with her tongue.

I grabbed her arm and pulled her into the back, trying to walk gently. I shut the door.

"Am I at least getting severance pay?" Carrie Ann leaned against a shelf, looking defeated. "Unemployment would be good, if a severance package is too much to ask."

What nerve. The woman, until recently, had been so part-time I wasn't positive she actually worked for me. Now she wanted a going-away package?

"I'm not firing you," I said.

"You aren't?"

"Nope."

"Then why all the drama about talking to me in private? Oh, I get it, you don't want your sister to hear what we are talking about. Is it about her?"

I plopped into my office chair and gestured for my cousin to take a seat in a metal chair next to me. I wondered how to begin.

The direct route seemed best. "I need the truth from you and nothing but the truth."

"I can do that."

"Good. So . . . I've been getting weird vibes."

"You and me both. That's what comes from talking to the universe."

"Huh?"

"Every day I talk to the universe. It's easy. You go outside, face up to the sky, and tell God or the universe or whatever energy source you believe in what you need or want. It really works, but sometimes you get weird vibes. Is that what you mean?"

I had to admit that Carrie Ann was much more interesting sober than she was in a drunken state. Glimmers of the young woman I'd chummed with in high school were starting to peek through from the depths of a hazy sobriety.

"That's not exactly what I meant," I said. "I get the feeling that people around here have been talking about me

behind my back. It sounds paranoid, but I'm pretty positive I'm right. Especially at the funeral yesterday." I didn't
break eye contact with her. "Now I'm sure they're wondering about how Clay and Faye and I fit together, since the
divorce happened one day, then right away Faye was killed.
Is that it? Are they curious and want to ask me questions
but they don't know how so they come up with their own
theories?"

Carrie Ann looked off, but not before her eyes gave her
away.

"You *do* know something." I shook her arm to get her to
look back at me while putting on my best pleading expression. "You have to tell me. We're bound by blood."

I don't know where that came from. It just popped out.
However, my Mom-like comment, laying on the guilty
family responsibilities thing, worked.

"You won't like it," my cousin said. "You'll wish you
hadn't asked."

"Try me."

"Please don't make me be the one to tell you," she whined.
"I hate this."

Right when I was considering intimidation tactics and
torture techniques, Carrie Ann caved. "It's about the affair
you were having with Manny Chapman," she said.

My mouth dropped open. Of all the different ideas that
had gone through my head, that wasn't one of them.

"That's exactly how I must have looked when I first
heard the rumor," Carrie Ann said. "You were a little wild
in school . . . okay, a lot wild, but I thought you had settled
down. Imagine my surprise to find out something like this.
At least you kept your personal business quiet, not like
that slinky husband of yours who sat at Stu's bar with one
woman after another bragging about his sex drive. Sorry.
That just slipped out. And I don't blame you one bit for

spending intimate time with Manny. I'm the last one to cast stones, let me tell you. I have my own secrets."

Carrie Ann would have kept up with the nervous chatter if I hadn't raised my right hand and held it out like a stop sign.

"That," I said, clearing my throat, "is the most ridiculous thing I've ever heard."

"So you're denying it? Good idea. We can pass that around and maybe it will stop all the talk. Or else it might fuel the fire. What should we do?"

"No wonder Grace and her sister-in-law treated me so cold," I said to myself, but out loud. "They heard what was going around and believed it."

"Should we confront the issue head on or hope it dies out? Or we could spread something new to distract them."

"Who started such a nasty lie?" I wanted to know.

"P. P. Patti," she said. "But don't tell her I told. And you better get some ice on your neck. It's swelling up like a balloon."

Twenty-five

When I was in high school, I wasn't the nicest person on the planet. Looking back, I realize that now and I'm not proud of everything I did. I was popular enough to be nominated for prom queen, but I didn't have enough real compassion for those less fortunate on the popularity scale. And I suppose I deserved to suffer for past actions, for every time I hurt someone else. What goes around, comes around, as the saying goes. And I should feel some of the same pain I'd dished out.

But why on earth would Patti Dwyre have said such a thing? Had she found out that I referred to her as Pity-Party Patti? Was this retaliation? I certainly wasn't the only one who called her that. She'd earned it all on her own. I couldn't even remember who'd started it.

Had it been me?

What if my mother and Grams had heard about this so-called affair? While I had given up on a meaningful relationship with my mother, deep down I didn't want her to think worse of me than she already did.

So I asked Holly if she knew about the latest gossip while we freshened up the vegetable bins. "There's a rumor flying around," I said, restacking vine-ripened tomatoes so they looked their very plumpest, "that I had an, ah, er . . . intimate relationship with Manny Chapman."

"I heard that," Holly said, not looking up from the garlic bulbs.

"From P. P. Patti?"

"From Mom. That's one of the reasons she wanted me to stick around here. Grams agreed."

"Oh, gawd. Mom knows?"

"Yup."

"So you're here to comfort me in my grief at the loss of my lover?"

Holly started cleaning up husks and silk lying around the corn bin from customers shucking their own corncobs. Something about peeling the husks away and exposing all those juicy yellow kernels appealed to our shoppers. Corn on the cob was one of our top sellers this time of year.

"Mom wants me to protect you from yourself, and Grams wants me to protect you from Grace."

"Grace wouldn't even have a right to be mad. She was sneaking around with Clay."

I told my sister about confronting Clay and how weakly he'd defended himself and Grace against my claim.

Holly shook her head. "Is it something in Moraine's drinking water that's making everybody so horny?"

"This is turning into a soap opera. You have to believe me. I was *not* having an affair with Manny," I said.

"Right," said my sister.

If your own family doesn't believe you, who will?

"Grace, open up," I called, peering through the screen door. I could see a pot boiling on the stove, steam rising from it. "I know you're in there."

I tried the door. It was unlocked. I opened it and called again. "I'm coming in."

"Stay right where you are on the porch," Grace said from someplace in the back. "I'll be right there."

Grace left me outside for a while before she appeared. She looked tired. It was only the first day after Manny's funeral. Life in Moraine had become complicated for both of us.

"I need to talk to you, Grace. About several things."

She didn't invite me in, just leaned against the porch and folded her arms. I started with the easy stuff first, since I'm a confrontational wimp.

"I tried to look up Gerald Smith so I could talk to him about the bees. He isn't a member of the beekeepers association and I can't find him in the phone book. Do you have his number?"

"No," Grace said, her lips in a thin line.

"Do you have any kind of contact information at all?"

"No."

"Did you see him when he picked up the bees? What does he look like? Did you see his truck?"

"No. Don't know. No."

Jeez. She was making this hard for me.

"Come on, Grace. You must know something."

"The bees are gone. That's all I care about."

"So this guy came after dark, loaded them up, and drove off? And you didn't see a thing?"

"That's right. Are we done?"

"Does Stanley have them?"

"Stanley Peck? Why would you think that?"

I sighed, disappointed. This was going worse than I expected.

"I heard about the robbery. Did they catch whoever did it?"

"No. The camera was old anyway. And they didn't get much money."

I wanted to ask her about the dead yellow jackets in the honey house and the pieces of nest and the bee blower out of place like someone had borrowed it and didn't put it away properly, but even if she'd known anything about those things, she obviously wasn't in a chatty mood.

"Will you consider selling the honey house to me?" I asked instead. "I'd like to keep raising bees, keep the honey business going."

"No," she said, and all hope of salvaging some of what was left of Manny and my honey-producing business faded.

Maybe I should have started with the hard stuff first. By now my palms were sweating. "The things they are saying about Manny and me? They aren't true. We were friends and that was the extent of it. I'm sorry you had to hear such awful lies."

I couldn't help thinking that Grace owed me something, too. An apology back would be nice, since she'd been with Clay and that fact was real, not just made-up gossip like the story about me. My ex had even confirmed it in his pathetic way.

"I didn't hear any lies," she said.

We did one of those stare-downs that I usually reserve for the police chief.

"You know what I'm talking about," I said.

"No. I don't."

"I said what I came to say." I backed off the porch, forgetting about my sore feet until I felt the pain, but didn't take my eyes off of her because the hairs on the back of my arms were standing up and I was getting a weird impulse to get the hell out of there. I've always been slow to think the worst of people, mainly because I want to believe that people are basically good. But recent events should have turned on my caution lights.

If Grace had killer instincts, what would stop her from attacking me? I had arrived without a protection plan in mind. "My sister knows I came out to talk to you," I stammered. "Carrie Ann knows, too. That I'm here. I better get back to The Wild Clover."

Grace didn't move. She watched me walk back to my truck, scoot in, and leave for what I assumed would be the last time.

On the way back, I was more convinced than ever that Grace had killed Manny. She had the means and opportunity—she could've turned on the bee blower, released the yellow jackets she had trapped in their nest, then run to the house and locked the door, leaving Manny to die an agonizing, venomous death. Why? Because she thought she would spend the rest of her life with that snake Clay, that's why. And when she saw him with Faye she went *buzz-erk* with rage and killed the girlfriend. Getting rid of me, the ex-wife, and thus a potential threat to her future would have been easy if her plan to frame me had worked out. Unfortunately for her, things went wrong, and Johnny Jay had arrested Clay instead.

How did she feel now?

And all along I thought Grace was a meek and mild woman with a simple case of low self-esteem.

I'd underestimated her.

Twenty-six

🐝

Ray Goodwin's delivery truck arrived at the market right behind Trent and Brent Craig, who reported for work at three o'clock on the dot. For the time being, I put aside my visions of death and intrigue.

Holly headed for her red Jag while I stood out in back, surveying the unloading. "Hunter called for you," she said. "Twice. He said it was important. My man Max is home tonight, then he's leaving again tomorrow on another business trip. We're going out to dinner." She giggled like a new bride. "Then we might try some of that water that's making the rest of this town so sex-minded."

"Very funny," I replied before turning my attention to Ray, who looked neater than usual. He wore clean jeans and had shaved nice and close, a rarity for him. "New woman in your life?" I asked him.

He gave me a Mona Lisa smile. "Maybe. Why? What gave me away?"

"I can just tell, is all." I changed the subject. "I'm still searching for Manny's bees," I told him. "Have you seen anything different? Someone with a bunch of new bees? Or a beekeeper with more hives than usual?"

"You're still on that kick? Besides, from what I hear, nobody wants you raising honeybees in town. Isn't that why you got rid of yours?"

"Right, yes, but—"

"How about me and you go out together Friday night?"

That stopped me in my tracks. Actually it was more like full impact with a moving train. Ray, apparently, thought *I* was his new woman. Oh, no. One of the worst things about being single was deflecting unwanted attention without destroying any fragile male egos, and I didn't want to be the one to reduce Ray's.

Usually, I had some kind of warning. This one took me totally by surprise.

"Uh, I'm busy Friday, but thanks for asking." Ray opened his mouth to say something, and I rushed in before he could speak. "The whole weekend I'm busy."

"Okay, then, I'll check back with you next week."

"Okay," I said. I'd worry about it then. "Thanks for asking." That was dumb, thanking him, which he would certainly take as encouragement, but I was flustered. "By the way," I said, "could you stop at Grace's sometime this week, go into the honey house, and get whatever honey you need to fill orders?"

Ray stared at me like I had two heads. "You mean, go into the sacred honey house by myself?" he asked.

I smiled at that, remembering Manny's main rule. Most of the time he was easygoing, but this particular one was a requirement. Or else. And that was that no one was allowed in the honey house unless one of us was along. It

was Manny Chapman's territory, and while he was alive I
had respected his wishes.

Competition among honey producers was friendly, but
as Manny said, not *that* friendly. "Grace isn't speaking to
me at the moment," I said, explaining why I was breaking
the rule this time. "She might take a shot at me if I do it."

"Isn't the honey house always locked up tight?"

"She'll let you in. Just make sure you let her know that
she's getting all the proceeds from the sales."

"Aren't you splitting sales from the business?"

"Not anymore." I went into the store through the back
door.

Under normal circumstances, I would have gone for
a long, soothing kayak trip on the Oconomowoc River
tonight after work, but these weren't common times.
Besides, I had no floatable transportation.

After careful consideration, I rejected the idea of sharing my recent thoughts with Johnny Jay until I had more
to go on. Instead, I called the police department to find out
when I'd get my kayak back. I'd already decided to trade
it in. I'd never be able to use it again without seeing Faye's
dead, staring eyes or some other unpleasant images.

No one at the cop shop could give me an answer. They
said they'd call when it was released.

Ray's date offer was on my mind. Not in the let's-give-
it-a-try way, because Ray has never been on my list of
potentials and never would be. His sitting in my backyard
had been almost too much personal closeness for me.

But there were a few things I really missed as a single,
unattached woman with no current prospects. They were:

- Knowing I had plans for a Friday night, even if it was
  something simple like a burger at Stu's.

- Not having to think about how everybody else seemed to be coupled up. I'd never noticed how many lovers held hands until I was alone and didn't have a hand to hold.

- Having a warm body to cuddle with while watching movies on a rainy day.

- Mainly the human contact—a hug, light fingers running up and down my arm, a foot massage, naked contact with someone special.

That last bullet point was part of my ongoing romance fantasy. The special *someone* part, not just the *naked* part.

I thought about what Holly said as she left the store, that Hunter had called twice looking for me. I considered returning his call but I still suffered from total embarrassment and didn't have anything to say to him. I was done apologizing to other people for the day.

I called Holly instead.

"I'm sort of in the middle of things," she said, quietly.

"It's only four o'clock."

"Love is timeless."

"One quick question, then. Why did Hunter and I break up in high school?"

"Isn't that something you should already know?"

"I can't remember. Everything about the man screams 'perfect,' but if that's true, why did we split up? I'm drawing a complete blank."

"You dumped him."

"I did?"

"You said he was too small-townish, that you wanted to see the world, and you were leaving the bumpkins behind."

"I said that?"

"Yup. You broke his heart."

Jeez!

"Did you return his phone call?" Holly asked.

"Not yet."

"He said it was important. Don't forget."

After we hung up, I thought about my youthful need to get away from Moraine. Not that I ended up traveling the entire world. Far from it. I only made it to Milwaukee, forty miles down the superhighway, but compared to my hometown of Moraine, Milwaukee *was* the world.

What would have happened to my life if I hadn't left Moraine? If I hadn't met Clay in Milwaukee and married him? If Hunter and I had stayed together?

Analyzing the past is a dangerous, slippery slope leading into quicksand, so after I closed the store and went home, I stopped in the garden, pulled a bunch of fresh red beets, and spent the evening in the kitchen, creating my special version of beet soup, which would go into this month's newsletter. I added ginger this time for a walk on the wild side.

Twenty-seven

By early the next morning, I couldn't ignore a growing feeling of unease about Moraine's two recent deaths. The little voice in my head was getting louder, tapping on the inside of my cranium like it was trying to get my attention. It didn't help matters that I'd dreamed about Manny and Faye right before I woke up.

In my bizarre dream, Manny and Faye were walking down Main Street together. And I mean really together, like sharing the same body. They rotated in and out of the dream sequence, first Manny's face and body, then Faye's. They kept on walking, not uttering a single word, and somehow I knew they had come for me.

That's all I remember after waking up with tears on my face.

The same voice insisted that Manny and Faye's deaths were linked. Too many coincidences were stacking up.

They had both died within the same few days, in the same town, both under unusual circumstances.

And that same little voice in my head told me that Clay was innocent. Not innocent of most things, as I know all too intimately. In fact they could charge him with any other crime and I'd go right along with it and hope my vote was the one that brought him down. But when it came to murdering Faye, I'd have to vote not guilty.

That left Grace. Meek and mild Grace. Her husband was dead and Clay's girlfriend was gone, too. How convenient and sinister. There were so many connections a fuse was going to blow.

The tricky part would be getting the right people to believe me. That was the challenge. I'd have to outline the interpersonal relationships for Johnny Jay and convince him that Manny's death hadn't been an accident.

Then I asked myself an important question that changed my tune. Where was I when Manny died? He must've died pretty early Friday morning, before Ray found his body. I'd opened the store that morning, but when Carrie Ann had finally shown up, I'd cut out to spend a little time alone before the champagne celebration started. Now I remembered. I'd walked along the Ice Age Trail that bordered the Oconomowoc River. Holy crap. I didn't have an alibi.

Which meant I better wait until I had all the facts, which I was determined to get. I owed it to Manny, my dead friend, and on some level I felt I owed it to Faye, too, since my kayak—and my ex—was involved.

After selecting a funky pair of yellow sunflower-studded flip flops and accessorizing with jean shorts and a pale yellow tee, I walked the two blocks to The Wild Clover.

I arrived at the store with a honey-coated bagel in my hand and enough concealer under my eyes to hide the evidence of another bad night's sleep. Carrie Ann came in shortly after and took over at the register while I worked on inventory in the back. When I came out, she was gabbing with Stanley Peck as she bagged up his purchases.

This time, I was going to stick to Stanley like lint on fleece when he left The Wild Clover. If he had Manny's bees, he'd lead me to them eventually. I had my thermos of coffee and my anything's-possible attitude back. And I had a plan.

"If Patti Dwyre comes in, tell her I need to talk to her," I said to Carrie Ann. P. P. Patti and I had some talking to do.

"Where are you going now?" Carrie Ann called out when I bolted for the door after giving Stanley a three-second lead. "I thought you hired me because you needed more help. Not that I'm complaining or anything, but I never see you anymore."

"Be right back," was all I had time to say before I bumped right into my grandmother, who'd chosen that exact moment to enter the store. I almost knocked her to the floor.

"Grams!" I exclaimed, attempting to rearrange my grandmother in an upright position and still keep one eye on Stanley as he opened his car door.

"I came to visit you," she said.

"Well, come on then. We can chat on the way." I grabbed her elbow and off we went.

"Where are we going, dear?"

"An errand."

"I'll drive."

"Oh, no, you won't. Get in the truck. And hurry. We'll lose . . . uh, never mind. Come on." I gave her a boost up.

I was a little delayed by my unexpected meeting with Grams, but we blew through town and caught up to Stanley on the outskirts of Moraine.

"That's some driving, Story dear," Grams said. "NASCAR stuff."

"I'm practicing stunt-car driving techniques. I'm thinking of trying out next time they make a movie around here."

"Looks to me more like we're following Stanley Peck."

My grandmother was one sharp cookie. So I told her about the bees and how I couldn't find them, and how Stanley had checked out a beekeeping book, and was acting sneaky.

"He's not heading for his farm," Grams observed.

"No. I followed him yesterday and lost him on the rustic road."

"Seems to me, you'd want to check out his farm rather than chase him around the countryside."

I glanced over at my petite, gray, sweet grandmother. We did a U-turn. "You're right, as usual. This is the perfect opportunity to find out if the bees are at his farm. You're a genius."

Grams grinned as if I'd made her day. But then she lived with my mother. You learned to appreciate any kindness that came your way when you spent too much time defending yourself against Mom's constant criticism.

Stanley Peck's farm was called, unoriginally, Peck Farms. Once upon a time, the Peck family worked the land themselves, growing acres and acres of corn and soy beans and raising dairy cattle. Stanley had opted for the same course as Grams, preferring not to sell out to big developers when they'd come calling. Instead, he rented most of his land for others to do the work and kept whatever part he felt he could manage for himself, such as the house, a few outbuildings, and enough space for a vegetable garden. When his wife, Carol, was still alive, the place was spruced up, but now a certain scruffiness had settled in. The grass was a little long, the garden a little weedy, and the house could use a paint job.

After parking, we walked around, hunting for beehives.

There weren't any. Not a single one anyplace. Believe me, I'd know if there were hives close by. I have built-in bee radar, aka bee-dar, and it doesn't miss.

Nada. Disappointing to say the least.

"I'm going to do some breaking-and-entering, if you don't mind waiting in the truck," I said to Grams, who was right on my heels the whole time. I wanted to do a quick peek in case Manny's bee journal was sitting out in the open on Stanley's kitchen table.

"You know, it's not breaking-and-entering if the door's open," Grams commented. "It's not illegal to check up on a good friend if we're worried that something might have happened to him."

"Oh, look," I said, testing Grams's open-door theory. "It's unlocked."

"There you go." Grams passed me up. "Now, if you'll give me a hint so I know what we're looking for? I assume we've exhausted our search for beehives and are now onto the subject of . . . what again?"

"Manny's missing bee journal." We walked in and I lowered my voice, not sure why. "He kept all his bee notes in it. It's black, spiral-bound, about the size of a hardcover book, and as thick. Scraps of paper are stuck in the back of it with odds and ends. Newspaper clippings and so forth."

While I described the notebook, I opened kitchen drawers searching for the junk drawer. Every house has one, right? I quickly found it, which was in fact totally filled with junk. It had everything imaginable inside it except the kitchen sink. Or Manny's journal.

Damn.

"Stanley needs someone to help him out with his home," Grams noted. "He isn't much of a housekeeper."

"Why don't you check his bedroom dressers while I search the rest of the kitchen," I suggested.

"Let's trade. I'll take the kitchen. You can do bedroom drawers. I'm too old for surprises."

We rooted around like two snoops, which was exactly what we were. If Stanley had secrets, we hadn't found them yet. The man seemed to be an open book, which made me even more suspicious.

"Ah-ha!" Grams said, picking up a kitchen utensil and brandishing it. "He borrowed my apple corer last month and refused to admit he still had it. 'I gave it back,' he said, letting me think I was losing it. Here's the proof."

At least something came of our efforts. Grams got her apple corer back.

"This is why you wanted to come here, rather than following him?" I said. "For your apple corer?"

"I needed it," Grams said after we left the house and I had boosted her back up into the passenger's seat of my truck. "I'm making apple crisp today with a ginger-snap crust."

Grams was the official baker in our family, and this dish sounded like a real winner, but that wasn't the point.

"You couldn't have mentioned the apple corer earlier?" I said with a tiny whine. "We couldn't have stopped to get it *after* we found out where Stanley was going?"

"We wouldn't have had the opportunity to shake down his house. Where's the fun in that?"

Driving back, I made a mental list of suspicious characters, or as Johnny Jay liked to phrase it in cop talk, "persons of interest." Suddenly, everyone in town seemed to be acting strangely, like they had hidden agendas. Except my family, who always acted a little strange and really did have hidden agendas.

I distrusted Clay Lane on principal, Stanley Peck because he was sneaking around reading bee books, and Lori Spandle for being anti-bee, and trying to get Grace to sell Manny's house.

Then there was gossipy reputation-ruining Patti Dwyre. If I tried, I could work all of these people into a powerful theory of murderous intent.

But it was Grace Chapman who had my full attention.

"I'm taking you home," I said to Grams.

"My car's at the store," she reminded me. We drove in silence for a few minutes, then she said, "Want me to check up on your bees when I get back?"

"You know about them?"

Grams nodded. "But my lips are sealed."

Twenty-eight

Why minding my own business (or as Holly would say, MYOB) was the best advice Mom ever gave me (even if she never took it herself):

- You won't have to find out about nasty rumors targeted directly at your back because you'll be too busy with your own life to notice.

- You won't feel the compulsion to go out of your way to learn who started said rumor.

- Then you won't have to worry and fret about why that person would tell such a lie (assuming it is a lie, which in this case, it definitely was).

- And you won't develop a case of extreme paranoia manifesting itself into the belief that everybody in town is against you and that they all believe the rumor.

- Then you won't feel like crawling in a big hole to hide and you won't consider wearing a sign that says, "I didn't do it."

- Plus you'll sleep better and wake up less crabby, and you won't have to apologize for your whacked-out behavior.

"I'm sorry," I said to P. P. Patti when she walked through the store and we met up in front of the wine rack where I was restocking Wisconsin wines. "I apologize deeply and sincerely for anything and everything I ever did to you or said or implied about you."

"Okay," she said, though hesitantly, like she was waiting for the punch line.

"I mean it. I'm sorry—past, present, and future."

"You're saying you're sorry for something you haven't done yet?"

"If that's what it takes."

"Am I missing something here?"

"I'm with you," Carrie Ann said to Patti, running her fingers through her choppy yellow hair, a sure tipoff that her nerves were frayed from all her recent lifestyle changes. "Totally confused." Then she looked at me, not too kindly. Or was I being overly paranoid? "You could apologize to me, too, while you're at it," she said.

"For what?"

"You don't pay me enough, for starters."

"Nobody else complains about the wages I pay. I never did a thing to you worth apologizing for, Carrie Ann, and you know it." That was a big lie. I'd propositioned her boyfriend after a funeral, of all things. Had he told her about that? "And besides, shouldn't you be watching the cash register?"

"I can see it just fine from over here." She swiveled her head to check out the counter.

"Can we find someplace to talk?" I said to Patti. "Do you have time?"

"You could buy me an Italian ice at the custard shop. I'm allergic to dairy, I get a horrible stomach ache, but the ices are pretty good."

"Fine. Perfect."

On the sidewalk, walking to Koon's Custard Shop, Patti brought me up-to-speed on her most recent problems, of which she had plenty.

"The raccoons are trapped and gone, but now squirrels are chewing through all my power lines. My cable's out. So is my landline. You haven't been trying to call me, have you? I better give you my cell number. The doctors are still looking into my shaking problem." She paused to prove her point. I detected a slight twitch in her hand, but nothing a little anxiety medication wouldn't fix.

She went on and on, working hard to uphold her Pity-Party Patti title. By the time she ordered her Italian ice and I ordered a dish of vanilla custard, and we parked ourselves at an outside table, I was ready to commit suicide. Or murder.

"Patti, we need to have a serious discussion," I said around spoonfuls of custard. My stomach was doing flips; I hated confrontations and conflicts and I was about to launch into exactly those things with Patti. "Someone," I began, "has been spreading rumors, lies that are hurting people, things that are mean and vicious and I'd like to know how to put an end to them."

"Me, too," Patti said. "One thing I hate is that kind of mean-spirited behavior."

I almost swallowed my spoon. "But," I managed to say, "the person I just described, the one spreading nasty lies is . . ."

I couldn't say it. Patti was watching me with intense

concentration, expecting to get the goods on some mean old gossip. She had no idea I meant her!

"I have to go to the bathroom," I said.

"But you were going to tell me something really juicy!"

"Be right back."

In the restroom, I washed my hands and stared at myself in the mirror. I'd never been good at this sort of thing, calling someone out when they did me wrong. Sure, I could stand up to my family in a passive-aggressive sort of way and I could go to bat for another person if I felt they were treated unfairly, like when Johnny Jay used to bully other kids or even now when he pushed around adults. But when it came to face-to-face confrontation, I wasn't nearly as confident.

In one enlightened moment while I stared into the mirror, I realized exactly why Patti was the way she was. I understood her perfectly, scary as that was.

Patti knew people didn't really like her too well. They didn't want her around, but she wanted desperately to be noticed and accepted. Gossiping got attention. Whether good attention or bad attention, she didn't really think it through that much, so long as she had her tiny little share of limelight.

She just wanted to be part of the community but she was going about it all wrong, driving people away instead of to her.

Or at least that's what I came up with.

When I sat back down at the table, she said, "It was nice of you to apologize to me, before, at the store. And I accept your apology. You weren't very friendly in high school. In fact, really rude and insensitive, is more like it. Hanging out with that clique of yours. Maybe now that you've grown up we can be real friends."

"Sure," I said, not sure at all, wondering what I was getting myself into, sensing a new direction I didn't want to explore. "But I'm pretty busy with the store and my bees. I don't have much time for girlfriends."

Which I realized was absolutely true. I didn't have any close female friends unless you wanted to count my younger sister or my cousin. How pathetic was that? I hadn't had time for a personal life while I'd been living in a bubble while struggling to save the store from ruin during my marital split.

Even so, Patti wasn't exactly my first choice for a new best friend.

"Now that we're buddies," Patti said, seeming to have forgotten the thread of our earlier conversation, thank God, "I didn't get a chance to finish telling you what I know about Grace and your ex-husband."

"Something important?"

Patti nodded. "I saw them through my telescope."

"Your . . . telescope?" *Jeez!*

"I have it set up in the window facing the river so I can watch birds and water fowl and, you know, whatever."

"Right." I tried to picture which window she might be referring to. And whether that same one looked out over my yard and into my windows. My compassion for her socially inept manipulations was fading fast.

Patti leaned forward, conspiratorially. "Anyway, I saw them together last Thursday night right before dark. You were at the store, I think, because I couldn't see you moving around inside your, uh, I mean your lights weren't on and I know you work late some nights."

P. P. Patti had been watching me through a frickin' telescope? Oops, there went my sympathy, completely gone.

"Grace had parked in the library parking lot so no one

would see where she was going." Patti was in her element, her eyes shiny. "I know because I followed her afterward to see where she went. That's how I found out where she'd parked. Anyway, she knocked on Clay's door, looked around to see if anyone was watching, and when he opened the door, she slipped right in. And this was the very night before her husband was killed by bees! Of course, she didn't know he was going to die. Later on, she must have felt pretty bad about her timing."

"Are you sure it was Grace?" This was the proof I was looking for! Grace and Clay really were having a clandestine affair! If Patti could be believed. From her detailed account, it had to be true.

"Like I said, I followed her about an hour later when she came out, dabbing at her eyes with a hanky. She'd been crying! I'm not sure why. She could have been calling it off with Clay, or he'd dumped her, because I haven't seen her back and believe you me, I'd know."

"That was the only time you saw them together?" I asked.

"That I know of, but I wasn't on high alert until that Thursday."

"Did you mention any of this to the police chief?" I asked.

"Should I have?" P. P. Patti said. "I didn't think it mattered. I'm only mentioning it now because of our new friendship. This should stay strictly between you and me."

"Carrie Ann heard about it through your fast-track grapevine, so we aren't the only ones who know. Who else did you tell?"

Patti's eyes shifted to the left, blinked, then her eyes moved to the right. "Maybe I did mention it to a few other friends. But I didn't tell anybody about your own little secret."

There! She'd brought it up. I felt my blood pressure

spike. "Oh, really," I said, "you mean the story you spread about Manny and me, saying we were lovers? Is that the secret you've been keeping to yourself?"

"Shhh," Patti cautioned. "Someone will hear you. It'll be all your fault if it gets out."

P. P. Patti was impossible—crafty and cagey with a knack for twisting the truth to fit her plan. This entire dramatic moment was reminding me of high school and how relieved I'd been to graduate and get away from Moraine and its small-town mentalities.

"I heard from a reliable source that you've been spreading that lie yourself," I said. Finally. Some guts.

"I don't lie," Patti said, narrowing her eyes. "All my facts are backed up with evidence."

"You are so full of it. You don't have any proof."

"That isn't the way to talk to a friend."

"You aren't my friend, Patti. Friends don't tell horrible, spiteful lies about each other."

"Is this the future event that you apologized for at the store? Because if it is, I'm not accepting this time."

I blew steam out of my nose and ears. I even saw red. "You took an innocent friendship between Manny and me and insinuated that it was something nasty and dirty. If you don't care about my feelings, you could at least try to care about Grace. How do you think that made her feel?"

"Grace was getting hers with that ex of yours."

"I know you lied about me. Are you lying about Grace and Clay, too?"

Patti glared at me. She had her arms crossed. "I'm done talking to you," she said. "Keep on bullying me and I'll call the cops all right."

The bullying part stopped me in my tracks, because I had an aversion to bullies and wasn't exactly sure I hadn't been acting like one, "I'm sorry," I said. "But you put me in a serious position when you spread that."

"Go away. You're acting like a nut case. I know you've been through a lot lately, but don't take it out on me."

I left her sitting there and headed for Stu's.

I needed a drink.

Twenty-nine

I was on my second Diet Coke.

After heating up to the boiling point, then cooling down some on the short walk over, the thought of drinking my lunch hadn't been nearly as appealing. Not to mention that Stu had refused to serve me.

"I'm cutting you off," he had said.

"I haven't had a drop of alcohol yet. You can't cut me off."

"You're my friend. This is my bar. I get to make the rules." Stu gave me one of those smoldering looks of his. Then he grinned, making it hard to be angry.

"A Diet Coke then," I said, pretending the switch to a nonalcoholic beverage was entirely my idea. "And make it quick. How's Becky?"

"Great."

"When are you two getting married?"

Stu opened my Coke and put it down in front of me. "And spoil our fun? No thanks."

As I said, I was on drink number two when Hunter strolled in the door. I couldn't help noticing he had a sexy strut. He and Stu gave each other knowing glances, and I picked up on the message going back and forth.

"You called him?" I accused Stu. "You told Hunter I was here? This is the last time I'm patronizing this establishment."

"Yeah, yeah," Stu said, flipping a towel over his shoulder and going back to work.

"You've been dodging me," Hunter said, sitting down next to me at the bar. "We need to talk."

"I'm all talked out, thanks to Patti. And I'm never apologizing to another living soul again as long as I live."

"Why didn't you return my calls?"

"What calls?" I said, shifting the blame to my little sister. I *had* been avoiding him.

Hunter gave me a look, like he knew I was dodging.

"Besides," I said. "You know where to find me. If I'm not home, I'm at the store." Which wasn't exactly true. Since I had Holly to help out and Carrie Ann was actually showing up for a change, I was freer to come and go than I'd been in a long time.

"Your store," Hunter said with a snort of amusement. "That place is a hotbed of intrigue and misinformation. I wouldn't want to give your customers even more to talk about."

"Not to mention that your girlfriend works there."

"Come on. Let's go."

"Where?"

"My place. I'd like to introduce you to Ben properly this time."

My heart was pounding. I shouldn't go to Hunter's house alone. The man was hot and sexy and so not mine.

"You want me to meet your dog again?"

"Humor me."

Hunter had ridden over on his Harley. He swung a leg across the machine, settled into the seat, scooted forward to make more room for me to climb on, waited for me to situate myself properly, and we were off.

I loved the ride. All the sensations of the machine under me—the firm grip I had on Hunter's waist, the smells of the countryside that you just don't experience inside a car, the wind whipping my hair, the absolute and exhilarating sense of freedom.

When we arrived at his house, I didn't want to get off. Ben was in a kennel on the side, alert as usual. Hunter dismounted, opened the gate, and let him out. Reluctantly, I got off the bike.

"Story, meet Ben."

"I've already met Ben." Where was this going?

"I know, but I was remiss, considering your past history and Ben's intimidating presence. But Ben isn't anything like the dog that attacked you. He would never hurt you."

Hunter had to bring that up! When I was ten years old, a German shepherd had attacked me on the street, pulling me off my bike and mauling me. I still had scars on my right thigh to prove it. Hunter knew all about it.

"Tell Ben to sit," he said.

"I don't want to."

"Come on, Try it."

"Fine. Sit, Ben."

Ben glanced at Hunter, then back at me. The beast sat. He watched me in case I had another command ready. I looked at Hunter, still wondering what was up.

"Ben knows all the basic obedience commands," Hunter said. "Sit, down, come, stay, heel. He responds to my orders one way, and to commands from others a little bit differently. He's been trained to attack and to back off when I tell him to, but only if I give the command. That part of his job is between him and me. We're partners."

"You trust him?"

"Completely. He keys in on aggressive behavior and can read body language better than any human I know."

"He's creepy," I said. "Like he knows what I'm thinking."

Ben the dog didn't move a single muscle, still waiting.

"Try giving him another command. Tell him to come."

"Ben, come."

He came to my side and stood at attention.

"Nice dog," I said, impressed in spite of myself.

"Ben has been trained to remain focused even during distractions," Hunter said. "Crowds don't faze him, neither do other dogs. He's a working dog and takes his job seriously. He would never attack unless he was called to assist me in a dangerous situation. So what do you think? Can you try to work out a truce with Ben? Give him a chance to prove himself?"

"I don't see why it matters to you," I said. "I'm not the one who is hanging around here with you. Carrie Ann is."

"Story, Carrie Ann isn't my girlfriend."

That wasn't what I expected to hear. A big fat grin spread across my face. I fought it down. "She's not?"

"No."

"But I thought—"

"Yeah, you thought wrong. And I'd like the misconception cleared up so we can move forward."

"But you and Carrie Ann were riding your bike together, and she said she couldn't come to the town meeting because she was with you. I automatically assumed you were a couple."

Hunter didn't say anything for a while, then he said, "Let's go sit down."

Hunter released Ben from further obedience and led me

over to a wooden glider. We sat side by side not speaking, watching the dog search for the perfect spot in the sun until he found it and flopped down. My heart was doing some kind of palpitation thing and my palms were sweaty, not because I was afraid of Ben but because I realized something serious was coming. I wasn't used to that from Hunter. He'd always been light and silly with me.

"Story," he finally said, "I've been avoiding you ever since you came back to Moraine two years ago. You came back to town married, and I, well, I had to stay away. I couldn't stand to see you with that creep, and to hear the stories circulating about him. I wanted to kill him with my bare hands."

I gulped. How had I ever walked away from this hunky man?

"I'm sorry," I said, racking up another apology, "if I hurt you in any way when I left Moraine."

"That was a long time ago."

"Well, I'm sorry anyway."

"Do you think we could give it another try? See where it goes this time?"

Oh. My. God.

"What about your relationship with Carrie Ann?" I wanted to know. "We haven't quite cleared that up yet."

Hunter let out a heavy sigh like he was hoping we could skip this part. "Carrie Ann came to me because she wanted to stop drinking. And I said I'd help her."

"What could you do to help her that she can't do for herself? I'm confused."

"She asked me to be her sponsor."

That hit me like a ton of bricks. I knew enough about AA to know that sponsors were recovering alcoholics themselves. That meant Hunter had his own personal demons to deal with.

"Nobody told me you were a recovering alcoholic."

"I've been sober more than ten years. It's old news."

"Did I do that to you?" I said, thinking maybe he'd found solace in a bottle after we split up. "Did I drive you to drink?"

Hunter laughed. "No. Don't you remember how much I drank in high school?"

"We all did."

"Yes, but everybody else slowed down or quit altogether. I couldn't stop. Finally, I took the big step and joined AA."

That explained the close connection between Hunter and Carrie Ann in a way I could understand. "So you were at an AA meeting together the night of the town meeting?"

"Yes. It's an important step for Carrie Ann, admitting her problem and attending these first meetings."

"Someone said they saw you making out with Carrie Ann," I said, figuring I better get everything out in the open.

Hunter laughed. "Let me guess. Patti Dwyre?"

"So it's true."

"Not at all. Patti saw me giving Carrie Ann a hug of encouragement and she misinterpreted it."

Figures! "I can't stand that woman," I said.

"She's a real trip to the beach, isn't she? But tell me about the town meeting."

So I did—about how the topic of killer bees went absolutely nowhere because of the false alarm, and about moving my bees to a safe location without revealing where. I also told him about Manny's missing journal and the elusive, possibly nonexistent, Gerald Smith. And about Stanley Peck's sudden interest in beekeeping.

"Bees all across the world are being affected by Colony Collapse Disorder," I explained to Hunter. "And honey producers have seen big declines in their bee populations. Manny and I were lucky we didn't have to deal with CCD, at least not yet. Bee colonies are going for premium prices, and I think this Gerald Smith, who might even be Stanley for all I know, stole Manny's beehives and now he wants Manny's journal because it has all his research notes in it. I need to find it first."

"But the man isn't stealing if Grace sold them to him. Just because you can't find him doesn't mean he isn't legit. Maybe you should let it go and move on."

"How would you feel if someone took Ben?"

"That's different."

"No, it isn't. Getting up every morning and remembering that all the bees Manny and I raised have vanished feels exactly the same as if someone took your dog. It left a big empty hole in my life."

"Are you telling me you're emotionally attached to those bees?"

"Of course! They aren't *just* a business. You train police dogs, right? Are the dogs you work with simply weapons to you?"

"I see your point. Tell you what, I'll see if I can find the guy for you." Hunter's leg rubbed against mine. He'd moved nearer, put an arm around me, pulled me closer. "So what do you say? Are you willing to try again? Pick up where we left off?"

"What about starting slow?" I had some healing to do before I dove into the relationship waters again without knowing exactly how deep they were. The last time, with Clay, I'd hit my head hard. Trusting a man again, even one I'd grown up with, would take time and effort.

"You don't even know me anymore," I said to Hunter.

"I know you."

"I've changed."

"For the better."

A pause, while I absorbed that last comment, not sure it was altogether complimentary.

Then he said, "Slow is okay with me. I'm not going any-place fast."

And that's how, in the middle of rumors flying every-where and dead bodies appearing too close to home for comfort, I ended up with a hot, sexy almost-boyfriend.

Unfortunately, when Hunter dropped me back at The Wild Clover and took off, I found Carrie Ann tied up and the cash register empty. We'd been robbed in broad daylight.

Thirty

Here's how it had gone down:

- Holly had called the store to say she'd be late coming in, so Carrie Ann stayed on to cover for her.

- During a lull in business, someone snuck up behind Carrie Ann and struck her on the head with enough force to knock her unconscious.

- She woke up to find herself tied to a shelving unit in the back room.

- When Carrie Ann heard noise from the front of the store, she called out for help.

- No one responded, but she heard someone hurrying past the back room, then a door slam.

- Holly arrived to find the front door locked. Since she had keys, she was able to open the door, but didn't see anyone inside the shop.

- Holly found Carrie Ann in the back room.

- I arrived on the scene in time to help her untie Carrie Ann, then called 9-1-1 while Holly applied ice to Carrie Ann's head.

- Holly discovered the empty cash register, which we estimated had contained four to five hundred dollars, counting the two hundred in various bills the drawer contained at the beginning of the day.

- Police Chief Johnny Jay chalked the whole thing up to a random robbery.

- Waukesha County and Moraine law enforcement were on high alert, but without a description, they didn't have much hope of apprehension unless the criminal struck again.

- End of story.

Except it wasn't that simple. Nothing ever is.

"If I'd been here like I should have been, instead of out at Hunter's house, Carrie Ann wouldn't be in the hospital with a head injury," I said to Holly.

"IMO (*In My Opinion*), if I hadn't been late," Holly said, "I'd have been here and creamed the guy with one of my special moves."

Okay, then. Both of us were having guilt pangs, blaming ourselves for what happened to Carrie Ann.

"She'll be all right," I said. "All our family members have thick skulls."

"The way she was joking around with the paramedics, she'll live," Holly agreed.

Holly had been leaning against the counter. She straightened up. "What were you doing out at Hunter's?"

"Nothing much."

Holly stared into my eyes and sucked out the truth. Or close enough. "You've got the hots for him!"

"I do not."

"Liar. I can see it in your eyes. Is he your BF (*Boy Friend*) now?"

"Here comes a customer. Time to get busy. We'll talk later."

I hid out among the shelves, straightening, putting in order the only things in my life that I could control at the moment. I felt the weight of responsibility.

"She's going to be just fine," I said to one customer after another, trying to reassure myself as much as them.

"You tell that police chief you need extra protection here," one suggested. "He should do more drive-bys."

Hunter called, having heard the bad news. I reassured him that I was fine and Carrie Ann would be, too. We made a date for Saturday night. He said he'd pick me up at seven at home, not at the "bed of intrigue," as he called the store.

The attack on Carrie Ann was foremost in my mind, of course, and every time I had a second, I worried over it.

Would it have taken place at all if both of us had been at the store? Probably not, was my guess. Knocking out a lone woman was much easier than incapacitating two people at once. And getting the timing right would have been harder.

So how did this person know that Carrie Ann was alone?

People had been coming and going from the store all morning. Every single customer could have noticed that Carrie Ann was working alone.

Holly raised another big question. "Why didn't the robber just grab the money and take off? If it were me, I'd have emptied the till and cleared out fast before Carrie Ann came around. Why drag her into the back and tie her up?"

"To gain time?" I reasoned, adding jars of honey to a display. "To make a clean getaway without anyone alerting the police?"

"MOS!" Holly suddenly called out.

"MOS?"

"Mother over shoulder!"

I cracked my head against the display shelf coming up, then spotted Mom right behind me.

"Oh, hey." I straightened up, rubbing the sore spot and looking around. "Where's Grams?"

"Baking."

Darn! Grams was my best ally when Mom was after me. I saw Holly slink away. No help there.

"Your cousin could have been killed today," Mom said in an accusing voice.

"We're all at risk every time we cross the street," I countered. "Besides, I feel bad enough as it is."

"Where were you?"

"Away."

"From now on, two of you have to be in the store at all times. And keep that back door locked. What were you thinking, leaving it open?"

"Nobody in this entire town had a reason to lock up anything until recently," I said. "I bet you left your car unlocked when you came in here, didn't you? Grams's back door is wide open right now, isn't it? What's this town coming to if we have to go around afraid?"

"Johnny Jay better get on the stick and clean up this town, or we'll fire him and get someone in who can do the job."

Ooh, good. Get her mad at the police chief.

"I hear you were out at Hunter Wallace's house."

"Who told you that?"

"One of Grams's friends saw you riding on the back of his motorcycle, heading toward his house. Please don't tell me he's back in the picture after all these years."

"Nobody's in the picture."

I heard Holly snort from the other side of the aisle where she was listening in.

"We still need to have a talk," Mom said.

"Not while I'm working."

"What are you going to do until Carrie Ann can come back?" Mom wanted to know. "You and your sister will have to cover mornings and afternoons until the Craig boys can get here. Do you hear that, Holly? You both are opening the store tomorrow first thing."

I heard a gasp and blathering.

"Or," Mom said, "I'm going to have to pitch in and do it right. I could rearrange this store so things are laid out much better than they are."

She had her hands on her hips and was studying the store with a sharp eye. Not good.

Not good at all.

Thirty-one

By the time the Craig twins came into the store at three o'clock, they, along with the rest of Moraine, already knew about the robbery. With a huge sigh of relief, I turned the front of the store over to them so Holly and I could go straighten up the storage room.

"What was our thief looking for back here?" I wanted to know, after checking the store's small safe and finding it undisturbed. Thank God!

"More money in a drawer?" Holly suggested. "Lots of store owners keep extra cash in the back that isn't as secure as ours is."

That made sense, but my inner voice suspected there was more to it. Too many disturbing things had happened recently to ignore anything.

I called the hospital to get information on Carrie Ann's condition. My cousin was resting comfortably.

"You'll have to pay her for time off," Holly said. "Since she was hurt at work."

"Carrie Ann's been nothing but trouble," I said, sounding like my mother the second the words were out of my mouth.

Holly giggled. "But she's a ton of fun."

"That she is."

"I'll run up to the hospital and see for myself how she's doing. GTG (*Got To Go*)."

"Let me know. And see you first thing tomorrow morning."

After Holly left, I made a minor dent in a pile of paperwork, hating every minute of it. Bookkeeping was not one of my strong suits, but a few invoices needed immediate attention or the electricity and phone service would be disconnected. The market paid for itself and more, so money wasn't the issue. Getting myself to sit down and do the work was the biggest problem.

After groaning through that chore, I walked down to Stu's.

"Can I borrow the canoe again?" I asked him.

"You can take the canoe anytime you want."

Stu was a great guy. Becky needed to land him for good one of these days before some other woman made a move.

"How come you didn't tell me Hunter was an alcoholic?" I asked him.

"Didn't know you didn't know. Besides, wasn't any of your business."

"I guess not. Is he okay?"

"Better off than most of us. His head's in the right place. Sometimes personal struggles make a person stronger and better."

"My problems haven't done a thing for my self-improvement," I said, thinking of my struggles with my mother and my marriage. "At least, not that I've noticed."

"It might sneak up on you someday when you aren't looking."

"How did you get so smart?"

"Born that way."

I went around to the back of the bar and grill, shoved off in the canoe, and lost myself in the river's action where life was simple and easy and smelled so sweet and fragrant.

Soon the migration would begin, birds flying south for the winter. They'd stop over at Horicon Marsh, a national wildlife refuge, which wasn't too far north of Moraine. Then they would fly over our Oconomowoc River, resting in the trees and on the water. I needed my own kayak for that big event.

For now, red-winged blackbirds swayed on cattails along the marshy side and called to each other. I gazed up into white, billowing clouds, the kind I almost think you could float on. Marshmallow clouds. I changed my usual path to avoid encountering the spot where we'd found Faye, instead heading downstream toward my home. I wondered how long it would take before I could paddle in the other direction without thinking of Faye lying dead in my kayak, water streaming over her face, her eyes looking nowhere.

I passed by my house, moving quickly with the current, noting that from the water, my backyard looked like its own wildlife refuge. I could see a rabbit chewing something on the edge of my garden. Darn.

The journey back upstream would be harder, especially in a larger vessel like Stu's canoe. I didn't go much farther before turning around, but I had enough personal private time to do a little self-evaluation.

I was more of a loner than I liked to admit. Sure, I needed people and conversation, and the market supplied those two daily requirements. But I craved as much alone time with my bees and nature and waterways as I could get.

Was it good to be that way, or bad, or both? How could I be with someone else when I wanted so much personal space? Between the store and bees and my own needs, did I have anything left to give to Hunter? Did I want to make the effort?

What if I was wasting my time? That was a huge issue.

When I paddled back to the bar, Stu was watching from the river's edge, taking a break from his work. "It's peaceful out there, isn't it?" he said.

I nodded in complete agreement. Stu took one side of the canoe and helped me bring it up on shore. "I need to get another kayak," I said. "I really miss my daily river trips."

"That old canoe is a hot commodity lately. I should start charging an hourly rate. It's seen some real action over the years," Stu said.

"I can imagine." I laughed. "Or maybe I shouldn't try to imagine. This old canoe has been around as long as I can remember."

"Just about every butt in town has sat in her. Even Manny took her for a ride just before he died." Stu paused, thinking it over. "I can't remember which day exactly; they all blend together when you tend bar every night. But it was that same week he died, sometime around dusk."

"Did I hear you right? Manny actually took this canoe out on the river?"

"He did."

"That's really strange. Manny didn't like water. He wouldn't even fish from the shore."

Manny had had a bad experience with water, to match the one I had with the dog that attacked me. He'd almost drowned once when he was a kid when the fishing boat he was on capsized in Lake Michigan.

I typically stayed away from canines; Manny usually kept off bodies of water.

"He did seem nervous, now that you bring it up," Stu

said. "Jittery, not like most people who want to take it out. I offered to find him a canoe partner from the bar patrons—one of them would have gone along—but he refused, insisted he was fine, and took off, heading downstream. I don't know when he came back. He didn't come into the bar, just left the canoe where he'd found it."

"Huh," I said. Stu went back inside, and I stared at the boat.

"Canoe," I said to it once we were alone, "if you could talk, what would you tell me?" I must be losing my mind, talking to an inanimate object. I glanced around. Nobody was near. "Manny, what the heck were you doing out on the river? You were afraid of water."

Manny didn't answer me. Neither did the canoe.

I walked back to The Wild Clover to say good night to the twins and check on things. I'd left the envelopes containing bill payments on my desk, planning to pick them up after the canoe trip and put them in the mailbox on my way home.

The envelopes were right where I'd left them.

But so was something else. Lying on top of the stack, perfectly centered, was a dragonfly earring. The dead-on match to the one Faye Tilley had been wearing when we found her body.

Thirty-two

"We *are* investigating, *Missy* Fischer," Johnny Jay said after my back room had been examined with a police microscope, the earring had been removed, and I'd accused our police chief of stagnation. "It never occurred to me to keep you informed as to our progress. I didn't know you were a member of my team. Oh, wait, you aren't." He rolled his eyes. "You have a serious problem with interfering where you aren't welcome."

"Interfering! Come on. I'd love to be out of this whole thing. This isn't something I have any control over."

The very last thing I had wanted to do was call the police chief. But after finding the earring, I'd shouted to the twins who had been waiting on customers. Once I'd blustered and blurted and blundered, too many people knew about my discovery. The secret was out in the open before it could go covert. Unfortunately, Lori Spandle had been one of the customers, so she was already on the scene, ready to report and cause trouble.

"I should take you in and hold you until we clear this whole thing up," the police chief said to me.

"You'd like that, wouldn't you?"

"That might be best, Chief," Innocent Bystander Lori said.

The police chief shot her a shut-up look before eyeing me up again. "Exactly where were you when that earring appeared out of thin air?" he asked.

"Oh, give it up and go after the real killer for a change."

"We have a suspect in custody, and you know it."

"So how could he have planted the earring?"

"That's my job to find out, not yours. Butt out."

"This is *so* my business. The damn thing was found on my desk!"

"Settle down now," Johnny Jay said, holding out both hands, palms to the floor to show me how to settle in case I didn't know how.

Lori now wore a smug expression instead of a bee veil. I have to say the veil was more flattering.

Brent Craig stepped forward with his own theory on how the earring got there, which happened to be totally obvious, but at least he broke up the argument. "Someone must have snuck in the back door and put it there." His brother, Trent, agreed. "We made a list of customers' names for you, Chief," Brent said, handing over a newsletter with the names written down on the back of it. "The usuals anyway, though some customers were passing through on the rustic road. We'd never seen them before."

"It wouldn't necessarily have to be a customer," I said. "The back door wasn't locked. Anybody could have come through it."

My mother better not find out that that door was still an

entryway. Old habits die hard. I'd forgotten to lock it when I left for Stu's.

Johnny Jay wasn't about to give up on me as his main source of stress and trouble. "Where were you when all this happened? Wait, do you hear the same echo I do?" He cupped an ear and listened. "Seems like I already asked you that question once."

"I was on the river. I borrowed Stu's canoe and went downstream."

"Anybody see you?"

"What does it matter? I'm the injured party, the victim, not the perpetrator."

"Did anybody see you?" he repeated.

"Stu did."

"If Story was on the river," Lori added, "we better start looking for another body."

I had my feet up on the patio table, a glass of red wine in one hand, and a kitchen knife under a newspaper in front of me just in case my tormentor sprang from the bushes. I wasn't taking any more chances. It took every ounce of my fading courage to even sit outside, but I refused to let anybody drive me into hiding. Besides, I probably had Patti watching me right next door in case I had problems.

After scanning Patti's windows without seeing a telescope pointed my way, I called Hunter with my wine-free hand, punching numbers with my thumb.

"Can't you take over the investigation into Faye's death?" I said to him. "Johnny Jay hates me."

"It's that prom thing. He didn't like you turning him down."

"How did you know about that?"

"I took you that year, remember. How could you forget? The ridge after prom in my old car . . ."

He let the rest of the sentence drop off the ridge, but I remembered. Clearly. Like it was yesterday. Amazing how memories come back.

The silence hung. Then Hunter said, "When Johnny found out we were going to the dance together, he wanted to fight me over it."

"I didn't know that!" I smiled to myself, imagining the two of them scuffling over me. Lardy Johnny, who had slimmed down since then, and scrappy, toned Hunter. No match. Hunter would have taken him no problem. "He can really hold a grudge," I added, wishing the police chief would get over it.

"You made a serious impression on him."

"So, now what? Please, please, I'm begging you, take over."

Hunter's rich laugh came through. "I work for Waukesha County and the local Critical Incident Team. Johnny Jay is Moraine's police chief and very territorial, in case you haven't noticed. I don't have any jurisdiction in Moraine, and he has stopped sharing information with me since he found out we've resumed our friendship with each other."

"Oh." That would have been my fault, bringing up Hunter's name every time Johnny Jay and I got into it.

Then I realized Hunter probably didn't even know about the earring showing up in my store, so I related that little bit of fresh terror.

"Maybe you should move out here until this whole thing is resolved," Hunter said, not suggestively. More worried than anything else.

"I'm fine," I said, now more worried than ever because *he* was. I took a sip of wine.

"Sure you don't want to come out here for a while?"

"I'm sure." While the thought of Hunter's protection appealed to the romantic side of me, I had a store to run and a bee business that was disintegrating before my eyes.

I couldn't let him sidetrack me with his sweet masculine musk.

Besides, we were supposed to be going slow, not moving in together.

After that we talked about the store robbery and Carrie Ann. He had stopped at the hospital to see how she was doing, but she'd been asleep. The hospital staff said she could probably go home tomorrow.

"I think someone might have murdered Manny," I told Hunter.

"Story, that would be quite a trick, a murderer conspiring with bees to kill a human. A real stretch."

"The killer recruited yellow jackets," I correct him. "Not bees. And it's possible. I could do it."

"Really! This I have to hear."

"I'd find a nest and come back at night. It would have to be a nest in a tree, not in a hole, one I could remove and trap in a container. I'd have to wear bee-protection clothing and move very fast. After that, I'd wait until Manny was in his honey house and I'd lock him in."

"From the outside?"

"It has a padlock on the outside. And I'd make sure he didn't have his own bee suit or any way to defend himself. Then I'd release the yellow jackets inside the honey house."

"Your theory needs polishing. For example, how would you release them?"

"I'm still in the early stages of development, but it could be done. Remember, I'd be wearing protection."

"Let me know when you pull it all together."

"You'll be the first to know."

"And if Manny was murdered, why?"

"I'm working on that, too." I wasn't ready to tell Hunter about Clay and Grace. Not yet. Better to give him small pieces at a time.

We said good night to each other, adding more affection to our tones than usual, with a last warning from him to be careful.

It felt good to have someone care.

After talking to Hunter, I walked through the garden, inspecting everything. The tomatoes were ripening, winter squash was sprawling in the paths, the buttercup squash seemed to grow larger right before my eyes, and my fall crop of lettuce was bursting forth, some of it chewed down by the rabbit I'd seen from the river. But my philosophy was, critters need to eat, too. I just planted more than I needed and shared the abundance.

After that I drove to the Waukesha jail.

"He doesn't want to see you," said a cop behind a glass partition after delivering my request to see Clay Lane.

"He can't do that. He doesn't have a choice. He's my husband." I'd be thrilled never to have to say that again.

The cop shrugged, not impressed.

"Tell him I'm going to help him get out of here."

That got me a second look and a raised eyebrow.

"I don't mean break him out tonight," I said. "I'm going to prove he didn't murder his girlfriend. Tell him that."

My message was relayed down the channels and eventually I was allowed in.

"What?" Clay said, looking like a convicted man who'd lost hope.

"I know you didn't kill Faye," I said. "And I'm convinced that Manny was murdered, too."

"Why do you think that?"

"I just do."

"What does that have to do with me?"

"I think whoever killed Faye probably killed Manny, since the odds of two murders by two separate killers in two days would be so low as to be almost nonexistent. And that person is after me for some reason. The store was robbed, and Carrie Ann was hurt. Then I found Faye's missing earring on my desk in the back room."

"What missing earring?"

"Don't they tell you anything in here?"

"Nobody tells me anything. My lawyer hasn't even been in since I hired him."

So I told Clay about the one earring Faye had been wearing when Hunter and I'd found her, and how the police hadn't been able to locate it until it showed up on my desk. And how Clay had to talk to me, tell me the truth, if I was going to be able to help him.

When I finished, Clay said, "Sounds like you want to help yourself, not me. In fact, I'm not sure why I'm in here and you're out there."

"You'll benefit from anything I find. Why do you care why I'm doing it, as long as it helps you get out of jail?"

"What do you want from me?"

"The whole truth and nothing but the truth. Let's start with why you and Faye were fighting and why she left your house that night?"

"We were fighting about stupid stuff, and I got mad and said the only reason I was going with her was because she reminded me of you. She didn't like that and stomped off. We would have made up if she hadn't been killed."

"Tell me the rest. What's going on with you and Grace Chapman? I want confirmation one way or the other."

What I heard left me without any forward steam. My stack of theory cards had fallen. The scoop I got was that:

- Grace had called Clay last Thursday night, sounding desperate and upset, and had said she needed to meet with him, but didn't want anyone to know.

- He invited her over to his house, thinking maybe in her weakened state they'd get it on (his own words).

- Instead, Grace had wanted information on Manny and me, all the sordid details, as she called them, and she thought Clay would be honest and direct with her.

- She obviously didn't know Clay at all.

"I was surprised that you'd want to be with another man," Clay said. "But I let her think I knew something about it, in case she needed a shoulder to cry on."

Ugh. I was so glad I'd dumped this slime ball! "You weren't having an affair with Grace Chapman?"

"Not that I wouldn't have given it a go, once or twice."

"That's the rumor going around. That you two were an item, sneaking around behind Manny's back."

Clay smiled like he was proud of himself.

"What about you and Manny?" he asked. "She seemed to think something was up with you and him."

"Never happened," I said. "Who told Grace that tall tale?"

"Probably Patti," Clay said.

"No one should ever believe Patti," I said. "Ever. She's the one who started the rumor about you and Grace, after she saw Grace go into your house. That's all the so-called proof she needed to start circulating lies. Did you know she has a telescope and spies on us inside our homes?"

"Sure, I know. That's why I strut in front of the window naked."

"I thought you were trying to impress me."

"It is impressive, isn't it?"

"Very funny, but get serious for a change. I need a promise from you if I'm going to traipse around the countryside, risking my life."

"Anything, honey."

"Don't call me that ever again."

"That's it? That's all I have to do for you?"

"No. When you get out, you have to move away, out of Moraine, even out of Waukesha County."

"You're breaking my heart with your coldness."

"Is it a deal?"

"Deal," Clay said. "I don't especially like it here anyway, and if you're not coming back to me—"

With that, I made a hasty exit.

Thirty-three

Friday morning, my sister did *not* arrive in time to help open The Wild Clover per Mom's orders, which wasn't much of a surprise. Between working the cash register and giving everybody updates on Carrie Ann's health, the robbery, and the dead woman's earring found on my desk, I had a hectic few hours without her.

Not to mention all the effort of trying to reverse certain reputation-damaging rumors. Holly would be proud of me. Not that I was going to tell her that I had bought into the gossip to the point that I thought Grace had murdered Manny to be with Clay.

Holly did manage to walk in the door by ten o'clock, one whole hour earlier than her regular shift. By then Ray Goodwin had already made a large delivery, in spite of my constant reminders to deliver after three o'clock in the afternoon when strong young male workers were around to help stock shelves. Ray seemed to hate anything smacking of authority and so instead, wasted time doing the opposite of whatever he was asked to do. He had a you-aren't-the-boss-of-me attitude, which clearly hadn't taken him very far, career-wise.

"Did you pick up that honey from Grace's?" I asked him.

"Didn't know you needed it right this *minute*." He put special emphasis on the last word like I was nagging him.

"I don't really, but soon, okay?"

Ray shrugged. "I'll get to it."

I rolled my eyes and went back inside. "Call over to the Craigs," I said to Holly, noting how great she looked. Rested and carefree. "See if one of the twins can come in early to help stock, ASAP."

Holly gazed at the boxes of produce still waiting to be moved to the bins and shelves and nodded. "Better them than me. I didn't sign on to do heavy lifting."

"Right. Since the boxes are strategically placed right next to where they need to go, you must be referring to hefting those two-ton tomatoes from box to bin."

"That's right."

"I love you," I said, surprising myself. I floored Holly, too, because she stopped and stared. "I couldn't have managed this last week without you," I told her.

I've never seen my sister smile quite that wide. "Thanks. It's nice to be appreciated."

"Don't I know it," I agreed. "Hey, guess what? Hunter and I have a date tomorrow night."

"I knew something was up! Where are you going?"

"I don't know." Which was true. We hadn't discussed it. Saturday night was coming up fast and I had a real date. Where we went didn't matter one bit.

Lori showed up for her two or three items as usual,

making her one of our daily customers, which had to be intentional on her part. The woman was so annoying, she liked to irritate me on a regular basis.

"Any luck selling Manny's home?" I asked her, really hoping this particular sale went nowhere. Manny hadn't wanted to sell and I wished everybody would respect his wishes, at least for a while.

"As a matter of fact, I *am* negotiating a deal on the Chapman property," Lori gloated. "But I can't talk about it at the moment."

"Then why are you?" Holly said, earning a glare from Lori.

"Who's making the offer?" I wanted to know.

"You wouldn't know the name."

"Try me."

"Confidential information," Lori said, flouncing toward the door. "Once the deal is done, you'll be one of the first to know."

I called Grace.

"I want to rectify any wrongs," I said to Grace when she answered her phone. I wanted to ask her about selling out, but first I had to mend fences. "Once and for all, I want to squash both rumors going around—the one about you and the one about me. And I'd like your help."

"What rumor about me?"

I took a deep breath and plowed in. "That you and Clay were having an affair."

"Are you spreading lies about me?" Her voice had risen to a range unknown to humankind. "Haven't you done enough damage?"

"NO! Wait! It was P. P. Patti who's been spreading it, after she saw you at Clay's house. But I know why you went there and I'm going to fix the damage Patti did."

"How? Are you going to tell people the real truth? That I only went to Clay because I wanted honesty about you and Manny and I thought he might answer my questions? Maybe you could start with telling *me* the truth about you and my husband."

This wasn't going well.

"Patti started that one, too. She's a menace, destroying families and relationships. Manny was my friend and that's as far as it ever went. He loved you."

Grace started crying.

"Look," I said, "I'll get Patti to tell you the truth, that she started the rumor and that it was all a lie. Okay?"

I thought I heard her say "okay," before she hung up, but her voice was so low and so anguished, I wasn't sure whether she'd agreed to my plan.

Honeybees work together in fine-tuned harmony, making sure their hives are functioning as they should. Humans could learn a few things from watching bees, since we spend as much time hurting each other as helping.

When a field bee comes in carrying pollen in her leg pouches, worker bees meet her at the entryway and help her unload. They don't have to be asked to pitch in. They just do it. Teamwork. Flowers and bees also form partnerships, helping each other out. The flower gives pollen to the honeybee so she can make food for her hive. The flower benefits when her pollen is moved along to other flowers for fertilization.

Teamwork. That's what I was hoping for.

Grace, Patti, and I sat in a tight circle inside the storage room, almost bumping knees. Grace wore pain and suffering on her plain face. Patti sported bold righteousness, and I was just plain worn out from pettiness and unnecessary lies when bigger, more dangerous events were playing out beneath the surface.

"As you know, we are here to speak the truth," I said. "Patti, you saw Grace go into Clay's house."

"That's right."

"And you told people that she was having an affair with him."

Patti squirmed. Not much, but I saw it in her eyes. The left/right thing she did when she felt cornered. "No," she said. "I didn't say anything of the kind."

"See?" Grace said.

"Patti, you tell Grace the truth or I swear, I'll never speak to you again."

What I wanted to say was I would kill her with my bare hands in front of witnesses.

"You don't mean that!" Patti said. "And I am telling the truth."

"Oh, yes, I do mean it. And you won't be welcome in The Wild Clover. Come on, Grace needs to know. Tell her."

Patti crossed her arms and set her jaw.

"You watched her through your telescope," I prompted.

That made Grace sit up and take notice. "You have a telescope?" she asked Patti.

"For bird watching," Patti said.

And peeping-Patti-ing, I thought, but didn't say. Instead I said, "Clay can tell you all about how she spies on him with her stupid telescope."

Grace pushed her chair back to get up. I gripped her arm. "Please don't go yet." I tried not to sound pleading, but I think I failed. Grace sat back down, though.

"Now then," I said, trying a different tactic. "Grace heard a rumor about Manny and me. Could we at least clear that up?"

"Okay," Patti said, still wary.

"Please tell Grace it isn't true."

"But it is."

I glared at Patti. My efforts to put things right had taken a left turn and were going south. "You can't really believe that!" I said.

"I believe my eyes," Patti said. "They never lie."

"You are totally making that up. Manny and I were never together in a romantic way."

Patti gave me a glare back. "Then why did he come up from the river and sneak up to your house?"

My mouth dropped open.

Grace got up and left, slamming the door to the storage room when she left.

I went for Patti but fell over Grace's chair, landing in the center of the circle of chairs.

Patti yelled for help when I sprang back up. Perhaps she saw the murderous look in my eyes because she hit me with her purse, which must have been loaded with thousands of heavy coins. I sat back down, but only for a second.

I staggered to my feet and grabbed the front of her top, hearing a rip.

My sister rushed in and wrestled me down.

Then I remembered what Stu had told me about Manny taking his canoe out on the river.

By then Patti had disappeared, running for her life.

Thirty-four

"I believe you," I said to Patti when she finally answered her phone. "Please don't hang up."

"That apology you gave me the other day about future apologies is worn out. I'm calling the police chief if you don't stay away from me. Assault is a serious offense."

"You're the one who struck first with that loaded purse of yours." I held an ice pack on my head, hoping to keep the swelling down.

"You tried to kill me," Patti said.

"Oh, yeah, right."

"I'm hanging up."

"No, wait. Please. I really do believe you."

"I said before that all my observations are based on facts. I have concrete facts on you and Manny."

She *had* said that she always had facts to back up her

claims now that I thought back on our custard stop, but I'd missed it at the time.

"If Manny came to my house, it's news to me," I said. "As far as I know, Manny hadn't been to my house since last spring when he helped me introduce my bees to the hives."

"I saw him. That's all I know."

"When?"

"About five or six days before those bees stung him to death. I was having my raccoon problem then. I probably told you how they destroyed my house and how much money they cost. I'd just set the trap, and gone back inside."

"Five or six days before he died," I repeated. That fit what Stu had said about Manny asking to borrow the canoe. It also gave the false rumor about us plenty of time to have reached Grace before her Thursday visit to Clay. "What exactly did you see? Tell me."

"It was almost dark. Good thing I was at the window at that same moment or I would have missed it completely. I saw Manny paddle up to your backyard, pull the canoe to shore, and walk toward your house, staying in the shadows. I couldn't see much after that, but believe you me, I tried."

"You could be mistaken, if it was that dark."

"You have that light out by the river. I saw him clear as day until he walked out of its beam of light. It was Manny Chapman and he was definitely sneaking around."

"Was I home?"

"You sure were and you know it. I saw you through your window, then you moved into a different room where my view was obstructed."

"You saw him go to my door?"

"I didn't have to. I'm not dumb, you know. And I don't lie."

Now that Patti mentioned the whole lying thing, I realized that I hadn't really ever caught her in any outright lies.

Mostly she just stretched the truth until it transformed into a completely different shape than it'd started out.

"I can't believe this," I said.

"I've got to go." With that, she hung up.

Even P. P. Patti didn't want to be my friend anymore.

But I had bigger problems to solve, because Patti might actually have had some basis for thinking that Manny and I were carrying on behind Grace's back. Flimsy, though, if what she said was based on real observations versus creative fiction. But Stu had pretty much corroborated it, saying that Manny had taken off in his canoe around the same time, heading downstream. That would have taken him right past my house.

So why didn't I know anything about it? Why would Manny come over without ever announcing himself?

This was too weird.

"How's the head?" Holly asked, coming into the back room. She pulled the ice pack away and fingered my head knot.

"Ouch," I said. "Don't touch."

"She really clocked you."

"You should have restrained Patti, not me. She was the menace."

"You looked more likely to do major damage. Now tell me the story."

My younger sister clucked over me like a mother hen while taking in the facts as I laid them out.

When I finished, neither of us had a clue what was going on.

"Anybody minding the store?" Someone called from the front.

Holly said, "BBL (*Be Back Later*)," and bounced away to take care of customers, leaving me with my dark thoughts.

What a confusing mess! And it all came back to the

same small circle—Manny, Grace, Clay, Faye, and me. One of us was in jail and two of us were dead.

And how did Stanley Peck fit in to the equation? An entire apiary was missing, and Stanley was studying up on bees with library books.

Then of course there was big-mouthed Patti and all the trouble she'd caused. Grace would never have thought anything bad about Manny and me if P. P. Patti hadn't spread it around. Was she up to more than just destroying reputations?

If Grace didn't kill her husband to be with Clay, might she have killed him because she thought he was having an affair with me?

That had possibilities, but how did that explain Faye's murder? Nothing was adding up.

Process of elimination. That was the only way. I'd start with Stanley, since he was much more approachable than Grace or Patti were at the moment.

When Stanley came into the market in the early afternoon, I said to him, "I'd like to get started in chickens." I knew that Stanley raised a few himself.

He looked surprised. "Don't you have your hands full as it is?"

"I'm busy, but how much work could a few chickens take? I have that little shed out back where we had chickens when I was a kid. They can stay in there at night and scratch around the yard eating bugs and laying eggs for me during the day. Chickens are the latest craze in the back-to-the-earth movement, in case you haven't been paying attention."

"I suppose I have a few you could start with, to see how you like them. If you don't, you can always bring them back. If you do, you can keep them or start your own."

Exactly what I'd hoped he'd say.

"Why don't I stop over at your place around three o'clock? After the twins come to cover for the rest of the day."

"Works for me."

I wasn't going to chase after Stanley Peck in my car anymore. This time, I'd go head-to-head with him, tackle the issue like a woman, and wrestle it to the floor until it gave me some answers.

I better take Holly along.

Thirty-five

"I remember back when Stanley had dairy cows," Holly said on the ride over to Stanley's farm. "He always smelled like manure."

"I like that smell," I said.

"And school groups would go out there and take tours. I got lightheaded from the strong odor and had to wait in the bus, I still remember."

"The days of local dairy farmers are almost gone," I said. "Someday, nobody will recognize the fresh, clean perfume of cow poop."

"The sooner, the better."

We pulled up next to Stanley's farmhouse. I turned off the truck.

"I forgot to tell you, Mom wants us to go over for dinner tonight," Holly said.

"Your husband Max out of town?"

"Foolish question. Of course he is. Will you come?"

I'd been expecting an offer, since I hadn't been over to Grams's for a while. Well, not all the way inside, at least. I could check on my bees, too, make sure nothing menacing was bothering them.

"Who's cooking?" I wanted to know.

"Mom. And we'll have Grams's AP."

My mental text dictionary couldn't keep up with her random abbreviations. "AP?" I asked.

"Apple pie. She said to come over at six o'clock and no later."

"Can I drink heavily first?"

Stanley came out of his house before Holly could endorse my strategy. We got out of the truck and followed him to his chicken coop on the side of the barn. He recited enough material on raising chickens to fill an entire textbook, beginning, middle, and end, until I knew more about the birds than I'd ever wanted to know.

"Pick out a couple. Three or four, for starters," he said, pointing to masses of hens pecking around inside a fenced area connected to the coop. "I'll find something for you to carry them home in." He wandered off in search of a way to transport them.

"They stink," Holly said, wrinkling her nose. "Worse than cows. And now you're stuck with chickens."

I'd filled Holly in on the way over so she knew the real reason we were visiting Stanley. The chickens were simply a cover.

"I've been considering getting chickens anyway," I said. "Now's as good a time as any."

"I can't believe you're going to put stinky chickens in your backyard."

"I like that smell."

"They all look alike."

On that, at least, we agreed.

Stanley came back with a big cardboard box and chicken feed. He and Holly watched me run around until I managed to snag three plump hens, then Stanley helped me get them into the box. "Tie this around it nice and tight," he said, handing me a ball of twine. "That'll keep them from getting out."

"Before we load them into the truck," I said after securing the box, "we have to clear the air."

Holly wrinkled her nose again and stifled a chuckle. The air, according to her silent smirk, needed big time clearing. "I feel dizzy," she said. "I'll wait in the truck." *From the fumes*, she mouthed to me so Stanley couldn't hear.

At times, it was hard to believe that Holly and I were from the same family; just like it was impossible to imagine Mom and Grams were related.

"What's up?" Stanley asked me.

"You've been studying up on bees. You checked out a bee-keeping book from the library. So you tell me what's up?"

"Can't a man read what he wants?"

"Sure he can. But he has some explaining to do if he's reading on a subject and that same subject seems to have vanished from Manny's beeyard right after he died. And especially since the town is upset about bees and certain residents don't want us raising them and are willing to make trouble over it."

"That's just Lori. She'll find something else to rail about eventually."

"Please, I need to know. Are you getting ready to raise bees?"

"What ever gave you that idea?"

"The book, Stanley. The beekeeping book."

"I was just reading."

Stanley refused to explain further. I phrased and rephrased the same question different ways without any luck. With nothing more to discuss, Stanley helped load the hens, feed, and a bale of straw into the back of the truck. Holly and I headed out.

"That man is hiding something," I said.

"No luck getting him to talk?"

"Nope."

Ten minutes later Stanley drove out of his driveway. We blew out of our hiding place and gave chase.

"Stay back or he's going to see you," Holly called.

"He's not going to check his rearview mirror for a tail," I said.

"How do you know?"

"Outside of the movies, what real person does that? When's the last time you glanced back to see if a vehicle was following you, one you recognized?"

"He's bound to notice eventually."

"Besides, last time I stayed back, I lost him. I don't want him getting away this time."

We left Moraine, following the rustic road, which was becoming more familiar to me from all the time I was spending chasing Stanley around. He wasn't in a hurry, going much slower than the speed limit. On the same stretch where I'd lost him before, he turned into one of the driveways I'd checked last time. Only last time I hadn't noticed that the main driveway went one way and a smaller, gravel drive went another.

Stanley followed the gravel one.

"GFI!" Holly shouted, getting excited. (*Go For It!*) "Follow him in."

Instead, I pulled over and parked. Hens squawked from the back of the truck. "Let's wait a few minutes, see if he comes out."

Fifteen minutes later, Stanley hadn't reappeared.

"Let's walk in," I said.

"ITA (*I Totally Agree*)," she said. "That will be less obvious."

The driveway was longer than we thought, ending at a small cottage tucked between a mature maple and an oak tree. A woman's home, with lace curtains peaking out, fresh flowers on windowsills, and tended daylilies all along the front.

Stanley's car wasn't parked next to the cottage, so I assumed he'd pulled into a small garage close by. That explained why I hadn't spotted his car the first time I chased and lost him on this same road. I remembered turning into this driveway then.

As we edged around the back I spotted beehives.

Not many. Five to be exact. Certainly not Manny's bees, judging by the beehive construction. And while you can't really tell one honeybee from another, completely different hives meant different honeybees than the ones I was searching for.

I moved closer to the back of the cottage, wondering who lived there. Holly stayed with me. Not a sound came from inside.

Holly tugged on the back of my top, gesturing with her head and her eyes. *Time to go. Let's get out of here.* I shook my head back. *Not yet.* Three feet to one of the back corner windows. I had to look in. We'd come this far. Two feet. One. Crouching lower than the window, easing up. Eye level. Holly right beside me.

It was a good thing the window was closed when I backed up, tripped, clutched my sister for support, and took her down with me. Holly let out a muffled yelp. We untangled and crawled out of sight.

I'd discovered Stanley's secret.

He had a girlfriend, one who was at the moment naked and entwined with Stanley on a bed right before our eyes.

And here I had been, peeking in at them like P. P. Patti

without a telescope. If I found time, I'd be ashamed of myself later.

Holly and I darted back down the driveway a safe distance before speaking to each other.

"Did you see that?" I asked.

"Yeah."

"Stanley has a girlfriend," I said, which was pretty obviously to both of us.

"He doesn't want anybody to know."

"It's our secret."

"Right."

"He's learning about bees because of her."

"Right."

"Stanley isn't Gerald Smith. He isn't the phantom bee thief."

"Right."

At the bottom of the driveway, we meet my new chickens running toward us, free as birds. At least, I assumed they were mine, since they looked exactly like the ones I'd picked up.

"Grab them," I said in a stage whisper, spreading my arms wide in hopes of driving them back toward the road.

Instead the hens banded together, dodged to my right as one unit, flapped their wings, and made it all the way to the cottage side of my blockade, still running on their scrawny chicken legs.

"Get them." I was right behind two escapees but couldn't help noticing that my sister wasn't. "We have to stop these chickens or I'm going to have some explaining to do. What will I tell Stanley?"

"I don't deal with live chickens," Holly called from close to the road. "They probably have all kinds of diseases."

The faster I ran, the faster the hens ran away from me. Within mere moments of giving chase, it was clear that I wasn't going to catch them. I couldn't do anything but give up and return to the truck.

My twine tying needed serious work. Somehow it had come loose and the chickens had worked themselves free.

Holly started laughing when I explained what had happened. "Once Stanley sees his chickens in his girlfriend's yard, he's going to know you were here spying on him."

"So were you."

"I'll deny it."

"Thanks a lot." I looked up the drive, hoping to see the chickens running back down. No such luck. "Chickens aren't wild animals," I said. "They won't last one night out in the open without shelter. A raccoon will finish them off. What should we do?"

Then I heard Stanley's voice coming from the general direction of the cottage.

"What the hell! Why, these look like. . . . they are! How did my chickens get all the way over here?"

With that, we drove off faster than a flying chicken, effectively ending my short-lived career as a chicken farmer.

Thirty-six

"What have you girls been up to?" Grams asked from her position at the kitchen sink where she washed fingerling potatoes I'd dug up from my garden.

"Nothing much," Holly said. "Just working hard."

"Or hardly working," Mom chimed in.

I'd had a nice big glass of wine to prepare myself for the ordeal. I could have used an entire bottle.

"How about a beverage?" Grams asked, wiping her hands on a towel. By beverage she meant, in her genteel manner, an alcoholic beverage.

"No thanks," Holly said.

"That's my girl," Mom said. "Booze ages a woman."

"I'll help myself," I said, pouring a generous glass of wine.

"See," Mom pointed out, casting me a look of disappointment.

That firstborn daughter thing was really getting to me. She wanted to control me or break me, or whatever mean people do. I planned on resisting until the bitter end. How could Grams stand to live with her?

The inquisition began immediately and continued through the meal prep as Grams fixed the potatoes, Holly and I whipped up an enormous garden salad, and Mom fried chicken. Here's the gist of the conversation, all pointed directly at me:

- That Carrie Ann, how anybody would trust her with a cash register full of money was beyond my mother.

- Speaking of the store, were we focusing on safety in numbers and doing as she told us to do or did she have to get more involved in the daily running of the store to protect us?

- How was the family going to recover from my sordid divorce and now rumors of my brazen affair with a married dead man, which happened to be the talk of the town? That poor woman, Grace. I should find my own man, not one already taken.

- Why was I seeing Hunter when he used to be such a drunk and those kind don't change their stripes. (That comment also proved that everybody in town but me knew about Hunter's former problem with alcohol.)

- Which brought us to that "nice boy," Dennis Martin, who'd had a crush on me since grade school and was still available and would make a perfect marital partner.

"He's gay," I said, drinking faster.

"You aren't taking any pills, are you?" Grams said. "We don't want a repeat of last time after the funeral."

"I was perfectly fine."

"That man slept over at your house," Mom said.

"He did not. Hunter escorted me home and left. Your sources are wrong."

"Now, Helen," Grams said. "You're being awful hard on Story. She a successful businesswoman and she'll get her personal life in order soon. She's just going through a transition, that's all. Aren't you, Sweetie?"

"And that dead woman's earring," Mom continued, not hearing anything but her own voice. "How did it get in your office?"

"I'm giving *you* a pill," Grams said to Mom. "You're getting worked up."

"I'm fine," Mom said, turning the chicken in the skillet. I wished she'd take the offered medication.

Why I'd arrived early to take all this abuse, before the dinner was on the table, was a mystery. It seemed an eternity but finally the meal was ready, and we took our positions, each of us having established a permanent seating arrangement as family members seem to do.

We squared off at Grams's table, Mom sitting directly across from me.

"Is it true?" Mom asked after Grams got a nice picture of her "three favorite people."

"Can't we have pleasant talk while we eat?" Grams asked, taking her seat.

"Is what true?" I said, wondering which one of the many accusations she'd hurtled at me she was referring to.

"Is it true that Manny Chapman was visiting you from the river so nobody would see him? I'd like you to tell me what's going on. Is it true?"

"I'm sure it's not," Holly said, finally speaking up and sort of coming to my defense.

I was reaching for a piece of chicken when it dawned on me—an epiphany. I'd been so dense until this very moment.

"Oh my God," I said. "Yes, that's absolutely right."

Unfortunately, I said that out loud when I meant to just think it.

Somebody gasped. Holly, maybe.

I dropped the piece of chicken back into the serving bowl, jumped up from the table, and flew out the door.

"Now look what you did," Grams said behind me, thinking I'd left because of my mother.

She was only partly right.

I wore my bee veil and gloves when I went in with the smoker. During one of my usual visits to my hives, I would typically just make sure the queen in each was doing well and that the workers were carrying on as usual. But this wasn't going to be a routine inspection.

Colony Collapse Disorder was an unsolved mystery yet to be unraveled and it was always at the back of a bee-keeper's mind. When this sad event occurred, adult bees simply vanished, abandoning the queen and brood. All the workers, including scouts and nurse bees, disappeared at once, every last one of them, leaving stores of honey and certain death for those remaining behind.

My bees were in fine health, judging by the activity around the two hives. The entrances looked like busy airports. I stepped gingerly around the nails spiking up through the board, having learned my lesson last time. I'd also traded my flip flops for a sturdy pair of work boots.

After settling the honeybees in the first hive with a few puffs of smoke to keep them docile, I lifted off the cover and removed each of the honeycombs hanging inside the hive box. Slowly, cautiously, with a little more smoke here and there, I slid out each of the frames and inspected under and around before replacing them. Then I did the same thing with the next hive, careful not to harm any of my bees in the process.

Everything was as it should be.

I stood back and pondered. Manny, even as afraid of water as he'd been, had taken a canoe down the river by himself and paddled over to my house. He must have had a very good reason. The only explanation I could think of that "held water," so to speak, was that he didn't want anyone to know where he was going. Or why.

I stared at the hive boxes. At home in my backyard, I kept the hives on concrete block bases so that they were raised off the ground, the theory being that the bees would be happier the farther their hives' entrances were from the dampness of earth. On the night I'd moved the hives, I hadn't bothered to also transport the heavy blocks. I'd had my hands full as it was.

Now that I studied the hives, I could see that one of them was at a slight angle. I'd assumed that was because I'd placed them on the edge of the cornfield where the ground hadn't been tilled flat.

Crouching down, I rather awkwardly raised one side of the tilting beehive about two inches. It was too heavy to hold with one hand and still check underneath with the other. If I'd been paying better attention to my bees, I would have noticed that they were getting excited. Usually they were the gentlest honeybees you could know, but like all bees, they were protective of their queen and territory and really tuned in to threatening behavior from outsiders.

Outsiders, like me.

Instead of tuning in to them (using my "mental awareness" as Manny had reminded me to over and over), I rummaged around on the side of the field until I found a fallen tree branch thick enough to use as a lever. I worked it in under the hive. That freed my hands, but the gloves were getting in the way.

I took my gloves off, and was promptly stung on a knuckle.

Ouch! That really hurt.

Quickly, I scraped the stinger away, crouched down next to the hive again, reached under, and began feeling around. I should have blown more smoke at the hive, because now the bees were getting rowdy. Bee colonies have quite a list of enemies—wasps, ants, mice, skunks, bears, and raccoons, to name a few—and I understand why they need to have their own special swat team. But you'd think by now the bees would know me well enough to give me a break.

That wasn't going to happen.

The next stinging attack came in the space between my right boot and my jeans. Then another, near that one. From the honeybees' point of view, they and their queen were under full attack. And I was a rookie beekeeper who hadn't been smart enough to anchor my jeans with elastic and was too excited to wear a bee suit. At least I'd had the sense to wear the veil so my face and neck were protected.

I gritted my teeth and forced myself to ignore the pain, not an easy thing to do.

Why was I putting myself through this torture and agony? Because Manny had been in my backyard, not in my house. He knew and loved bees, and he'd been up to something. I had to know what it was. It had to do with the bees, I was sure of it.

Another bee dove in, stinging my other hand. My throbbing fingers finally felt something other than pain: An object pressed against the hive that didn't belong there, anchored to the bottom of the hive with tape. I felt along, peeling it away by touch while the sound of pissed-off bees grew louder and louder.

By the time I scooted away from the hive, I had lost count of the number of stings I'd endured, mostly on my hands and ankles.

And they really, really hurt.

Bee-sting therapy, also called bee-venom therapy, is supposed to relieve the symptoms of MS and arthritis, among other ailments. The treatment involves allowing bees to sting the area in question as many as ten or twenty times. The venom is supposed to jumpstart the immune system. All it did for me was jumpstart my pain sensors. By the time I drove home and stumbled through my back door, my ankles had swollen beyond belief.

But I had Manny Chapman's missing journal clutched in my puffy fist.

Thirty-seven

In my opinion, personal journaling is just what it implies—personal, as in private. Like the diary I had as a girl. My little tidbits scribbled down while lying in bed in the dark weren't intended for an audience. I hate to think what would have happened if my mom had found mine. She would have had a bird's-eye view into my mind, which was never a good thing.

Which reminded me, I wonder whatever happened to that diary . . . ? I decided not to go there. It could only cause panic, thinking Mom may have had it all this time.

Holly keeps a journal where she writes down her thoughts and experiences. She says she does it to understand herself better, to work through her emotions and analyze their significance.

I'm not really sure I care to understand my actions better.

Analyzing them up and down and sideways would drive me nuts.

But Manny Chapman's journal wasn't a personal diary; it was an accounting of his honeybees' daily lives. It was a jumble of notes and clippings, all in reference to the community inside his colonies.

For example:

- What type of mite appeared when and what he did about it.

- Dates of harvests and hive splits.

- The times he caught swarms and the results.

- Which hives were most aggressive, which ones he considered best for raising more queens.

I'd had the exclusive privilege of accessing the journal, although I hadn't spent more than a few minutes on an occasional page, recording an observation of my own or adding an entry at his request.

The journal was very important to him, so when it went missing, I should have been much more clued in that something was off kilter. That said, I'd been pretty distracted by two deaths—two murders—in as many days, so maybe I shouldn't be too hard on myself.

But if the journal hadn't been stolen, if (as it appeared) Manny himself had hidden it under one of my beehives—why?

That was the sticky question.

He'd risked the river despite his water phobia to conceal the journal. And he'd never said a word to me about it being there. Did hiding it have something to do with the break-in at his home, the robbery that Johnny Jay had chalked off as a kid's prank? Had he been so worried about someone taking the journal that he had to get it off his property? Or had he been hiding it from Grace? Were the answers to my questions inside the journal? I sure hoped so.

Before I could explore the pages, I had to scrape out several remaining stingers that I'd missed the first time around, and I lay down on the couch with ice bags on my ankles and hands, not an easy balancing act. During my home-style stinger treatment, I heard a knock at the door and Hunter's voice calling out.

"I'm in here," I said, removing an ice pack long enough to tuck the journal under a pillow. "In the living room."

Hunter and his giant dog Ben appeared in the doorway.

"What happened to you?" Hunter wanted to know.

"Nothing," I said.

"Holly called me and said you'd had a fight with your mother."

"Just the usual. Nothing special."

Hunter lifted an ice bag and studied my ankle. "Bee stings," he announced.

"No way," I said, observing the beekeeper's secret oath. Never let anyone know you've ever been stung. "I've never been stung," I bragged.

Hunter made some kind of throat noise, a sure sign he didn't believe a word of it. "How many times?"

"Six or seven. Or ten."

"Weren't you wearing protective gear?"

"Partly. My head is okay."

Hunter sat down next to me. Ben stuck his nose on my shoulder and sniffed my hair.

"Hey, Ben," I said, and the dog actually wagged his tail.

"How long do you have to keep the ice on?" Hunter put my feet on his lap, readjusting the ice packs.

"As long as I can stand it."

"Need anything?"

I wanted to say I needed him. That I wanted him to lie

down next to me, wrap me in his strong arms, and cuddle me. But I doubted he'd stop at cuddling and I was in severe pain, or had been until I'd applied ice. Instead, I said, "I'm fine."

"You got that right." Hunter smiled.

I loved his smile. "You came over because my sister called you? Because you were worried about me?"

"In case you needed comforting."

"Nice."

"And to ask you a favor."

"Ask me anything."

"Anything?" Hunter was running a finger up and down my leg, sending shivers that felt like tiny electric shocks. "Anything?" he asked again.

"Almost anything," I clarified.

"You look pretty helpless at the moment. I'm not sure you're up to doing me a favor."

"I'm almost as good as new." Or would be soon. A few bee stings weren't going to keep me down for long.

"You're always great," he said.

One thing I'd really missed was sweet talk, not that I'd heard it often from Clay. Everybody needs to know they are appreciated, including me. I could almost feel my self-worth ratcheting up a notch or two.

"What's the favor?" I asked.

"I have a training session tomorrow. It starts early and finishes late. I hate to leave Ben alone for that long."

Oh no. I could see where this was going. "You're cancelling on me? Our first official date as adults and you're ditching me?"

"The training doesn't go *that* late. I'll be done by six o'clock. But six in the morning until six at night is twelve hours that Ben will be alone."

"Can't he go along with you? Isn't he part of the program?"

"These are C.I.T. drills. Hostage negotiations, weapons practice, the latest techniques and technology, that sort of thing. He can't come for this one."

"Then the answer has to be no."

"What happened to 'ask me anything'?"

"I said you could ask. I didn't say I'd agree. You know how I am about dogs."

"Ben likes you."

The dog stuck his nose on me again and sniffed. Then he licked the side of my face, one long-tongued slurpy lick.

Hunter and I laughed together. Then he became serious. "I'll feel better if you're with Ben. No one will bother you."

"Will he attack if someone totally drives me crazy?" Like Patti or Lori or my mother, I was thinking.

"No, but his presence will deter trouble."

"Deterring trouble is good."

"I also brought offerings of food," Hunter said.

"You did?"

"Pizza. I left it in the truck."

"From Stu's?"

"You bet. Holly said you fled the family scene without eating."

What a sister, setting me up like this!

"You better go get it," I said.

We stayed on the couch, eating pizza and talking while Ben made himself comfortable on the floor. It's amazing how fast pain can recede when you're in a good place with the right person.

And no, nothing extremely intimate happened. Not that that's anybody's business.

But when Hunter left, I had a canine roommate. How could I say no with him rubbing my legs like that? Hunter, I meant, not Ben.

I fell asleep right there where I was.

Manny's journal had completely slipped my mind.

* * *

"You're back!" I said when Carrie Ann walked into the market first thing the next morning. Her short hair was looking spiky and perky, and so was she.

"Saw a familiar truck in front of someone's house last night," Carrie Ann said, giving me a knowing smile. "Things starting to heat up?"

"Searing hot," I said, giving her a big hug.

"Who's the new employee? He looks vaguely familiar." Carrie Ann arched a brow at her competition. "And how could you replace me so soon? My feelings are hurt."

"Meet Ben. He's Hunter's K-9 partner."

Ben had stationed himself near the front door where he could keep an eye on the street and still know exactly where I was. He was smart. He'd sensed I was now a member of his pack, at least temporarily.

"Thought the four-legged guy looked familiar," Carrie Ann said, reclaiming the cash register. "That's where I know him from. Hunter's. We need someone like him around here on a permanent basis."

"Are you sure you're ready to come back to work? How are you feeling?"

"Pissed off. I'm going to catch the creep who tied me up after braining me and when I do, it won't be pleasant."

I believed her.

Carrie Ann didn't smell like smoke and her eyes were clear, indicating she was hangover free. In my opinion, new projects and missions are always handy ways to distract us from the same old destructive habits we tend to get bogged down with. So her plan for vengeance might help with her recovery.

"Johnny Jay hasn't been his usual efficient investigator lately," I said. "He could use all the help he can get."

"Well, I've deputized myself, and our robber better hope the police chief gets to him before I do."

"Too bad Holly the champion wrestler wasn't around to assist you," I said. "BTW, we're double teaming at the store from now on. It's safer."

Had I just said *BTW* (*By The Way*)? Was Holly's text-speak contagious?

"What's that all over your ankles?" Carrie Ann wanted to know after gazing at my flip-flopped feet. I had on a new pair of flip flops, black with a mini wedge. "Looks like bee stings."

"Giant mosquitoes in my garden," I lied, as any good beekeeper would. "They itch. I've been scratching them." I lifted and scratched an ankle for effect.

Holly called right as I finished restocking a bin filled with peanuts in the shell. I tucked the scoop into a pile of peanuts and answered the phone.

"What happened to you yesterday?" she said without so much as a hello. "Mom was speechless for the first time ever. She didn't say a word for at least fifteen minutes after you bolted."

"I thought of something I had to do. Then Hunter came over with a pizza, thanks to you."

"You're welcome if that's your impression of a thank-you. Oh, and just so you know, Max and I are going to Milwaukee for the weekend."

"Lucky you."

"I'll be in on Monday."

"Eleven sharp?"

"Was that sarcasm? If it was, you better take it back because I covered for you with Mom. Everything is cool, and you don't even have to explain your bad behavior to her."

"How did you do that?"

"I told her you always act erratic when you have your period."

Okay, then.

"TC," were her parting letters (*Take Care*).

Thirty-eight

Saturdays are always busy at The Wild Clover. It had rained overnight, but tapered off to a light drizzle by morning. The forecast called for sun by noon, if the weather team could be believed.

Wet weather didn't stop the tourists, although Main Street was a bit less traveled than usual. The fall months in our area bring out people from the cities to watch the trees change colors. Moraine is tucked between Milwaukee and Madison, an easy drive from both cities, which makes it a logical stop along the rustic road leading up to Holy Hill. People came through town, hunting in the antique store for buried treasures, with frozen custards in their hands and spare money to spend. Their brightly colored umbrellas disappeared as soon as the clouds parted and sunbeams replaced raindrops.

Customers picked out handfuls of old-fashioned penny candy from bins lining one wall of the market, scooped peanuts into paper bags, and selected fresh flower bouquets, which Milly Hopticourt had, as usual, brought in first thing when the market opened.

Milly also brought in a new recipe for the newsletter using the wild grapes I'd picked for her. "I need more honey," she said. "I'm working on something very special for next month's issue."

I handed a jar to her, free of charge, since she worked so hard on the newsletter and shared her creations with the rest of us.

"That's one scary dog," she said, watching Ben as he sat at quiet attention near the door.

"He's a Belgian Malinois," I said. "He tracks bad guys and hunts drugs for the police."

"You don't say."

We both studied Ben. He was acting more like a regular dog now that Hunter wasn't around, although he would never be a frolicking pup. I was still cautious when he was nearby but I didn't want him to sense any of my fear, which, as luck would have it, was starting to subside just a little.

"I heard you better not raise your voice around those attack dogs," Carrie Ann called over, raising her voice. "They hate that."

"What would he do if I yelled or screamed?" Milly wanted to know.

Carrie Ann shook her head. "I don't know, but I don't want to find out. Aren't you worried he'll hurt business, sitting at the doorway like that?"

By now a couple of kids were petting him. Ben maintained an attitude of tolerant indifference. "He's used to crowded situations," I said.

Another group of tourists came through, buying the caramel apples we got from Country Delight Farm.

Brent Craig showed up, saying his twin brother, Trent, would be along in a few hours.

I kept waiting for a slowdown so I could start reading Manny's journal, which I'd hidden in a box of honey jars in the back room. Unfortunately, I had no spare time, but that was a good thing as far as taking in cash was concerned.

A few locals showed up and gossiped. I listened in.

"When are they going to have that dead girl's funeral?" one of them said. "I haven't seen anything about it in the newspaper."

"They must be holding the body. It's a murder, after all," someone else commented.

"Has Story's rotten ex-husband been arraigned yet?"

"Shhh. She'll hear you."

"She knows he's rotten. And a murderer besides!"

"If you ask me, she's in on it. The police chief found that dead girl's earring in the back room of this very store. Right over there."

"That's not exactly how I heard it. Story found it and called the police chief."

"I'm sure it's the other way around. And what about the robbery?"

"She might have a partner who decided to go solo."

"You watch too much television."

"Shhh. Here she comes. Hi, Story. My, these tomatoes sure are nice and ripe."

Lori Spandle came in. She bought bratwursts and buns for grilling and six ears of corn, pulling down the husks on at least four times that many before making her final choices.

"Any progress on the Chapman deal?" I asked, convinced that Lori was just blowing smoke to make herself look important.

"It's progressing," Lori said, vaguely. "My new associate and I are working on it."

"What new associate?" Carrie Ann asked.

"My new real estate partner, my sister, DeeDee. And the name of the interested party is confidential, as Story well knows from all her efforts to pry it out of me."

"DeeDee's your new partner?" Carrie Ann snorted. "What kind of partner? Your partner in crime?"

"That hit on the head must have scrambled your brains, or you wouldn't be talking that way, Carrie Ann Retzlaff."

I stepped in. "Let's be nice."

Lori glared my way. "I heard what you did to my sister, accusing her of stealing from your store, and I think it's just terrible."

Stanley Peck came in at that moment and overheard the last part of the conversation. "Are you talking about how Holly caught DeeDee red-handed with stolen goods and how Story wouldn't let Johnny Jay book DeeDee for shoplifting?" he said. "Shame on you, Story. Next time, you let that girl have it with both barrels."

Lori stomped off down aisle six.

"Speaking of barrels," I said to Stanley. "You aren't carrying a weapon, are you?"

"Why?"

"Never mind."

"You're thinking I might be mad about how my chickens showed up way down the road from either my house or yours?"

"Sorry about that."

"And about how you must know my big secret, the same one I've been keeping to myself for very personal reasons?"

"Sorry about that, too."

"You know, I felt guilty that I was having so much fun. I felt terrible about it for a long time because of Carol being

dead and me carrying on like some kind of love-sick puppy.
I didn't want anybody to know. Still don't."

"I won't tell a single soul."

"If you do, I'll have to shoot you," Stanley said straight-
faced. Then he laughed. "Just kidding. But you are the
snoopiest woman I've ever known. You must get that from
your mother."

"Please don't tell me I'm just like her," I begged.

"You aren't. Not a bit. Except for the nosy part."

"Do you mind answering one more question?"

Stanley sighed. "Do I have a choice?"

"Did you borrow Manny's bee blower?"

"No, why, is it missing?"

"Not really."

"Story, you sure are acting strange these days."

"I know." I sighed.

With that, Stanley bought a newspaper and a pound of
Wisconsin coffee and walked off down Main Street, whis-
tling like he didn't have a care in the world, which he probably didn't.

"He's in a good mood," Carrie Ann said. "That's what
happens when you're getting lucky."

"What makes you think that about Stanley?"

"I can always tell," Carrie Ann said, proud of her gift.

Ray Goodwin came by without his delivery truck, which
was a first. I really hoped he wasn't about to try another
tactic to get me to go out with him.

"My day off," he said when I asked about the truck.
"And not a thing to do tonight."

Oh, jeez. "I'm sure something will come up. Otherwise,
hang at Stu's like the rest of us."

One place I was sure to avoid with Hunter tonight was
Stu's. The last thing I wanted was to hurt Ray's feelings by
showing up with another man.

"Did you get the honey from Manny's honey house?" I asked Ray, changing the subject fast.

"Sure did."

"Grace didn't give you any trouble?"

"She wasn't home when I stopped by and loaded up. I'll call her today and let her know, so she doesn't think somebody stole it. Not that she goes out there anyway. She'd never notice."

Just then I saw DeeDee Becker walk past the market. I came up with an idea right on the spot, ran out, and called her name, waving her back.

"What?" she said, shielding her eyes from the sun, which had finally decided to appear through the clouds.

"I'd like to cut a deal with you."

She looked exactly like her sister when she gave me her doubtful look. Except Lori didn't have pierced nostrils and eyebrows. "What for what? Exactly," she said in a demanding voice. Again, just like her sister.

"I'll lift your ban on the store," I offered. "All you have to do is tell me if someone really is interested in the Chapman place and if it's true, who that person is."

I noticed Ben, watching me intensely from inside the door, his ears pointed straight at the ceiling.

"Getting to go back into your establishment isn't such a big deal," DeeDee said. "I'm shopping at other places now. Cheaper ones."

Great. Just great. I didn't have anything else to bargain with. "Could you tell me for free?" It was worth a try. The worst she could say would be no.

"No," DeeDee said, shaking her head for emphasis. "I'd be taking a chance on getting fired. That's worth something."

"Lori isn't going to fire you."

My fountain of information turned to walk away, acting like she didn't care one way or another if I didn't get what I wanted. Without an offer on the table, I'd lose my chance.

"Wait," I called, "I'll throw in a twenty percent discount on everything in the store for one month."

My offer to allow a known thief entry to my store, and even throwing in a discount on top of it, might seem overly desperate to a casual observer. But knowing DeeDee, she wouldn't use the discount anyway, since she usually paid zero dollars for what she wanted. Holly would have her in another hold on the floor in less than a week. And this time, I'd let Johnny Jay do it his way and book her.

Ray came out of the store, gave a little wave, and drove off in a black Chevy with a crumpled back bumper and an obvious problem with the car's muffler.

"So what do you say?" I asked DeeDee.

She thought it over.

"Make it twenty-five percent and two months and we have a deal," the little shoplifter had the nerve to say.

"Done."

"You want to know who's putting in the offer?"

"So it's true?"

DeeDee nodded. "And you won't tell anybody who your source is, since it's what some might say is unprofessional?"

I nodded again.

Then she told me. Part of me almost expected DeeDee to say it was Gerald Smith, the phantom who took Manny's bees.

She didn't say Gerald Smith.

But I knew the name that slid off her studded tongue.

"Kenny Langley," she said. "I'm surprised you didn't think of that on your own. You know him? Right? The owner of Kenny's Bees?"

"No way! You mean to tell me," I said, "that the same Kenny who tried to hustle in on my territory wants to buy Manny's property?"

"It was him all right. But he withdrew the offer about an

hour ago. I'm actually looking for Lori to tell her the bad news. She isn't going to like it one bit."

"She was just in a little while ago." The rush of additional information was too much for my overtaxed brain. But I was talking to her back end as DeeDee strolled into The Wild Clover with her big suitcase purse.

Thirty-nine

Ben rode shotgun next to me in the truck. Business at The Wild Clover had finally slowed down enough around mid-afternoon for me to take a long break. Carrie Ann said she wanted to stay on, that she needed the money, and the twins were there, too. So everything was covered.

By now there wasn't the slightest doubt in my mind that Manny had been murdered. He'd been worried enough about something that he hid his journal under one of my beehives. It was a safe bet that one or more of the pages inside it played a significant role in his concern for its safety, and probably in his death.

I made a few assumptions:

- Manny Chapman's and Faye Tilley's deaths were both murders.

- The same person probably killed both of them.

- Clay had the opportunity and means to kill Faye, but he didn't have a strong motive to kill either her or Manny, at least none that popped right out at me.

- Grace had the opportunity and means to kill Manny, but no real motive. Okay, if she thought Manny was cheating on her, maybe she had a motive.

- Moving on to other possible suspects, Lori Spandle was a nasty person, but that hardly qualified her to be a multiple murderer.

- Stanley Peck had a beekeeping girlfriend, but so what?

- Kenny Langley wanted to take over my honey area and that was a fact. He had made an offer on Manny's property, but then withdrawn it.

Why? Was Kenny killing off the competition so he could take over more territory? That seemed extreme.

Who'd ever heard of such a thing in bee circles? If anything, we usually supported each other. Although Kenny had a streak of competition that had put some distance between us, a little too much testosterone to play nice with a "girl," as he called me.

I've been called worse.

I drove past Grams's house, noting that her car was gone from the driveway. Then I turned into the cornfield and bumped along the side of it, parking close to my beehives. Bees flew through the air, coming and going, having forgotten their quarrel with me yesterday. I found their buzz comforting.

While Ben sniffed along the tree line, leaving his dog scent on pretty much everything that didn't move, I stayed in the truck with the windows open and began to page through Manny's journal, starting from the back and working toward the front.

I skimmed the journal quickly, paging over my own entries, trying to make sense of Manny's notes. He had practiced selective breeding for years, hoping to extend honey production for greater yields, and he'd seen significant progress as seasons and time went by. He'd also been working on developing strong queens and healthy drones that were resistant to mites without the need for chemical controls.

The science aspect was way over my head. As a first-year beekeeper, I was more concerned about the basics, like providing food sources for my honeybees and making sure they had enough room inside the hives to keep filling honeycombs.

"If they run out of space to store their harvests," Manny had said, "they'll leave to find a bigger, better home. Keep an eye on them at all times."

I had been happy to leave the question of which queens and drones to mix together for more experienced beekeepers to ponder.

I turned to several pages that laid out all the numbers for our most recent honey harvest, which was up by 20 percent over last year. Every year Manny's percentages had climbed. He'd also included notes about the queens and royal jelly statistics. Bees needed royal jelly to survive. All I knew about royal jelly at this point in my beekeeping experience could be summed up in a few short bullet points:

- It's secreted from glands in the heads of nurse bees.

- Combined with honey, it is fed to larvae.

- When a new queen is selected, that special larva is fed only royal jelly and lots of it. That's what makes her grow into a queen.

- Royal jelly is supposed to do great things for humans—
  slow aging, lower cholesterol, strengthen the immune
  system, and a whole list of other benefits.

From conversations Manny had with other beekeepers,
he didn't plan to go into full-scale royal jelly production,
but the scientist in him couldn't help but include basic
observations.

It would take several days to go through the journal the
way I should, so after a while I closed it, called Ben back
to his seat in the truck, and almost sideswiped Johnny Jay
as I pulled out on the road.

He swerved, lost control, and ended up in the ditch
across the road, sideways. It was a rather deep ditch with
several inches of standing water.

Nothing good could possibly come out of this encounter.
Scotty, beam me up.

When I didn't evaporate into thin air, I knew I was on
my own.

"Hey, Johnny Jay," I said through the open window
when he got out and stepped down into the water before
noticing it. The police chief didn't look happy about the
situation or about seeing me. "Sorry about that," I added as
he sloshed toward me.

"Missy Fischer, even though our fine country fields
don't have their own special stop signs, it's implied that
those who don't stay on the roadways will yield to those
who do. I'm writing you up for reckless driving."

"Whatever gives you a thrill," I replied, noting his
smug, righteous air as he leaned on my truck, an authorita-
tive attitude that always brought out the sass in me. "But I
didn't see you. Perhaps you were speeding."

"Isn't that Hunter's dog?" he asked.

I nodded. "He's trained to attack."

"Are you threatening me?"

"Just telling it like it is."

"I'll need your driver's license. Then you can sit tight while I run your plates, see if you're wanted for anything. Let's see—reckless driving *and* threatening a police officer."

"I'm really sorry about prom," I said, stooping to an all-time low by apologizing to Johnny Jay. And twice in a row—first for the ditch, then for the dance. "I didn't mean to hurt your feelings."

Johnny Jay stared at me through the window, speechless. Then he said, "What are you talking about?"

"Prom. When you asked me to go, and I said no."

"What's that got to do with anything?"

"I thought that's why you're so mean to me, and why you aren't even going to listen to me when I try to tell you that Manny Chapman was murdered."

"Don't you have anything better to do than make up situations in your head?"

"I'm not making this up."

"Come with me." He opened my door. "We're going to have a little chat."

"What kind of chat?"

"Just get out."

Suddenly I realized that I was alone with a big bully. Holly wasn't here to act as my bodyguard.

My reaction was probably silly. Johnny Jay had done some pretty rotten things, but he'd never been accused of physical abuse. At least not since high school, when he had been implicated in several black-eye incidents, which had been his word against theirs and never solidly proven. Although I distinctly remembered a scene with me back in third grade when he'd rubbed my face in the snow. I'd gotten even with him later when I blasted him with mud balloons.

I didn't move. Ben was doing his thing, watching and thinking something only he knew about. Suddenly it felt good to have this big scary dog beside me, on my side. What secret words would trigger an active, go-get-him response? Later tonight when I had my hot date with Hunter, I'd have to try to get the magic words out of him just in case I ever needed them.

And why was I so afraid of Johnny Jay? He and I were supposed to be on the same side, too.

"I'm not getting out of my truck," I said, deciding I wouldn't go, no matter what. "But I'll follow you to the station, where I'll be happy to have that little chat with you. So do your business, write me up, read me my rights, whatever you need to do to make yourself feel like you're the boss. Then we'll go down to the station. Now close my door and MOVE back."

There was a long pause while we stared at each other.

Then Johnny Jay closed the door. "Okay," he said. "I'm letting you off with a warning this time."

"What?"

"But only if you swear you'll shut up and mind your own business. I know you're upset about the robbery at the store, and that earring showing up, and I'm perfectly aware that someone is toying with you, trying to scare you or worse. But what happened had nothing to do with Manny Chapman and everything to do with your ex-husband and his dead girlfriend. Christ, the guy's prints are all over the kayak. It's a given, he's going to be doing time. So do we have a deal? You let me do police work, and you mind your store?

"What's the alternative?"

"A court hearing and a fine you can't afford to pay."

"This is blackmail."

"I call it self-preservation. You're driving me crazy."

"Don't you want to hear what I have first? We could compare notes."

"Hand over your driver's license."

"I'll take the deal," I lied.

Forty

Just as I'd hoped, Grace wasn't home. In the past, whenever Manny and I got together on Saturdays to harvest honey, Grace would leave in the afternoon to visit her brother and sister-in-law and do a little shopping. It was one of her routines, and so I was counting on her being away.

Ben stayed in the truck. He licked his lips, pressed his nose against the pane of glass, and followed me with his eyes.

I was starting to kinda, sorta like the big hairy guy.

But I also wasn't too happy about continuing my investigation without a human backing me up. Johnny Jay was impossible to deal with, Holly was in Milwaukee for a romantic weekend with Money Machine Max, Hunter was in advanced C.I.T. training, and even Carrie Ann was busy at the market. Plus, I didn't want to expose my cousin to any more danger, since she'd already had one episode with violence at the store. That left my mother to ask along (no thanks) or Grams, who was so sweet I could count on her to offer the bad guy a brownie.

I desperately needed a best friend, one who was available when I needed her, one who didn't judge or criticize or think anything negative about me. A happy, positive, go-getting female, who wasn't afraid of my honeybees or taking risks. Was I expecting too much?

Pushing aside my worry about going it alone, I walked into the center of what used to be Manny's beeyard. Empty now, without the buzzing of activity I remembered so fondly.

I was back where it had all begun.

The image of Manny's body lying there with honey and bees all over him was almost as vivid as the real thing had been. I missed him so much, all his wisdom and passion and patience with my beekeeping inexperience.

Now that I thought about it, Manny was the closest thing to a best friend that I'd had in years. If I wasn't on a mission of justice at the moment, I might have sat down and cried over my huge loss. Instead, I headed for the honey house with key in hand, thinking about how Gerald Smith or whoever he was had Manny's strong, productive hives, which should rightfully belong to me. The best bees in the state, maybe even in the country.

The only other honeybees around as special as Gerald Smith's were my own. I had two perfect hives with great bees and queens, thanks to Manny's selective breeding techniques.

The implications suddenly became crystal clear, even to someone as dense as I had been recently.

Manny had been killed right in his own beeyard because somebody wanted his bees, and his journal. His home had been searched before he was murdered, and he'd seen the writing on the wall, maybe he'd even been physically threatened. So he hid the journal where he knew I'd find it eventually. Just in case the worst happened. And it did.

The killer had almost everything he or she wanted—strong colonies, special queens, maximum production of honey and royal jelly. Everything planned out precisely to steal what Manny had devoted his life's work to. Except that as far as the killer knew, the journal was still officially missing. Manny's research notes would keep the colonies' genetics sound. The killer needed them to ensure future success with the hives. Manny's killer must be frantic by now, wanting that journal enough to start taking more risks. That's why my market had been robbed in broad daylight; whoever it was had been searching for the journal.

Had the same person also come back and left the earring? But why do that? What did Faye have to do with any of this? Was it possible there *were* two killers?

It was time to admit the truth of the situation: I was in real danger.

Would anybody believe my story? Probably not.

The honey house had an abandoned feel to it when I inserted my key into the padlock and opened it up. I stood in the doorway looking inside, but not really seeing it.

Grace Chapman wasn't the murderer. Grace was a bitter, hurting woman, and I hadn't made her transition from wife to widow any easier. She'd had to deal with innuendos and lies at the same time she had to learn to live without her husband.

Gerald Smith had suspect written all over that fake, generic name. And Kenny Langley had something to do with this, too, trying to buy Manny's home. But why had he withdrawn his offer?

There was only one way to find out what was going on.

I'd have to ask Kenny.

* * *

Kenny's Bees had been in the Langley family for multiple generations, and every one of the eldest male heirs was named Kenny. This particular Kenny was the fourth son to take over the business, and according to rumor, he was grooming his own son Kenny to take over for him. Their honey farm, in rural Washington County, was located on twenty acres of rolling fields. An ideal location to raise bees.

I pulled into a gravel driveway and parked next to a white corrugated building with a sign hanging from a metal awning that read "Honey for Sale." An "Open" sign hung on the inside of the door. As with some other small businesses in the area, Kenny hadn't bothered posting the hours he was open. Some people just didn't want the additional commitment of getting to work at a specific time. That always amazed me. I couldn't imagine opening The Wild Clover whenever I felt like showing up. What bad business sense was that?

Yet Kenny had a thriving honey business.

Ben waited in the truck again. He gave me a disappointed stare. I could tell he wasn't happy with my decision to leave him behind again by the way his pointed ears sagged ever so slightly.

Kenny was a tall, large man in his late fifties, with soft, flabby features. In my opinion, he needed a daily run or he'd go the same way the other Kennys in the family went—out quick with major heart attacks, dropping right on the spot, and never getting the chance to find out what life might be like in their sixties.

Too much bacon grease will do that to a person.

Now was a good time to reaffirm where the lines had been drawn with Kenny and our honey distribution. It was a good excuse to start a conversation and lead it where I wanted it to go.

"Well, if it isn't the girl," Kenny said in greeting from a stool behind a counter, instantly rubbing me the wrong way and setting us on a rocky path right from the start.

"That's Ms. Fischer to you," I said."

"Sorry to hear about what's-his-name."

"His name was Manny."

"I guess your honey business is down the toilet. What a shame." Kenny didn't look sad, not one bit.

"I'm taking over Queen Bee Honey," I said, hoping it wasn't a lie. I still had my sights on the honey house and the possibility of raising enough colonies to continue producing our premium products.

Kenny laughed like he thought I was unbelievably funny. "Anything I can do to help," he said, "just ask."

"I do have a favor I need from you. I'd very much appreciate it if you would continue to honor the agreement you had with Manny about sales territories."

"Why? He's not around anymore."

"It's still a viable business, and you shook hands on it. I was there, remember?"

"Sure I do. But a girl like you can't run an operation like that. You're spread thin as it is with that hobby grocery store you run. I could help you out. In fact, why don't you come work for me? I could be the key to your future."

"I'm doing fine. And you haven't answered me about upholding the agreement."

Kenny shifted on the stool. "We can work something out."

"Ray can't sell your honey in Waukesha County. I already told him that."

Kenny glanced down at some papers on the counter like he had better things to do and was dismissing me.

"I'm looking for a guy named Gerald Smith," I said, watching him closely. "Do you know him?"

"Never heard that name." But his head came up, and I saw something in Kenny's eyes before he answered. Or did I?

"He took all the bees and hives from Manny's yard," I said. "Then he disappeared."

"Then you *are* out of business." Kenny tried not to look pleased. Or did he? I'd never be much of a detective if I couldn't learn to read people better than this.

"We had a great production year," I said. "All our honey is bottled and ready for sale, and once I get the rest of our bees back, it'll be business as usual."

"You never overwintered by yourself before. They'll all be dead before spring."

"I'll manage."

"We're heading for Florida with ours. Leaving in a week or two. You want, I can take what you have left along."

I'll just bet he would! "Thanks, but no thanks. I have another question."

"You're full of them, aren't you?"

I wanted to tell him exactly what I thought *he* was full of. Instead, I said, "You offered to buy Manny's land. I'd like to know why."

"None of your business. And Lori Spandle has one big mouth."

"She wasn't the one who told me." Why was I trying to make Lori's life easier when I owed her a dropkick to the back of her legs? "I also know that you withdrew the offer."

"Changed my mind."

"Any particular reason?"

"Again, that's none of your business. Why don't you run along now? And flip that open sign around on your way out."

Forty-one

I wasn't finished with Kenny Langley, not by a long shot. He had a large beeyard worth further investigation.

By the time I found a place to hide my truck, stumbled through all the brush, and tramped in the low areas where water had accumulated in hidden little patches, my feet were soaked and poked by thistles, and I had branch scratches all over my face and arms.

I made a mental note to carry sturdy boots and a jean jacket in my truck from now on. Flip flops and a short-sleeved top just didn't cut it for fieldwork. Ben trotted ahead, then circled back to check on my progress. I couldn't leave the poor guy in the truck this time without feeling like I was abusing Hunter's four-legged partner. The fresh air would do him good, and he seemed to be a great listener whenever I asked him to pay attention.

I'd misjudged the distance from the truck's hiding spot

to the back of Kenny's beeyard by what seemed like miles, although I'm sure it wasn't more than one. The twists and turns and highs and lows and dodges around thick brush had made the hike take longer than I expected. But eventually I poked my head out of the brush line and gazed upon a field of beehives, for as far as my eyes could see. Beehives. Rows and rows.

Kenny had been increasing his apiary over the years, and I'm pretty sure he had downplayed its size when he met with Manny. But all I cared about was whether or not he had bees that didn't belong to him.

But what clues could I go on to determine whose bees were whose? That could be a problem. Manny's and my honeybees were strong, but that didn't mean they looked any different than any others. If I was another bee, I would be able to smell the difference between each member of a hive, but I wasn't. The best I could do was look for hive boxes that matched ours, and hope they hadn't been painted over already. Kenny's hives were all varying shades of white, ranging from bright to gray, depending on their ages. I'd painted all of Manny's hives and the two I'd hidden at Grams's an unmistakable bright yellow.

I'd been mentally going over the conversation I'd just had with Kenny as I traipsed through the bushes. My brain was telling me that something he'd said was important. If I could just remember what it was . . . Every time the scene rolled in my head, I stopped when he referred to me as "the girl." Then I'd get annoyed and lose focus.

I told Ben to sit. He did. "Stay," I said, before turning to the beeyard and crouching behind one of the hives at the end of a row. Bees flew over my head, a few checking me out before going off in search of nectar. They were too busy to bother with me as I ran in a crouch from hive to hive, always with an eye on the back of the white corrugated building where Kenny and I had had our little chat.

Running in a crouch is never easy. It's not a position one normally trains for. After the third row, I was feeling it in my legs and had to take a break. Ben stayed where I'd left him, obeying my request much better than most people would have.

I continued on. When I didn't find any yellow hive boxes, I headed for the side of the building where I could see extra supplies stacked up. Pails, hive sections, spare honeycombs.

Nothing yellow.

If Kenny had painted the hives, it would be hopeless. I thought about reinspecting the brightest white ones again, if my legs would ever manage a crouched position again.

Then I sat down hard with my back against the building. I'd just remembered what Kenny had said about him being the key to my future. That was it! It wasn't his comment that was significant, but it brought back another conversation I'd had recently with Ray.

When I'd asked him if he'd picked up the honey from Manny's honey house, he'd said he had. Nothing bothersome there. But then he went on to say that Grace hadn't been home and he'd taken what he needed anyway.

The honey house was always locked. Always, always. It had been locked up tight the few times I'd been back since Manny died.

So how did Ray get in? There was no way Ray had a key.

Was it possible I'd left it open?

No, I was absolutely sure I'd locked up every time. It was locked today. And Grace wouldn't have left it open. She never set foot in the place.

Ray had been out at Kenny's the day Manny died. And Ray had found Manny's body, or so he'd said. What if Kenny and Ray were in it together? Ray could have been the one who killed Manny, then stole Manny's key. What if Ray had been stung, not at the orchard like he said, but while he was transporting Manny's bees from Grace's house? The timeline sure fit.

Something about this whole thing smelled like rotten garbage.

Because of the way my luck was going these days, as in no luck at all, I heard a vehicle pull up in front of the building. I flattened against the metal wall, trying to imagine I was back in the only yoga class I'd ever attended, pretending I was between two panes of glass like the teacher taught me. I couldn't see the car from my position, so I hoped I was safe from the driver's view as well. I really didn't want to explain why I was sneaking around behind Kenny's Bees.

A car door opened and slammed shut, and I heard the door to the building open and close.

I felt something cold and damp on my leg and let out a squeal, which I managed to stifle before it had time to reverberate.

Ben had arrived without announcing his presence and stuck his nose against my leg. So much for perfect obedience.

"Go away," I whispered. "Get back where you were supposed to wait. Now."

The dog didn't listen to a word of it. He sat down next to me.

Jeez. I'd have to get out of here quick or one of us might be spotted. Before I left, though, I really wanted a quick peek at whoever was visiting Kenny after hours.

Just curious.

I'd come this far. Why not?

With that decided, I promptly tripped over Ben and fell to my knees. He scooted out of the way. I rose, ignoring the skinned knee that would go with my other scratches and scrapes. I sidled up to one of the side windows, wondering why these kinds of buildings always had such tiny windows.

With one eye peering through the window and the rest of me hidden from view, I squinted until I made out Kenny's backside, which as I said before, was pretty large. It seemed to loom even bigger in the shadow of the room. He stood with his hands on his hips, and his cigar-shaped fingers resting on his back like he had an ache or two he wanted to massage out.

Then I heard his voice rise and even without being able to hear the words, I could tell he was angry and yelling at somebody. I still couldn't see the other person, hidden from view outside of the room.

Then I heard the blast go off inside.

Forty-two

My knees almost gave out when I saw big Kenny topple backward. He'd stopped shouting when the shot went off. Based on his next moves, or un-moves, there wasn't any question in my mind that he'd been on the receiving end of the bullet.

I hunkered down with my arms around Ben.

"We have to get out of here," I told him, starting to crab-crawl toward the beeyard, which stood between me and the safety of my truck. Ben loped ahead, apparently thinking we were on a picnic or some other lazy-day outing. He reached the tree line and waited for me.

By the time I turned around to make sure we hadn't been spotted, I heard the car drive noisily away. That took a huge weight off my shoulders, even though I never saw a thing that would help identify the driver.

My knees were still wobbly.

I had to make a choice: either save myself from any further involvement, or go back and help Kenny, my nasty competition.

I'm a Wisconsin woman. We have principles. I couldn't live with myself for the rest of my life if Kenny died and I hadn't even tried to save him.

"Come," I called to Ben, who had a puzzled expression when I started back the way we'd come, but he galloped up and paced me as I ran for the front door.

"Stay, Ben." I knew enough not to let a dog inside the building to possibly mess up a crime scene. I even used a piece of my top to open the door in case the shooter had left fingerprints.

Kenny's eyes were closed, which made me think he was still alive, but I couldn't find a pulse.

I'd barely crouched beside him before I heard another vehicle stop outside. I rose and saw Ray get out of his car and come toward the door.

And it all came together for me.

A speck late to help, though.

Ray's muffler had been loud at the market. And the car that drove off a few minutes ago had been louder than normal. That's why I could hear it from across the field.

I ran to the door and threw the lock in time, but he'd seen me.

"Story, open up," Ray said, pressing his face against the door's windowpane. "I saw your truck down the road on my way here. Did you break down?"

I felt sick to my stomach. Ray had shot Kenny, driven away, then saw my truck. He assumed, rightly, that I'd been in the vicinity and might have seen what he did.

So he came back.

Wonderful. And where was Ben? He'd been right outside a minute ago. I backed away from the door.

"I'm calling the police," I said. "Kenny's hurt."

"Open up." Ray jiggled the doorknob. Then he shot through the door lock.

I forgot all about my knees, all my aches and pains, and ran through the building to a back door, hoping it wasn't locked.

It wasn't.

I burst out into the open and ran for the beeyard. Ben came from my right, passed me up, and kept going.

Ray fired shots from behind me, but I kept running, because I knew that it was better to take my chances on the outside than stay inside. His odds of hitting me weren't great.

As long as he didn't catch me.

Ben had stopped up ahead at the same spot as before, alert and ready, but for what?

"Ben," I screamed when I saw Ray take off after me. "Attack!"

Ben perked up, totally ready, but he didn't move.

"Ben, help!"

Nothing. For all he knew, this was one of many simulations, a pretend assault to test his ability to follow orders precisely. What had Hunter told me? That Ben wouldn't attack without the proper command, and even then, only if it came from him. *Damn!*

Just then, my flip-flopped right foot hit a dip in the earth and twisted. Down I went between two hives, giving Ray enough time to catch up.

"Where is it?" he wanted to know. I knew exactly what he meant: the journal.

"Someplace where you'll never find it," I said.

I stayed on the ground. Ray trained the gun on me. "I'll kill you if you don't tell me."

"You're going to kill me anyway."

Ray grinned. It wasn't pretty. "It should have been you with your face in the water instead of that other woman. I screwed up once, but I won't this time."

I remembered standing at the window with my customers that day and the comments they had made about how much Faye looked like me.

Oh my God! He'd mistaken Faye Tilley for me!

I chanced a look at Ben. He still waited by the trees.

"Most of it went as planned," Ray couldn't help saying, sounding proud.

"Like what?"

"I have the hives. That's what's most important."

"Where are Manny's beehives?" I asked.

"My parent's farm out on Highway E. And I'll get yours, too. Good thing I phoned in the fire alert or those idiots would have destroyed your hives. The board was going to vote against you, you know."

"All this extra trouble just to get my two measly hives? Getting greedy will do you in."

"You always had such a smart mouth." Ray came closer.

"What did Kenny do to deserve to die?"

"We had a bargain. He was going to be my silent partner, buy the property, since Manny was dead and Grace would be easy to convince. I would raise strong bees using Manny's research notes. We'd take over the entire territory. Then Kenny started getting suspicious, asking too many questions about Manny's death. When I couldn't produce the journal, he tried to back out. But a deal's a deal."

"So you shot him?"

"I call it tying up loose ends. Just like I'm going to tie up this one."

"You're the one who sent the e-mail to the cops, trying to frame me for Faye's murder."

Ray smiled and I wondered why I hadn't ever noticed before how nasty his smile really was. "After I realized I killed the wrong woman, I thought it might be fun to see you in jail. Too bad the police chief didn't bite."

I had been scooting backward on the ground and

circling so I could see Ben, all the time thinking of command possibilities while bees flew overhead like clouds. I noticed when Ray said that last sentence about the police chief not biting, Ben had reacted by perking up even more, to extra-high alert.

I could tell by Ray's eyes that he was tired of talking, that he was building up to the moment when he raised the gun and fired.

This was my last chance to activate the K-9 cop.

"What did you mean," I said, "the police chief wouldn't BITE?!" I yelled the last word at the top of my lungs. Ray looked startled and confused. "BITE!" I yelled again, not screaming hysterically like I wanted to, but trying to sound loud and commanding.

Ray had his back to Ben. He couldn't see that the big dog was on the move. Ben came at a dead run and hit Ray like a freight train, taking him down and attaching his jaw to one of Ray's arms. I saw the gleam of sharp teeth.

Ben stayed down with Ray as I waded into the action and came out with the gun. Unlike my fear of dogs, guns didn't scare me. Although I wasn't sure where the safety was. Or if it was on.

Ray kept begging for my help, the rotten creep, but even if I'd wanted to, I had no idea how to stop Ben.

Finally, I heard a voice calling from behind me, from close by the building.

"Off!" Hunter shouted, and I turned my head to see he had a gun trained our way. It was as simple as that. Ben let go. "You're supposed to be primping for our date," Hunter said to me.

"Something came up," I said. "How did you find me?"

"Tracking device under your truck. I got worried about you when the truck stopped in the middle of nowhere and didn't move."

"That is just too sneaky," I said, more grateful than I

ever thought I'd be to discover my movements had been followed without my knowledge. "Remind me to file a complaint later."

And that's how I was saved by a dog and his man.

Forty-three

As it turned out, Hunter and I never did get to go out that night. The paperwork, aka the red tape, took forever, and afterward we spent time piecing together what happened. It helped that Ray Goodwin was in a talkative mood, telling so many lies as he tried to pin the illegal stuff on his ex-partner that he tripped himself up and eventually the whole truth came out.

Especially when he found out that Kenny Langley was still alive.

I guess I'm not the world's best pulse-taker after all.

Kenny, as it turned out, wasn't guilty of more than choosing bad friends and offering to front money for a bad business deal.

Ray, on the other hand, had:

- Made anonymous, threatening phone calls to Manny, which was a stupid way to handle a hostile takeover.

- Pulled off the robbery at the Chapmans', stealing a camera and some cash to mislead the police, but making it obvious to Manny that he needed to hide his journal.

- Captured a large yellow jacket nest, which agitated them into attack mode, surprised Manny inside his honey house and locked him in with the nest until he was stung to death, then dragged him into the beeyard and covered him in honey to make it look like the docile honeybees had killed him.

- Decided to kill me, too, for good measure, since he was afraid I would talk Grace into giving me all the beehives. He killed the wrong woman instead.

- Hired one of Kenny's beeyard helpers to pick up all the bees from Manny's, but still couldn't find the journal, which was an important part of the future of his new business.

- Sent the false tip, burglarized my store looking for the journal, and left the earring, still hoping to frame me.

- Shot Kenny when he backed out of their deal.

And for all that, Ray would spend the rest of his life in prison. Good riddance.

A week after the truth came out, I walked down Main Street to open The Wild Clover and found Grace Chapman waiting for me in the blue Adirondack chair outside the store. She hadn't been around much since Ray was arrested.

I could understand her pain. It was one thing to lose your husband to a freak accident. It was quite another to find out he was murdered. I could sympathize with her, because I'd loved Manny, too, only in a different way than she did.

"Sit down," Grace said, and I cautiously seated myself in the yellow Adirondack, leaving one chair between us.

I really hoped she wasn't armed.

By some miracle my cousin Carrie Ann arrived early, greeted us as though Grace and I always sat outside the store together, and disappeared inside.

"We've both been through a lot," Grace said, making a point of studying her hands instead of looking directly at me. "And it's time to clear the air between us."

"I couldn't agree more."

"You start," she said, putting me on the spot.

And so I did, telling her everything that had happened along the way, starting from the day of Manny's death through the confrontation I'd had with Ray in Kenny's beeyard. I told her about my hopes and dreams regarding Queen Bee Honey, about how the honeybees meant as much to me as the financial end of the business. I even told her how much I had cared about her husband, and what a great friend and mentor he had been to me.

"I found Manny's journal hidden under one of my hives," I said, wrapping up my story. "Patti really did see him in my backyard, but he was hiding the journal to keep it safe, not visiting me in some clandestine affair."

When I was through, Grace dabbed at her eyes with a tissue and said, "Thank you for sharing with me. The journal is yours. It was special to Manny, and maybe you can get some use out of it. And I called Mr. and Mrs. Goodwin to make arrangements to relocate the bees. They're yours, too, if you want them."

I couldn't believe my ears. "Yes!" I said, leaping up and giving her a hug right where she sat, which almost resulted in both of us tipping out onto the grass.

"We'll have to sit down and figure out the rest later," she said, getting up as soon as I backed off. Without another glance, she headed for the front door of The Wild Clover.

The bees were mine! All eighty-one hives. Eighty-three, to be exact, including my two. The enormity of the project suddenly overwhelmed me. Could I do it alone? Run the store and the honey business?

After all I'd gone through to get Manny's honeybees, I'd better be able to handle it.

I went inside to call my sister. We had some bees to move.

As for the rest of the story:

- Clay, for the first time in his life, honored a promise he'd made to me. Once he was released—thanks in no small part to my efforts—he put his house up for sale and moved back to Milwaukee. The only part I didn't particularly like was that he used Lori Spandle as his real estate agent.

- The house is still on the market.

- I still avoid Mom and think Grams is the best.

- I haven't paid Holly back yet, but she likes being a part of The Wild Clover so much, I asked her to stay as long as she wanted.

- Carrie Ann's sober most of the time.

- Plans are under way to move the honey house, which I now own along with the rest of Queen Bee Honey.

- I have a new kayak. Yellow, of course.

- Hunter and I have started spending a lot of time together.

- Ben likes to come along.

The Wild Clover
❧ September Newsletter ❧

SEPTEMBER IS NATIONAL HONEY MONTH!

Notes from the beeyard:

- This year's batch of honey has been bottled and is on the shelves!

- Our honeybees are preparing for winter.

- Watch for news about upcoming honey tastings.

Here are a few simple honey concoctions:

- Honey lemonade—stir ½ cup honey into 1 quart hot water. Squeeze in 4 lemons.

- Honey dressing for fruit salad—half honey, half lemon juice. Yogurt and cinnamon to taste.

- Caramel corn—heat ⅓ cup honey, ¾ cup brown sugar, 2 tablespoons butter. Pour over popcorn.

- A tasty appetizer—slice of pecorino or parmigiano, slice of pear, drizzle with honey.

- Old-fashioned cough remedy: equal parts honey, lemon juice, and whiskey.

Honey Frozen Custard

The secret to Wisconsin's famous frozen custard's creamy texture is egg yolks and 10 percent butterfat. Here's my take on this special regional treat.

6 eggs
⅔ cup honey
2 cups milk
2 cups heavy cream
1 teaspoon vanilla
Ice Cream Maker

Whisk together eggs and honey. Heat milk and 1¼ cups cream until almost simmering, stirring. Important! Unless you want honey scrambled eggs, make sure to SLOWLY add 1 cup of cream mixture to egg mixture, whisking. Add to pan and simmer until thick enough to coat spoon; continue to stir. Cool; chill in fridge at least one hour. Add 1 teaspoon vanilla and remaining ¾ cup cream. Pour into ice cream maker, and follow those directions.

Honey Candy Bites

½ cup butter
1 cup flour
¼ teaspoon salt
¾ cup honey
2 tablespoons milk
1 teaspoon vanilla
1½ cups grated coconut
2 cups Rice Krispies (or Cornflakes), slightly crushed

In a large saucepan, melt butter and blend in flour, salt, honey, and milk. Cook over medium heat, stirring constantly until dough pulls away from sides of pan. Remove from heat. Stir in vanilla and 1 cup coconut. Cool for a few minutes and add cereal. Shape into 1-inch balls, roll in remaining ½ cup coconut. Store in refrigerator.

Apple Gingersnap Crunch

This is the best! It includes sugar *and* honey.

> 1 cup gingersnap cookies, crumbled
> ½ cup sugar
> ½ cup flour
> ½ teaspoon salt
> ½ cup butter
> 4 apples, cut into chunks
> ½ cup honey
> ½ teaspoon cinnamon
> ¼ cup pecans, chopped

Preheat over to 350°.

Mix cookie crumbs, ½ cup sugar, flour, and salt. Cut in butter until the mixture is crumbly but holds together when pressed. Spread half over the bottom of an 8 x 8 inch baking dish and pack down lightly.

Mix together apples, honey, and cinnamon. Spread in pan. Add pecans to remaining cookie mix and spread over top.

Bake 50–60 minutes or until fruit is tender and topping is well browned.

Serve with frozen custard or ice cream.

Wild Grape Jam

At this time of the year, grapes are growing wild along Wisconsin back roads. They are free for the picking.

3 pounds wild grapes, a mix of ripe and partially ripe
½ cup water
1 cup honey per cup of juice (or to taste)
3 ounces liquid pectin

Stem and wash grapes. Slightly crush in the bottom of a pan, using a fork or potato masher. Add water and bring to a boil. Simmer for 10 minutes. Strain mixture through cheesecloth. Measure juicy pulp into a saucepan and add honey. Boil for 1 minute, then add pectin. Boil again for 1 full minute.

Notes from the garden:

- Don't forget to dry seeds from your flowers and vegetables for next year's seed swap!

- One zinnia pod contains as many as one hundred seeds—and honeybees love zinnia nectar.

- Jalapeños are technically fruits, not vegetables.

- Use beet greens from your garden early and the beets will grow more tops.

Salsa to Die for

20 tomatillos
1 onion, quartered
2 jalapeños (or to taste)
4 Anaheim peppers

Cilantro (optional)
Salt to taste

Preheat oven to 425°. Roast tomatillos, onion, and peppers for 15 minutes. Put in food processor with cilantro until coarsely chopped. Add salt.

Story's Summertime Beet Soup

1 pound beets, peeled and diced
1 medium onion, diced
1 large carrot, diced
1 clove garlic, minced
3 tablespoons ginger, minced
1 Thai chili pepper (optional)
2 tablespoons sugar
2 cups water
2 cups chicken broth
½ teaspoon salt
½ teaspoon white pepper
Whipping cream
Chives

Put all ingredients except salt, pepper, cream, and chives into pot and bring to a boil. Reduce heat and simmer for 15 minutes or until tender. Add salt and pepper.

Cool slightly, strain, and reserve liquid from the pot; puree cooked vegetables in food processor. Combine liquid and vegetables, stir in a little whipping cream to taste. Serve warm or chilled. Garnish bowls with chives.

**Subscribe to the online edition of
The Wild Clover newsletter
at www.hannahreedbooks.com.**

Wisconsin Resources

Honey Acres
www.beekeepersbestinc.com

Kallas Honey Farm
www.kallashoney.com

Gilles Frozen Custard
www.gillesfrozencustard.com

Kopp's Frozen Custard
www.kopps.com

Wisconsin Made
www.wisconsinmade.com

Basilica of Holy Hill
www.holyhill.com

Rustic Roads
www.dot.wisconsin.gov/travel/scenic/rusticroads.htm

Harley Davidson
www.harley-davidson.com

Ice Age Trail
www.iceagetrail.org

About the Author

Hannah Reed lives on a high ridge in southern Wisconsin in a community much like the one she writes about. She is busy writing the second book in the Queen Bee Mysteries. Visit Hannah and explore Story's world at www.hannahreedbooks.com.